Praise for Adam Cesare

"The best new writer I've read in years."
—Nate Kenyon, author of *Bloodstone*

"A cunning, cinematic redmeat feast for weird film lovers and horror freaks, Adam Cesare's *Tribesmen* is a first-rate literary midnight movie, and a blistering debut. Bring your friends!"
—John Skipp

"Sick and sardonic and just plain brilliant."
—Duane Swierczynski, author of *Fun & Games*, on *Tribesmen*

Video Night

Adam Cesare

SAMHAIN
PUBLISHING

Samhain Publishing, Ltd.
11821 Mason Montgomery Rd., 4B
Cincinnati, OH 45249
www.samhainpublishing.com

Video Night
Copyright © 2013 by Adam Cesare
Print ISBN: 978-1-61921-227-5
Digital ISBN: 978-1-61921-178-0

Editing by Don D'Auria
Cover by Kendra Egert

First Samhain Publishing, Ltd. electronic publication: January 2013
First Samhain Publishing, Ltd. print publication: January 2013

Dedication

This book's for best friends: past, present and future.

Chapter One

Tuesday

The night was cool and clear: the perfect night for being young, drunk and unemployed.

Jake liked to get high while they did it. Rhonda didn't, but she had no complaints. Jake was a big, tall, sandy-haired Irish beach bum who probably took in more sun than was healthy. Rhonda just wanted to do it, period.

The night had been a serviceable, if unspectacular, date. First they stopped at one of the last drive-ins left on Long Island. The movie was *Friday the 13th Part VIII: Jason Takes Manhattan*. It had already been open for months, but the drive-in ran its movies until the film dissolved. Jake was upset that Jason didn't take more time killing "city trash", but Rhonda enjoyed it. After that they parked in the woods and had a few beers, Jake ate something out of a plastic Baggie (mushrooms, she assumed) and then turned on the stereo for a little late-night hanky-panky in Jake's van. The park after closing was a favorite place for the couple to end a night. After the sex they would usually turn the music down and listen to the crickets and look for falling stars through the sunroof.

"Little Dolls" boomed on the cassette player, rattling the windows and sending pleasant vibrations up her buttocks and lower back. Jake had his drugs and Rhonda had her Ozzy. *Different strokes for different folks*, she thought, as long as they were both getting hot.

For a few minutes it was great. Heavy metal, sweet sweat and warm hands mingled with Jake's rough-but-sincere gyrations. Rhonda smiled and let loose a tiny moan.

It started to get weird when Jake's beads of sweat became less morning dew, more rushing river.

The night was chilly. Fall was already here and the heat in the van hadn't worked since they had started dating, years ago now. Jake shouldn't have been sweating so much, even in the throes of passion.

"Are you okay?" she asked.

He just grunted and kept pumping, a soft wheeze in his breath. *Must be the drugs*, she thought. It was getting so good now that she didn't care.

His nails dug into her back. "Not yet," she moaned. He didn't. The song was now Alice Cooper's "Poison". Not as good as Alice's earlier stuff, but Jake was cute for putting together a mix tape for her.

They kept at it, but something was wrong. Jake was unusually quiet. He was not muttering his usual foulmouthed compliments, the kind he picked up from dirty movies. Instead of telling her how "hot" she was, he remained silent, his stomach audibly grumbling.

The gurgles were distracting. What they were doing stopped feeling good and began to feel gross.

"Let's stop, honey."

Jake just shook his head. She could see even in what little light there was that he had gone pale. Jake kept his mouth shut, his lower lip trembling like a nauseated person trying to stay with it. He began thrusting harder, and things went from uncomfortable to painful.

"I said stop!" She pushed his hips away just as he opened his mouth to vomit. Liquid sprinkled her naked belly as she tried to crawl away from him. He was sick all over the carpet. Rhonda despaired for a moment over how difficult the van was going to be to clean, then snapped back to reality.

"Hold on, baby." She threw a blanket over his shivering body and placed the back of her hand against his forehead. He was burning up, but that wasn't the most alarming part. There were dark swirls of blood in his puke and a bulge forming in his neck.

"Oh Jesus," she said and wrapped her arms around him from

behind. Whatever was stuck in there, she had to clear it from his airway. She had her CPR certification and had spent summers as a lifeguard at Jones Beach. Even though she'd spent most of her time at work sipping vodka cranberries and chewing spearmint gum to hide the scent from her boss, she still knew the Heimlich.

She put her hands at the proper position and pulled up and in with a quick jerk. Jake groaned but the bulge didn't move. Blood dribbled down his chin.

Rhonda put one blood-streaked hand to her mouth. Tears stung her eyes and she tried to wipe them away. *You had to keep the patient calm.*

The bubble in Jake's neck got bigger, looking like an enlarged Adam's apple, slowly shifting higher and higher. Blood started running from his nose and eyes.

He needs a hospital. She began searching through his balled-up clothes for the keys to the van.

Jake made a sound like he was trying to clear phlegm; she stopped and stared at him. The bulge looked like it had almost passed now. She figured the hospital would be too far away if he was choking to death. Wrapping her arms around him again, she gave another tug. Tearing at his ribs with all her might, she finally elicited a sound like uncorking a bottle. He made one last wheeze and collapsed facedown, his head bouncing off the floor of the van.

When she turned him over, she got her first look at the obstruction. Between his half-parted lips she could see it moving inside of his mouth. Tiny wet tendrils cautiously licked out at the corners of his lips. The appendages felt the air outside and then darted back in, as if it were some kind of hermit crab with Jake's head as a shell.

Rhonda screamed. Jake lay still. She checked his pulse: nothing. She was momentarily relieved when his mouth started to move, but then came the realization that it wasn't Jake moving. The thing in his mouth was moving *him.*

One spiny leg and then another jutted out from Jake's mouth. They worked their way to his cheeks, where they slipped and left streaks of slime before finding purchase. Small pearls of blood appeared beneath the legs' sharp points as they pierced his skin.

Rhonda pressed herself against the door of the van, staring aghast. She choked back tears and tried to remain quiet as she fumbled for the door handle.

The creature began to push against the corners of Jake's mouth, its legs forming a grotesque, impossibly wide smile on her boyfriend's face as it pushed itself free. Rhonda heard a crack and winced as she thought of Jake's crushed jaw and destroyed teeth.

It was a form impossible to fathom. A giant cockroach blended with a squid and a porcupine writhed and shook its way free from Jake's mouth. It was about the size of a loaf of bread and was something no biology class could have prepared her for. Smooth and slimy on its belly, yet jagged and angular along its back: at once insect and reptilian. Even in all of her little sister's "Zoobooks", the ones the two sisters had been so fond of growing up, there was nothing like the thing in the van.

Rhonda let out a surprised, pained scream as she opened the sliding door and tumbled to the ground outside. Dead leaves broke her fall when she landed with a puff of dust and dirt. She rose to her feet, keeping her eyes on the creature. It was standing on Jake's chest and shaking off its myriad spines like a wet dog. Blood and meat sprayed the van's carpeting and splotched against the nearest wall.

She slid the door shut and looked in the van's circular window. The creature appeared disinterested in Rhonda. It wandered around Jake's body, occasionally making a loud clicking noise that she could hear even from outside of the van.

Something in the back of her mind screamed *run*. But she stayed and watched as the bug, or whatever it was, clumsily tiptoed around Jake's body. When it had made several rounds, it stopped and produced a long, spiked tentacle from under its mouth. A nightmare of a hypodermic needle attached to what looked like an umbilical cord. She screamed for a second time as the tentacle dug into Jake's chest with a squirt of blood.

Retracting the blade, the creature turned to sense where the sound had come from. Two flaps on either side of its body rose up, like ears or satellite dishes. It then tossed itself at the van's window with suicidal abandon, thudding against the glass and leaving a splotch of mucus and blood behind. That was all the incentive Rhonda needed to start running.

She was only a few feet away when she heard a second thud and the glass cracking. She did not turn around. *Run and don't look back.*

In junior high she had been on the varsity track team. Once she got to high school and began dating Jake Connolly, her afternoon run had been replaced by a steady diet of heavy metal radio and cigarettes. Now that she had been out of school for a year and was no longer required to take basic phys ed, she became winded just walking down the block.

Suppressing a cough, she heard the glass shatter in the distance. She turned instinctively and instantly regretted it. The creature used its barbed tentacle to dig into the metal door of the van and catapult itself after her. It sailed ten or so feet and hit the ground running. All six legs galloped in perfect formation, no four touching the ground at the same time.

She whipped her head forward and commanded herself to focus on getting away. Her bare feet pounded the grass and dirt. Twigs and leaves snapped as she prayed she would not stomp all of her weight down onto anything sharp in the darkness. She remembered the movie from earlier that night, how those types of movies always had a scene just like this. That girl in the movies was always scantily clad. She always fell when chased. Rhonda Krieger would not fall.

The sounds of the creature's pursuit were gaining too fast. She turned again, just in time to watch as it crouched low to the ground and hefted its bulbous body with unbelievable speed and grace. It passed a low-hanging branch and shot out its prehensile feeler, wrapped it around the limb and swung for a few feet.

Too fast was the last thought she could muster before it was upon her, hitting her with the same force it must have used to break the window. Its sharp body scraped up her abdomen as it knocked her over. The ground kicked the wind out of her as she landed on her back.

By the time she caught her breath, the thing was already standing on her stomach. It clicked its small jaws together inches from her face. She tried using her fists to knock it off of her chest, flailing against it with all the strength she could muster, but her attempt at self-defense resulted in nothing but pain. She put her hands in front of her eyes to protect her face from the creature's small, foul-smelling mouth. As she raised her fists, she could see that she had broken off several of the animal's sharp quills. The spines stuck through the flesh in her hands, sending waves of sharp pain up her arms.

She saw all of this by the lights of the distant parking lot. The fluorescence of the bulbs filtered through the trees of the park and illuminated the thing's oozing body. It was a grotesque, pointed and clattering mess. The needle-tipped appendage glinted as it hovered above her for a moment. The creature's clicks and screams accelerated, reaching a crescendo as it shot the stinger down into Rhonda's chest.

Pain. There was pain between her breasts. The creature's clicks subsided and she could hear the beast suckle at her insides. Before the pain stopped completely she felt a rush of cold...as if the creature were leaving something dark there inside her body.

Chapter Two

Wednesday

Being fifteen had been difficult, Billy Rile remembered, but being seventeen was a hell of a lot worse. Billy often thought about things of this nature while playing video games, his head filled with deep, existential musings during his extended sessions on Nintendo. Meditations on how tough things were now, accented with the fear of how much tougher they could get once he left for college. He wouldn't call himself self-pitying; he was only a realist.

Billy's fingers fit naturally on the blocky controller in his hand. He was barely paying attention to the television, and yet he made Mario run, jump and eat mushrooms with the physical acumen of a short Italian plumber half his age. The game and cartridge were two years old. Its levels were so familiar that Billy could play through them by rote muscle memory. The ease of the game afforded him this time for abstract thought.

Thoughts about how he knew his mother and father were going to be able to help him pay his way. Thoughts of how he would balance a job to help them pay for a car and college. Thoughts of supple and full breasts. He wondered if he would ever get to cup and nuzzle real ones before he died.

These were the big questions in a teenage geek's life.

Mostly, though, he thought about his friend, Tom Mathers, and what the hell they were going to do without each other.

Tom was not going to college, nor did he want to. Tom would be lucky to be attending their high school graduation at the end of this year. Billy felt a mix of concern and anger toward his lifelong friend. He knew that articulating such concern would land him a punch in the arm and leave him labeled a "homo" by Tom, but he worried for his friend's future all the same. Billy wasn't entirely goal-oriented, but he knew that a person should have higher aspirations than working in his uncle's liquor store for the majority of his life until he saved up enough to buy a secondhand muscle car. That—best-case scenario—was exactly the path that Tom was on.

He also felt anger over the fact that Tom's crappy academic performance, on the few days that he did attend school, might soon drive the boys apart. Billy went down the list of reasons he hated this: Tom would no longer be there to sit with him at lunch, play video games, pull snatch and grabs at the 7-Eleven for dirty magazines, or be there to make sure that he only got mildly bullied. But aside from all of that, it was the least outwardly significant of things that seemed the most important to Billy.

There will be no more video night, he thought, letting Mario fall to his death in a pit of lava.

He was on the second-to-last castle in the game, but the loss of a life did not faze him; he was too troubled. Every Friday, Tom would willingly forgo whatever party he had been invited to that night and watch a movie at Billy's house instead. It was tradition, and traditions weren't supposed to end.

Way back in his elementary school days, Billy's family had been one of the first in town to get a VHS player, making 1982 the height of Billy Rile's popularity. His dad had even converted the basement into a well-lit, carpeted family room, with a nice TV set and ample comfy seating arrangements. In the years since that top-loading home entertainment monstrosity (and Billy's glory days), the Rile family had upgraded to a hi-fi player, but the monster movies at Billy's house had long ago lost its appeal with his classmates. All except Tom, of course. For the past few years video night had consisted of just the two of them, and more recently Darcy Roberts, whom Tom had started fooling around with during the summer before their senior year.

There was a single knock followed by the front door opening downstairs. Billy paused his game. He heard muffled voices as Tom exchanged his usual brief pleasantries with Billy's mother and then ran up the carpeted stairs, his boots thudding as he took them two at a time.

"Hey, dickwad," Tom said as he opened Billy's bedroom door without knocking. The taller boy slung his leather jacket behind his back, as he always did upon entering a room, even if he did not intend to stay. It was an old, black, leather motorcycle jacket, the kind that the punk kids at school would have loved to tear up, sew patches on and poke metal studs into. Tom's was in its original condition, though, with enough wear to show that it had seen some action. Tom glanced at the small television and pointed. "What castle is this?"

"Second to last," Billy said. Tom could not tell which level it was, not because he never played Super Mario Brothers (he actually played at Billy's house quite frequently), but because he lacked the skills necessary to be familiar with such an advanced level of the game. Tom might have the lady skills, but Billy had the Nintendo skills. This was more depressing to Billy than it was a point of pride.

"Wow, good job, nerd. Finish up; we gotta go. I got shit to do today." Tom talked like this all the time, but the use of "nerd" was meant to be a term of endearment despite being glaringly, painfully true. Billy's bedroom teemed with proof that he was indeed a nerd. Even his coolest personal possession was still slightly nerdy: an authentic samurai sword that he'd received as a gift from the World Showcase gift shop when his parents had taken him to Epcot Center a few years earlier. The tempered steel was for display only, but that didn't stop Tom from occasionally whirling it around. These impromptu samurai training sessions made Billy anxious, but they did make Tom look cool.

Sword excepted, everything else in Billy's room screamed "spoiled geek": his *Empire Strikes Back* bedsheets, piles of *Starlog* and *Fangoria* magazines, the collection of Gobots and Transformers on his dresser (he prayed that Tom didn't know he still occasionally played with them) and a bookshelf that sported a mix of Stephen King and some Doc Savage paperbacks that had been hand-me-downs from his father. Add to that his string-bean arms, perpetually damp hair and profuse

15

sweating habits, and it didn't take Crockett and Tubbs to deduce the state of Billy's virginity.

It was nothing like Tom's room. If Billy's was the room of a boy, Tom's was that of a man. A square-jawed, stubble-faced, tousle-haired man, complete with badass leather jacket. Tom's room was much smaller and the wallpaper was ripped and faded, but instead of toys and kid's stuff, Tom had the accoutrements of an adult—or at the very least a late adolescent. On his walls Tom had *Hustler* centerfolds and posters for bands like Dio and W.A.S.P., and atop his dresser he kept cassette tapes and drug paraphernalia.

"What do you have to do today?" Billy asked and pressed the "Power" button on the Nintendo. He was no longer concerned with finishing his game. He had rescued the princess before and it was never that exciting.

"Darcy's coming over later, so she's what I'm doing." Tom stuck out his tongue and wiggled it, putting his hand up for a high five. Billy gave it to him with little enthusiasm. It wasn't just talk. Billy knew that Darcy Roberts was putting out regularly for Tom. Billy was jealous, of course, and it made his friend even more of a hero to him, but he was also mystified as to why. Tom treated her well, but a girl of Darcy's standing should have been dating football players, not mildly drug-dependent teens who rarely attended school.

"Oh, speaking of Darcy, I almost forgot to tell you that she's going to come Friday to, you know, video night." Tom said the words hurriedly and nonchalantly, trying to defuse the effect he knew it would have on Billy. Billy winced. It was understood between the two friends that Billy and Darcy didn't get along, especially when it came to video night. Darcy would come over and be on her best behavior for about ten minutes. After that she was either forcefully making out with Tom, or she would ask to use the phone and then talk for hours to her friends. The kissing was nowhere near as bad as the talking.

As part of the plush conversion of the basement, Billy's parents had installed an extra phone line. It was a line that Darcy used liberally and without fear of pissing off Billy's folks. Her loud Long Island accent and heinously annoying laugh would drown out all the dialogue, thus robbing the film of suspense and making the gory parts far less enjoyable.

Billy forced his face to look as dejected as possible and pursed his lips to speak. Tom cut him off before he could get a single word out.

"But, but, it won't be so bad because I'm going to get her to bring a friend," Tom said, smiling widely and putting a hand on Billy's shoulder.

"Oh, no, you don't have to do that. It's fine, really. Darcy can come alone. No problem." Billy wanted to stop this guest list from ballooning any further. He didn't need Darcy's voice in stereo. He got chills thinking about the way she pronounced coffee. *Caw-fee.* It was a stone-cold fact that the more annoying people were, the more pronounced their Long Island accent.

"Don't be a jerk. Darcy has lots of hot friends. I'll make sure she brings one of them. Not a cow." Tom held up his hand as if he were in court, swearing on a Bible—as he had done on numerous occasions. "I promise."

Billy rolled his eyes, and Tom continued, "Maybe even someone special." He crossed Billy's room and stopped at the window, parting the blinds with two fingers. "Has she been dancing around in her room naked lately?"

"No, you goddamn pervert."

"You say that with such certainty. You've been watching closely to make sure she doesn't, eh?" Tom gave him a quick slap on the stomach with the back of his knuckles. Billy prepared himself too late and the blow really hurt, but he tried not to let it show. "Oh, don't put on that face. I'll try my best to get the girl here, okay?"

The possibility, however distant, of rubbing up against something warm and female, especially if that something was Rachel Krieger, was so compelling that Billy surrendered without another word of protest.

"Now let's get this show on the road," Tom said, and put his jacket back on with the same flourish and style with which he had taken it off mere moments ago.

Billy couldn't stop himself from thinking about how he wanted to be as rude, as unstable, as *cool* as Tom, even if it was only for a day. Then he followed his friend out the bedroom door.

Rhonda Krieger awoke to the warmth of the sun rising high above the Heckscher State Park trees. She was naked, hurt all over and didn't feel like herself. It wasn't necessarily a bad thing.

Leaves and grass tickled her back and caught between her ass cheeks as she lifted herself up. She looked down at her body, more intrigued with her own nudity than she was with the quarter-sized hole that had been drilled into her chest.

After she carefully plucked the spikes from the oozing wounds in her hands, she cupped her breasts. She pressed them together, then traced a manicured fingernail around her prominent tan lines and down to the wound between them. A small discharge of green pus leaked down her chest. *Very nice. That should scab over in a few hours.*

The thing inside her, using Rhonda's body and mind, realized that she would need to cover herself in order to avoid attention. She would need the girl's clothes back. Judging from the height of the sun, it was already past midday. It was a miracle that no one had stumbled upon either her or the van and thereby Jake's body.

She walked over to the van, placed one cold hand on the door, and paused. The sun had warmed the entire side of the van. She pressed herself against the door, trying to get every bit of exposed skin onto the metal. It felt more than exquisite; it felt energizing. Once she had sapped all the heat from the surface, she threw the door open, her new body moving with enhanced vigor after absorbing the heat.

Jake was starting to stink. The smell of his voided bowels was nothing compared to the sun-warmed gore dribbling down his crushed jaw. She could smell him, but she didn't much mind. Rhonda—the real Rhonda—retched and cried. Locked deep down inside of herself, a prisoner in her own mind, she could do nothing but watch. She was offering all the resistance that she could muster, but nothing strong enough to manifest itself physically. The real Rhonda was being swallowed up, engulfed. She had lost the struggle. The thing that had won climbed into the van, quickly found her clothes, and slipped them on. Something would need to be done about Jake's body.

Destroy all evidence; that's the first part of the plan. The thought was not her own, but she found herself agreeing with it. Jake's face was the evidence: his mouth a mangled hole, jaw shattered, lips torn apart and teeth broken out. Yes, this would definitely raise suspicion.

Rhonda rummaged through the mess in the van's glove compartment. Inside she found a lighter, but no accelerant. The lighter had been Rhonda's, one of the few gifts Jake had ever given her. It was a no-frills, faux-gold Zippo that had lost its luster from constant use.

The thing in her head began scanning through Rhonda's memories, like a nimble clerk searching a file cabinet. The real Rhonda's attempts to hide the memory, to shuffle it around in her mind, only drew attention to the cardboard box at the rear of the van. Rhonda opened it up and found the couple's paltry camping supplies. Sitting beneath a small bag of match-light charcoal, a rolled-up sleeping bag, a clump of napkins and several ketchup packets (both from McDonald's) was a small tin can of lighter fluid.

She undid the plastic stopper and began to squeeze the canister, making sure to evenly distribute the liquid on the walls, floor and ceiling of the van. Lastly she covered Jake, crossed his arms over his chest and stepped out of the van. She lit a bit of shag carpeting by the edge of the door and then slid the door shut. The thing that was now Rhonda Krieger walked away with a cautious spring in her step and a giggle in her throat. At the back of her mind, the tiny part that was crying grew softer with every step she took away from the fire. The real Rhonda and her memories had been absorbed entirely by the time the sun set and the thing walked up the back steps of the Krieger residence.

"One second," Billy said as they exited the front door. Tom nodded and kept walking to the street as Billy took a left to the garage. Tom's bicycle lacked a kickstand, so he had just thrown it half on the sidewalk and half on the Riles' well-manicured lawn. Tom parked this way every time, and it left a ring of dead grass that pissed off Billy's parents more than any other questionable lesson Tom could teach their only child.

"You coming, Alex P. Keaton?" Tom yelled from the end of the driveway. Billy hated being called that.

"Keep your skirt on, Mallory," Billy said as he walked his bike out of the garage.

Billy's bike was a brand-new ten-speed his father and mother had bought for him last Christmas. Tom's bicycle was a size-too-small knockoff brand bought off the rack at Toys"R"Us five years prior. It had a slightly bent frame and only patches where the original obnoxious neon blue paint still remained. Flecks of paint clung to the bike like a stubborn moss, while the areas around them had turned rusty silver: the most pathetic form of metallic sheen. Instead of feeling sorry for his friend's poverty, Billy was envious of the bike. It was earth-worn and rugged, qualities which it passed on to its rider. *Or was it the other way around?* Billy wondered.

The two boys saddled up and set off for the video store. It was only Wednesday, but the rental would last for a full week before Billy would be charged a late fee.

The ritual hadn't changed much through the years. Wednesday afternoon Billy and Tom would ride their bikes to VideoLux. VideoLux could have been considered a mom-and-pop rental store if it were run by anything resembling a mom and pop. Instead, behind the counter sat Russ, a jolly, middle-aged loser who subsidized his business by selling pot to the neighborhood kids and their parents. "Jolly" was the word that Billy used to describe him, but Tom's assessment of "fat and creepy" was admittedly more accurate.

The store was a short but scenic bike ride from Billy's house.

The five-minute ride from Billy's house included samples of both Long Island's natural beauty, in the form of Connetquot State Park, and its tendency to destroy such beauty with concrete and big, ugly houses. The boys rode their bikes on one of Sunrise Highway's many overpasses. The highway was the Island's long main vein, coursing with a constant stream of moody, sun-beaten, and sometimes intoxicated motorists.

Once over the bridge, Billy looked up at the blue-and-white sign for Union Boulevard. "Think we should stop by Darcy's house? See if her mom will bake us some pizza bagels?"

Billy had gotten into the habit of saying something like this every time they passed Darcy's block. Tom had once shared with him a raunchy story about Darcy, an unlocked bedroom door, her mother, some pizza bagels, and interrupted mutual masturbation.

"Sure. That sounds delicious, fuckface," Tom said, the joke having long ago lost its ability to offend.

Beyond Sunrise Highway, past Union Boulevard, lay one of the Island's many "Main" streets. This particular Main Street was home to the Bayard Strip Mall, which housed Bijou Nail Salon, Berg's Pizza, a Waldbaum's supermarket and VideoLux.

A cobbling of sleigh bells tied above the glass door announced the boys' arrival at the video store. The insignificant sound brought feelings of excitement, nostalgia and elation—or at least it did for Billy.

"Hey, dudes." Russ barely looked up from staring at his hands to greet his most consistent customers. He wore an Alice Cooper T-shirt stretched over his considerable beer belly. On the faded shirt, Alice's face was superimposed over a clenched fist. Billy had the same shirt, from last year's tour, and he was amazed by how shitty Russ's already looked. Russ's shirts always had stains and rips; as an ex-flower-child burnout, that was to be expected. But this one was downright wrong. The black shirt somehow looked green and mossy.

The pair gave Russ a friendly nod and walked straight to the back right corner of the shop. Above the last rack of videos there was a hand-drawn sign that warned, "Beware: Horror." The letters were drawn in red marker and outlined in black. The waviness of the penmanship on the sign could either have been intentional or the result of Russ's constant tremors. A cardboard cutout of Elvira, Mistress of the Dark, stood guard in the corner, advertising not videotapes, but Coors Light. As per the ritual, Tom gave Elvira's flat breasts a quick imaginary squeeze.

The majority of the horror-section tapes had been rented and re-

rented by the pair throughout the years, *Dawn of the Dead* and *The Texas Chain Saw Massacre* being perennial favorites, if a tad overexposed. The really good stuff, though, lay in the big plastic boxes. Movies that nobody but Billy, Tom and Russ had ever heard of. *Maniac, The Prowler, The Deadly Spawn, The Burning, Abomination, Just Before Dawn*. Their packages and lurid covers promised—and only sometimes delivered—buckets of blood and gore.

Since Darcy and maybe her friend (*possibly Rachel*, Billy allowed himself to hope beyond hope) were coming, the two decided that traumatizing the girls into a state of shock was the only way Billy was going to get into anyone's pants.

"How about *The Dead Pit*," Billy said with a hint of glee in his voice. He grabbed the box and inspected the art: a mummified zombie with red, glowing eyes. Placing the box right up to Tom's face, Billy pressed the button on the box and made the eyes of the zombie glow red. In Billy's opinion, the gimmick alone made it worth a rental.

"Nah, everything's too fake-looking in that one," Tom said, pushing the box away. Tom was always less involved in picking the movies to rent than he was in the ones *not* to rent.

"What about *Friday the 13th Part 3*? A classic." Billy held the box up for Tom's approval, as if the cooler boy was working quality control…which he was.

"Not bad, not a bad one at all," Tom said. "But there are too many people screwing and then being killed in that one. I don't think it sends the girls the right message. Do you? We want to assure them that screwing is safe and healthy."

After numerous tries, Tom finally approved *Re-animator*. Billy thought that the scene involving a severed head that was also giving head was pushing it, but Tom claimed that it would make the girls "hot and bothered, even if they don't want to admit it".

By the time the two friends approached the checkout counter, Russ had nodded off. A string of drool connected his bottom lip to the pages of the magazine in front of him. Billy noticed that it was not only Russ's shirt that bore a mossy look; the side of his head also had what appeared to be patches of lichen clinging to it. The mammoth ex-hippie resembled a zombie straight out of one of Billy and Tom's movies. Billy glanced over at Tom, who either didn't notice or wasn't visibly bothered by what appeared to be Russ's decomposition.

Tom coughed something that sounded like "asshole" and Russ sprang awake.

"Hey, dudes, are you all set?" Russ took the tape from Billy and wrote the boys a receipt, folding up the carbon copy and placing it inside the tape's clamshell packaging. "Two bucks," he said. It was strange. Russ went about his actions mechanically and made no reference to their pick. When handed *Re-animator*, Russ usually made some comment about how Jeffery Combs should have been nominated for an Oscar or what a shame it was that Barbara Crampton didn't make more hits.

Bewildered by Russ's brevity, Billy paused in a stupor before digging into his back pocket for the money (the rental was always Billy's treat). Russ took the bills, made change with some difficulty and then stopped before handing back the video. Here it was: now they were going to get a lecture on what a genius Stuart Gordon was and how criminally underappreciated his last two films had been (although Billy had to agree with him about *From Beyond*).

"Hey, do you guys like to get high?" Russ asked. That was unexpected. There was still no friendliness in his voice, but at least the tone of his words finally sounded like the Russ that the boys had known since childhood. Russ wasn't usually this public with his drug pushing, though. Billy had never even known about the pot dealing until Tom had told him last year.

Drugs weren't Billy's thing, and he felt his cheeks flush. The tips of his ears were no doubt bright red, and that made him even more embarrassed. He stood silent, rendered immobile by the thought of anything illegal (besides underage drinking, but Billy didn't consider that full-on illegal). His friend, though, was less inhibited. The edges of Tom's mouth curved in a mischievous smile.

"Why?" Tom asked.

Russ ducked his head under his desk and came back up holding a shoebox. He looked at the door and then around the shop to make sure that no other customers were in sight. VideoLux was empty, as it always was. Russ lifted the top off of the box and tilted it toward the boys.

"If you like to get high before watching a movie, then these'll knock your socks off," Russ said with a slight twitch. Billy noted that Russ only blinked with his left eye. The right one was red and engorged, pushing against the eyelid and jamming it open.

Billy peered down into the box, while Tom offered a more cursory glance. It was empty except for one corner, where there lay four small, black pills.

Billy knew that he was crazy, imagining things. But he could have sworn that he saw one wiggle.

Chapter Three

"Come on, babe." When whining, Tom's tough-guy persona all but disappeared. Getting Darcy to bring a friend to video night was proving harder than he had anticipated. The couple sat on his bed, his small bedroom not having many other places to get cozy.

"Who am I supposed to get?" she said, using her fake Brooklyn accent. Tom had noticed that she never said nice things about anyone in this voice. "The kid's a fuckin' loser."

"Watch it. That's my loser. My friend," he said, injecting some hurt into his voice. Begging wouldn't work this time, but sympathy sure would. Darcy was like that; not normally an openhearted person given to charity, but for Tom she was Mother Teresa. He knew that it was because she felt bad for her "poor boyfriend from the wrong side of the tracks", but why not use that to his advantage?

When an overzealous frown appeared on Darcy's face, Tom knew he had won before she could say the words. "Awww, baby, I'm sure I can find someone."

"How about Rachel Krieger?" Tom said, trying and failing to ask his question without sounding too rehearsed.

"Ha!" Sometimes Darcy's sentences weren't even words. From this noise, Tom was supposed to get, "No, dear. Try again. And this time aim lower."

"Why the hell not?" Tom, while not showing much initiative in school, could be a master of debate when he put his mind to it.

"Because Rachel—this Rachel," she made a wave over her face and then cupped the air in front of her own modestly sized breasts, "is out of his league. Besides, now that her sister is getting with Jake

Connolly, she's looking for something bigger and better."

"Rachel may be hot, but she's still no Rhonda. Besides, what's bigger and better than a rich kid?"

"Billy Rile is not rich," Darcy said. "You use that word too much. Calling everybody 'rich' all the time. I'm rich, Billy's rich, your neighbor's dog is rich. Billy doesn't even have a car."

"He's going to college," Tom said, and then added, "out of state." He scooted closer to Darcy's end of the bed, sliding his hands up under the sheets and pinching her thighs. "The kid has had a crush on her forever. Just ask if she'll come hang out."

"Everyone has a crush on her; that's the point. Therein lies the an-ing-ma."

Tom, who was no genius, knew this to be a gross mispronunciation of the word enigma, but thought it would be better if he didn't point that out. "She doesn't have to marry him, she just has to watch a movie." He grinned. "And maybe touch his pee-pee." Then he fell on her, tickling her stomach and that spot behind her knees, sending her into what looked like an epileptic fit accented with laughter.

"Stop, I'll try, I'll try!" she screamed.

Tickling gave way to groping. Groping to heavy petting. Heavy petting led to Tom throwing the lock on his door and opening the underwear drawer where he kept his rubbers.

"What's this shit, and why am I here?" Lieutenant Todd Darl of the Suffolk County Sheriff's Department took an exaggerated look at his watch, squinting to make it out in the darkening woods, and then glared at the park ranger. The sheriff's department was responsible for all crimes on government property. This rule meant lending the occasional helping hand to the parks department, a helping hand that tonight Darl would have preferred to use to flip them the bird.

"Well, I think that it's a Dodge Ram Van by the looks of it, sir," the ranger—a stammering, pimply-faced kid in his midtwenties—said.

There was no doubt in Darl's mind that the kid had applied for the job in order to start a grow operation in Long Island's largest park. He must have been unaware when he signed up that he might have to do actual work from time to time.

"Why did you call the sheriff? On a burned-out car you call the police and give them the plates."

"But, sir—" The kid was interrupting him. Darl hated that.

"No, son, you let me finish. After you call the plates in, then you call a tow truck and have them get this hippie POS off this fucking dead-grass dirt pile you call a park."

"It's the start of fall, sir. The foliage changes color." The young officer looked patently ridiculous trying to talk back to Darl while wearing his puke-green rent-a-cop uniform.

"Just lead the way, Smokey," Darl said.

The old lieutenant and the young geek walked through the trees to where the van was parked. Darl put a hand up to his salt-and-pepper mustache and plugged his nose with calloused fingers.

"Son, do you know what I hate more than the smell of burned-out car?" Darl asked, but continued on without allowing time for an answer, unconcerned with how ridiculous he sounded with his nose plugged. "That's rhetorical, because what I hate more than the smell of burned-out car is the youth of America. I hate the fuckers. They drive too fast, they dress like shit, they talk during movies and they set vans on fire, thus causing those vans to smell like burned-out car." He paused for a deep breath, becoming winded from the walk and talk. Darl really wasn't this much of a prick, but having to answer this call had pissed him off and he was on a roll. This kid was just the unlucky target of his aggression.

Removing his fingers from his nose, he wiped the sweat from the stubble on his chin. "From the age of eleven to twenty-five," he said, "we should keep you kids all in special camps or something, for our own protection and the protection of our five senses."

He continued with his diatribe, not even noticing that he was following the ranger's lead right up to the still-hot door of the van. The ranger took a cloth from his pocket and wrapped it around his hand.

"I'm twenty-seven years old, sir," he said, and pried open the van's sliding door, standing aside to reveal its contents.

"Mother. Fucker." Darl looked into the eye sockets of the body's charred, destroyed skull and thought about all the paperwork he would now have to fill out.

Chapter Four

Darcy gathered her clothes up and left shortly after the sex, leaving Tom alone with his thoughts. Tom's mind was always working when he was alone, contrary to what his teachers, principal, mother, father, and even his court-appointed therapist assumed. They mostly concurred that Tom's problem was that he didn't think. Not that any of them particularly cared.

Tom reached under his bed frame and pulled out his father's old flask. He had stolen it one night when his father had gone out and mistakenly left it on the kitchen table. His father was a drunk and a loser, but luckily he did not have abusive in his repertoire to complete the blue-collar dad trifecta. He'd simply assumed that he had dropped it, and considered it lost to that night's drunken festivities.

Tom ran his fingers along the scratched and dented surface of the flask. His father had written his name on the bottom in permanent marker, the way a child marks a favorite toy. Tom smiled, then unscrewed the cap and took a long pull, reaching over to turn on the tape deck. He kept the volume low, but compensated by lifting it onto the bed and pressing one speaker flush against his ear. The music vibrated against the flesh of his earlobe.

Billy was angry with him and he knew why: his friend wasn't a fan of drugs. Once Tom had insisted that they buy those pills from Russ, with Billy providing the cash, their bike ride back to his house had been too quiet. When Russ had described them as "crazy hallucinogens", he must have seen how the words made Billy cringe, because he added the disclaimer that they were also "totally safe and natural". Tom didn't buy that and he knew that Billy hadn't either. Billy didn't want the pressure of both girls and drugs at their "video night", and now, in retrospect, Tom felt terrible that he had forced the issue. *We don't have to be friends for that much longer anyway,* Tom thought. He let the numbing sensation of rage counteract his compassion. *I'm not the one saying 'fuck you' and leaving for college in a handful of months.*

He tried to calm himself down by thinking about Darcy, how she would be sticking around for college because she was going to Hofstra, a five-minute drive away. But it didn't make him feel any better. They weren't in love or anything. In fact, when she wasn't being sweet she was a total pain in the ass.

He turned the dial all the way to the right, cranking the music up as loud as it could go. He tried to make it loud enough that he didn't have to think. He didn't care who in the house he disturbed...or what they thought of him.

Deborah Krieger had been dozing in the living room after a long day of gardening when the clatter of the screen door woke her. "Digging in the dirt", as her husband liked to call it, was one of the best ways that she knew to calm down during a stressful day. And when your eighteen-year-old daughter hasn't returned home or even called after going out last night? It's been a stressful day.

"Rhonda Krieger, where the hell have you been?" Deborah's unlit cigarette bobbed up and down at the corner of her mouth as she jolted awake and placed her romance paperback on the arm of the couch, then hurried to catch her teenage daughter sneaking home through the back door. She looked at the wall clock and did some impromptu, incorrect calculations. "Twenty-one hours late for curfew. That has to be a new world record."

She stopped in the doorway from the living room to the kitchen, body-blocking the hallway and the stairwell that led to Rhonda's second-story bedroom. "Your excuse better include the words charitable, volunteering, Jesus Christ and Santa Claus or you are grounded, young lady," Deborah said.

"Hello, Mom," Rhonda said, her voice cracked and hoarse as she entered her mother's field of vision. "I'm sorry I'm late."

"Mom? What happened to always calling me..." Deborah started, but the words died in her throat as she looked at her daughter. Really saw her, looked into Rhonda's haggard face. Her little girl's arms and legs were covered in a layer of mud and grime. Her clothes were just as dirty and speckled with small copper spots, *dried blood*. Her hands were covered in dark red scabs, like she was recovering from a wild animal attack, or a deadbeat boyfriend with a knife. "My God. Where were you? Are you okay?"

"I'm fine. Jake and I were in a small accident."

"Accident, oh Jesus. Sit down, I'm calling 911. That bastard, that no-good little prick bastard finally tried to kill you."

"Mother, please, I'm fine. It wasn't Jake's fault."

"No," Deborah Krieger said, "you are not fine, dear. I think you're in shock. Sit down, please." She took the girl's dirty arm and tried to guide her down into one of the chairs at the kitchen table, but recoiled when she realized Rhonda's flesh was cool to the touch. "Oh God, baby, you're freezing."

Deborah screamed into the hallway for help, dropping all pretense of maintaining the calm in her voice. "Harold! Rachel! Come help me." She didn't wait for an answer; she knew that Harold was still at work and Rachel was God-knows-where. She ran to the wall for the phone, stuck her finger through the nine and spun the rotary.

"Mother, please, calm down. I am fine."

Deborah dialed the first one.

"You just sit down now, Rhonda," Deborah said. Adrenaline surged through her fingers, making it difficult to find the rotary again. She reached for the final number as Rhonda stood up. "Everything is going to be okay, baby."

"I know it will be, Mom." Deborah felt a sharp tug as Rhonda grabbed a tangle of her hair. Rhonda's strong hands ripped her backward for a moment before shoving her face into the wall-mounted phone with what felt like all her might. Deborah's senses went blank as the plastic of the telephone shattered into her face.

Billy's clock radio read 12:56 a.m. It was a school night and he usually would have been asleep for an hour or more by now, but he couldn't stop thinking about those pills he and Tom had bought. Smooth black ovals a little less than an inch long. What would they do to his brain when he took them? "Safe and natural"? *Bullshit.* Would the chemicals stay at the base of his spinal column for the rest of his life, like he heard that LSD did? Would he have a bad reaction and be a vegetable or, maybe even worse, unemployable?

The pills were currently tucked into his sock drawer. Russ had given him a small plastic Baggie to keep them in, and Billy had hidden the Baggie in a sock. Even lying in bed, waiting for sleep to come, Billy wanted to sit up and go check on them. He had spent a lot of time staring at them when he got home, stashing them in his room after Tom suggested that Tom himself not be the one to hold on to their purchase. "If Darcy finds out I have them, she'll want to have a hit, and then we won't have enough left over for video night," Tom had said. "We want these to be our ace in the hole."

Where Tom got an expression like "ace in the hole" was anyone's guess. That was the thing about Tom: even Billy, his closest friend, was unsure how much of Tom's bad-boy, anti-intellectual image was real, and how much was an act. There were times when Billy thought (maybe feared) that his friend was just as intelligent as himself, possibly even more so. For all Billy knew, Tom kept a secret stash of Proust and Hemingway under his porno mags and Judas Priest tapes.

The rest of the time since he got home from VideoLux had been spent finding ways to resist the temptation to part his blinds and spy on Rachel Krieger. To assuage this urge, he was repeatedly reading the back of the *Re-Animator* plastic videotape box. Billy and Rachel weren't lifelong neighbors; the Kriegers had moved in at the beginning of high school. But Billy had coveted her at school long before she literally could be labeled "the girl next door". Now that she lived directly across the street, Billy found it hard not to take the occasional peek out of his window to see if he could catch a glimpse of her going about her day.

He had never seen anything of note, but he got a shameful little thrill just knowing that the possibility of catching her changing clothes was there. If her sister's room hadn't been at the back of the house, he surely would have caught Rhonda fooling around with Jake at some point. He snapped himself away from thoughts of Rachel's underwear and Rhonda's sexcapades by shoving the videotape box so close to his face that it brushed against his nose.

Re-Animator, directed by Stuart Gordon, released theatrically in 1985, starring Jeffery Combs, David Gale and Barbra Crampton (who spent much of the runtime nude), loosely based on the short story by H. P. Lovecraft. He read the synopsis over twice, realized that he had known all this information since a year prior to actually seeing the film (*Fangoria* ran *very* extensive write-ups of upcoming movie releases), and turned his attention back to the contents of his sock drawer. He finally got up and opened the drawer, but instead of looking inside the sock, he lifted the false wood bottom that Tom had helped him install and took out two issues of *Hustler* and one of *Playboy*.

The October 1987 issue of *Hustler* ("America's Magazine") bore the headline: "AIDS Research Rivalry: Killing Chances for Cures?"

Nothing gets me in the mood better than AIDS. Thanks, Mr. Flynt. Billy threw it back in the drawer and grabbed the *Playboy*. This one had an interview with Michael J. Fox and a photo spread of Donna Edmonson. A "wank" was what they called it in Britain, but in gym class they just called it jerkin' off. It would have hit the spot and sent him quickly to bed, but even though it was late, Billy didn't want sleep right now, so he resisted flipping through the pages.

Instead, he slipped on a pair of socks to muffle his footsteps and slowly opened his bedroom door without a sound. On tiptoe he crept down the second-story hallway, past his parents' room and down the stairs. He didn't need to be so quiet; his parents had been asleep for a couple of hours, and wouldn't be able to hear him walk down the carpeted hallway anyway. Sneaking around, the stealth of the act of creeping downstairs, gave him a thrill at the base of his stomach. It was the flutter that a little kid gets when snooping for Christmas presents or stealing a sip of whiskey from the liquor cabinet.

Billy liked that feeling. It was the safe kind of rush that you could trick yourself into having without putting yourself in any actual danger. He used to get the same kind of feeling from horror movies, but not so much anymore as he'd grown too much of a tolerance. He walked down the salmon-carpeted steps to the basement, putting his arm against the walls to steady himself in the dark. When he got to the bottom, he flicked out his hand and caught the light switch on the first attempt.

He squinted to let his eyes adjust to the light. When he opened them, he walked from the bottom of the stairs and placed his hand on top of the long, white, oblong box that hummed in the corner of the basement. His father had bought the trunk freezer from a friend a year and a half ago. It was filled with frozen hamburger patties, frozen steaks, frozen bread, a whole chicken, bags of frozen veggies, even paper plates stacked with strawberries. Billy's mother never saw the point, but the freezer made his dad so happy that she didn't dare voice her opinion for fear of breaking his heart. From the freezer, Billy made an about-face and explored the rest of the basement.

Billy's parents had moved the old couch from the living room to down here in front of the television. The teal fabric of the couch showed slight wear at the corners of the cushions, but was still as vibrant as the day it was purchased. Billy poked his hand between the cushions and felt for the remote, found it where it was supposed to be. From the couch he walked to the television, another hand-me-down from the living room. The television was housed in a large wooden cabinet with doors that were held closed by magnets.

Under the TV sat the VCR—not a cast off, but a new, top-of-the-line machine. Billy pushed a finger against the automatic plastic door, squatting down to check if there was a tape inside. The machine was empty, and as he looked in he could see the tape deck's silver inner workings beyond the tips of his fingers.

In Japanese movies, the characters could always be seen bowing in front of wooden shrines just like this one, only instead of a television there was a stone statue of some spirit or whatever. The parallel amused Billy, who let the thought leave his mind as casually as it had entered. Amusement gave way to sadness, and Billy squatted for a few moments more with his fingers inside of the VCR. *I'm not going to cry over a VCR*, he thought, *I'm too young for a nostalgic cry.*

Once he regained his composure, he returned upstairs. After reading the Michael J. Fox interview in *Playboy* (and glancing at the centerfold, of course) he fell asleep.

After laying Deborah Krieger's body on the kitchen floor, the thing that looked like Rhonda Krieger slipped two plastic Waldbaum's bags over her mother's still-bleeding head. She had found two rubber bands in the Kriegers' junk drawer and used them to secure the bags to Deborah's neck. Rhonda then began to clean up the kitchen.

She took the broken phone off the wall, ran a bucket of warm water in the sink, and began wiping the floor and wall clean of the blood that had poured out of Deborah's head. Long after the woman was dead, the small gouges in her forehead had continued to ooze, so the blood had formed substantial pools on the kitchen tile. When the kitchen was passably clean, Rhonda put all the bloody rags into a garbage bag. She then turned her attention to what to do with Deborah.

The night was too cold and the yard too exposed for Rhonda to dig a grave, so she would have to hide the body instead. Closing her eyes and concentrating, she searched through the old Rhonda's neural pathways, checking the house for the optimal hiding place. She decided on the gardening shed outside, since it appeared that nobody else in Rhonda's family, Rhonda especially, had the slightest interest in gardening.

Being as careful as possible not to leave a trail of blood splotches behind her, Rhonda picked up the corpse, cradling it in both arms, and walked out into the backyard. She surprised herself with her own strength. The mother had at least thirty pounds on the girl, but Rhonda lifted her effortlessly.

Outside the air was cool and crisp, the scent of burned leaves and fertilizer carried on the occasional gusts of fall wind that pressed against her body. Rhonda did not like the breeze; it made her flesh prickle and stiffened her muscles. The cold sapped her newfound strength, causing her to feel as if she were moving underwater. She had to move as quickly as possible to avoid being spotted by any nosy neighbors up for a late-night snack or drink of water. Deborah now felt much heavier. The moment Rhonda left the warm, climate-controlled house, the old woman's weight seemed to triple.

The yard was small, with a green chain-link fence running around the perimeter and a large garden that took up most of the lawn. The fence was open on either side, allowing the neighbors (Dobsons to the west and Hanstrums to the east) a view of Deborah's garden, but blocked at the back by the Carlsons' tall wood-slat fence. The Carlsons were a young couple who had just moved to Long Island from upstate, and they enjoyed their privacy. Her mother's flowers were wilted, a result of seasonal change rather than neglect. There was a spot of freshly tilled ground toward the back where Deborah was attempting to grow some corn, but the stalks were all knocked over.

The shed sat against the western fence and had seen better days. Its pink paint had faded into a sickly pale flesh color, and the slats closest to the ground appeared to consist of more moss than wood. On the door to the small wooden shed hung a sign proclaiming, "Jesus Loves this Garden." Rhonda set the body down, opened the door with a loud creak and shoved Deborah inside. She put the body in upside down, with Deborah's feet resting against the rakes, hoes and other gardening equipment. Once she had positioned the body so it could not fall and kick open the door, Rhonda secured the shed and walked as briskly as she could back to the house, eager to warm up.

Once inside she turned the thermostat as high as it could go and took a look around the house. In the living room she lingered at the mantelpiece, inspecting the photographs and placards atop it. One picture showed the Kriegers: Deborah, looking smart in a neon green tracksuit, her balding/graying husband Harold and their two daughters. In the photo little Rachel, a year younger than her sister, still outshone Rhonda despite the fact that when the picture was taken, Rhonda was not looking quite as trashy as she had been lately. There were a few dusty medals from Rhonda's junior high track and field days, but the rest was a testament to Rachel's greatness. Pictures of Rachel playing the violin, trophies from Rachel's volleyball wins and four bumper stickers reading "My child is an honor student at IT High School." Looking through Rhonda's memories, the creature could only find feelings of anger and regret to associate with her sister's accolades. In a weird way, this family was both new and old to Rhonda. She had no particular affinity for them, but she was connected all the same, by Rhonda's memories and her knowledge.

In the glass of one of the picture frames she caught sight of her own reflection and realized she should clean herself up. In the bathroom she stripped naked, turned the shower knob as hot as it could go and stepped into the tub. She admired her body as she had in the park, using lavender soap and a washcloth to scrub off the tiny layer of moss that had started to form under her breasts and at the small of her back.

She turned off the water, stepped out of the shower and looked at herself dripping wet in the mirror. *Good as new*, she thought and smiled. She then turned her attention to the hole in her chest: it was still leaking green mucus as it scabbed up around the edges. Working her pinky finger around the edge of the hole, she clenched her chest muscles together to expel a small, wriggling seed. It bounced against the surface of the sink, and she caught it before it could fall into the drain.

Rhonda jumped in surprise as somebody opened the downstairs door. She glanced through the old Rhonda's memories and realized that it was only her father returning home from the night shift.

There was a knock at the bathroom door. "Who's in there? Deb?"

"No, it's Rhonda, Dad," the thing answered, looking into the mirror as she said her new name aloud. She had to suppress a giggle to properly form the sound.

"Why is it so hot in this house?" he yelled.

"I don't know. I didn't do anything."

"All right, then. Hurry up in there; I have to go to the bathroom," he grumbled from behind the door. "Don't know what you're doing up this late anyway..." His voice trailed off as he walked down the hallway into his room, dropping his work belt on the floor with a clatter. Rhonda picked up the seed from the corner of the sink with a wad of toilet paper and tucked it into her pants pocket, wrapped a towel around herself and grabbed her clothes as she left the bathroom.

"Where's your mother?" Harold asked from her parents' bedroom. He stood with his shirt off in the doorway, his potbelly covered with gray, wiry hairs.

"She's sleeping over at Aunt Mary-Kaye's. They had knitting club or something tonight." The lie slid easily out of Rhonda's mouth; she had composed it out of snippets of Old Rhonda's memories shortly after collapsing Deborah's skull. It was best to be prepared for exchanges like this.

"Oh, well, where's your sister?"

"Damned if I know." Rhonda shrugged.

"Jesus, you three girls can't stay still. Would it be a sin for the four people in this family to sleep under the same roof every once in a while?" Harold pried off his work boots while talking, taking his frustration out on the laces.

"I'm sure we will one of these nights, Dad. Don't you worry about her; she's a good girl." The thing was getting the hang of speaking like Rhonda, still Daddy's little girl after all her fuckups.

"Don't I know it," Harold said, but even he sounded unsure what exactly he meant by that.

"Just relax and go to bed. Since Mom probably won't be around, I'll cook your breakfast in the morning."

Harold looked a bit shocked at this last part, and Rhonda thought maybe she was pushing herself too far out of character with her dutiful daughter act. The big man stopped disrobing and looked the girl in the eyes. "That's real sweet, baby. Thank you. Now go to bed." He gave her a kiss on the top of the head and walked down the hallway to the bathroom.

"Good night," he said from down the hall.

"Good night, Dad," Rhonda said and peered out the window at the end of the hallway. It was starting to get light outside. She took the ball of toilet paper out of her jeans pocket and looked at the small black lump inside it. They were so cute at this age.

Chapter Five

Thursday

Billy had never once pressed the snooze button on his alarm. When he was up, he was up. The radio alarm blasted him awake at six thirty with equal parts static and music. He looked down at the dirty magazine still folded across his chest and put it back in the drawer, replacing the false bottom. He went to put on his socks and remembered the four black pills stashed inside one of his balled-up socks all the way at the back of the drawer.

Billy placed his hand on his bedroom door to make sure it was firmly closed. Then he crept back to the dresser to inspect the drugs. He took the Baggie out of the sock and held it up to the lamp next to his bed. No movement. Maybe he *was* crazy. There was a brief knock, the door opened and he dropped the bag.

"Hurry up, time's a-wasting," his mother called from the doorway, then shut the door again.

"Coming," Billy said. He hated having his mother drive him to school. They were a two-car household, but his father needed his car to drive to the train station in the mornings. It was either have his mother drive him or take the bus. While Billy was on the bus, Tom was not there to protect him from whispered insults and loneliness, so Billy opted for the safer but marginally more humiliating ride from his mother.

He walked down the carpeted stairs, through the dining room and into the kitchen, where his father stood propped against the refrigerator reading *The New York Times*. Even though *Newsday* was Long Island's local paper (written at a fourth grade reading level), his dad read the *Times*, not out of snobbish pretension, but out of habit. Billy's father had grown up in Manhattan.

"Good to see the Dems aren't even trying to run this year. Maybe next term," Billy's father said. He was looking at Billy but didn't intend to get into a lofty political discourse. Instead he rolled up the paper and gave Billy a smile and a light slap on the shoulder.

His mother was slouched over the stove working on some eggs, which was unusual because most of the time his dad handled the cooking. She did her best to keep the eggs in the pan in front her from having ruptured yolks, but as Billy glanced over her shoulder, it appeared that she was losing the battle.

It was nice to come downstairs and see the whole family gathered together. A lot of kids his age didn't get this chance, and Billy wasn't ungrateful. Billy never understood why many teens in similar situations felt the need to rebel. Kids who had parents who were still happily together wanted to yell and scream and say terrible things to the people who raised them. But Billy loved his parents just as they loved him. His father, Andy Rile, was a psychiatrist operating out of the city, and his mother, Gwen Rile, worked for Grumman Aerospace. Grumman was one of the leading providers of military and private airplanes, and they employed a high percentage of the competent people on Long Island.

"Shit," Gwen swore down at the frying pan, and Billy giggled. His parents cursed in front of him regularly, but it was very rare for him to do the same in front of them. Billy and his father took their seats at the kitchen's small table. They had a dining room, but it was used only when Andy and Gwen had adult guests. The couple hadn't made many friends since moving to the Island over fifteen years ago, so the dining room was rarely utilized. There was something about Andy and Gwen that native Islanders didn't take to, not that it seemed to bother them much.

Gwen slid the greasy eggs with popped yolks onto the plates in front of her husband and son. "That didn't turn out right. At all. Just use a lot of ketchup," she said, frowning, then walked to the fridge to toss the Heinz to Billy with a short underhand lob.

Andy cleared his throat, getting Billy's attention. "Not that it's going to be a problem, I'm sure, but I think your mom and I are leaving tonight instead of tomorrow morning," he said while salting his eggs. For the last few years nostalgia seemed to be taking its toll on Billy's parents, and they had begun taking semiregular weekend trips into Manhattan to visit their old college friends, all of whom had stuck it out in the city with various levels of success.

"Oh, I think I'll be okay," Billy said, pouring the watery part of the ketchup out onto his napkin before banging his fist against the side of the bottle and forming a crimson lake on the side of his plate.

"Just make sure that all the hookers come from a respectable joint and that you keep anyone who is vomiting off of their back. They can suffocate that way. That's how Bon Scott died."

Billy laughed uncomfortably. The joke would have been funny coming from Tom, but from his dad it just felt strange and dirty.

"Andy, cut it out. You love making our kid turn all kinds of colors, don't you?" Billy's mother rubbed his shoulders and gave him a kiss on top of the head. "Finish your toxic sludge quickly. We should hit the road soon."

Billy nodded and gobbled down his eggs. He loved his parents. He didn't care if that wasn't cool.

Lieutenant Todd Darl's head was throbbing. Last night he had run the license plate numbers on the van and positively identified the crispy Irish kid inside. He then paid a visit to the Connolly household, hat in hand, to tell Mrs. Connolly that poor Jake wasn't coming home. After that he had gone home and tied one on. Jim Beam and Coca-Cola. The Cokes were the kind in the glass bottles, which he bought at a Central Islip bodega on his way home from work. "Say what you will about the Mexicans," he would constantly tell the deputies, "but at least they make their sodas with real sugar instead of that high-fructose corn shit."

Once the little green bottles of soda were gone, he started drinking straight from the Jim. In his younger, rowdier drinking days, Darl used

42

to boast to his friends that he could remember everything, no matter how drunk he got. It was usually a blessing because it allowed Darl to hold himself responsible for any stupid shit he might do. Being cognizant of that made him less likely to slip up. Mornings like this, though, remembering was a pain in the ass.

He peeled himself off of the carpet a little before noon, once the sun had risen high enough in the sky to slice through the partially closed blinds into his apartment.

After Mrs. Connolly's sobs had begun to subside and she had poured him a cup of coffee, she had mentioned that Jake had been out with his girlfriend the night before. Darl's stomach churned when he thought about how there was only one body in the van. He was sad for the woman's loss, but petrified that the girl was still out there somewhere. Worst-case scenarios began to swirl in his head. Some serial-killer psycho with a gas can, a hard-on and an abducted twenty-something girl was just what he needed.

It was already getting late when he had left the Connolly residence, and against his better judgment he had gone home to his apartment and started pouring drinks instead of investigating the whereabouts of the girlfriend, Rhonda Krieger. He told himself that girls broke dates all the time, that the little pothead dirtbag had gotten a bit overzealous with his bong and had lit the shag carpeting of his van on fire. But he remembered the kid's fucked-up face and the chill that seeing his broken jaw line had first inspired. This was no simple fire.

Darl hated his job most days because, aside from the occasional burglary, nothing ever happened. Jake Connolly had helped him to realize that it was when the shit hit the Ram Van that the job really sucked.

Darl stood in his own apartment, one hand on his sore back rubbing a knot out of his old muscles, and stared at the walls of his television room/dining room/bedroom. The walls were mostly bare, but there were a few mementos tacked up. There were a couple of framed newspaper clippings ("Local Sheriff Foils Robbery" was his personal favorite headline, although the real story was much less exciting) and a movie poster. The poster was for the 1969 John Wayne/Rock Hudson film, *The Undefeated*. It wasn't even that great a movie, but Darl loved the poster. Two cowboys playing against type. He wondered whether Wayne knew about old Rock, that he was gay. Darl wondered how many people could figure it out without being told. Thinking about it just made him more depressed.

The knot in his back undone, Darl sucked in a big gulp of the apartment's stale air to try and fight off the impending hangover and began to shuffle through his laundry pile for a clean pair of underwear. It was time to pay a visit to the Krieger household. He reached for the top of the coatrack and took down *his* hat. The department issue was some cheapo brown felt job, so as soon as he could afford it, Darl had replaced his with a genuine-beaver Stetson. The New York suburbs were not the Wild West, but that didn't mean he had to walk around feeling like an asshole wearing a bargain-basement costume hat.

Hitching up his belt, he bowed his head and prayed silently. He was pleading with no specific god, praying that Rhonda had gotten home safe last night and would be there to answer the door when he came to call.

It was fourth period lunch by the time Tom arrived at school. Billy had already been slammed into two lockers and forced to answer which member of New Kids on the Block he would prefer to blow (he had finally settled on Donnie and then received two extra kidney punches for choosing poorly).

Billy was sitting alone at their usual lunch table when Tom and Darcy came over to sit down. Billy had been busy reading when the overpowering smell of Darcy's hair spray heralded the couple's arrival. He closed his book, *The Great Gatsby* for his advanced-placement English class, and looked around the lunchroom. From Billy's perspective it was sixty-something years after the first printing of Fitzgerald's story and Long Island was basically the same: the bigger an asshole you were, the more friends you had. At least that was his assessment thus far; he was only a few chapters into the book.

The cafeteria was filled with the usual suspects. It was a football-field-sized room with two-story ceilings and about fifty round tables. Roughly speaking, each table contained a clique. In some cases two or three tables were pushed together to hold the larger groups (the football team, wrestling squad, etc.). Along with the stereotypical "geek" and "jock" tables, there were even more specific subdivisions: there were tables with the goth kids who liked The Cure, the goth kids who *hated* The Cure, the stoners, the rich girls, the girls who pretended to be rich, the table of guys who joked about sex all the time but had yet to have it. It was as if a John Hughes film had exploded inside the room, coating the walls with hormones, poor decision-making skills and insecurity.

"Who pissed in your mom's face this morning? You look like the world's saddest plus-sized tampon." Tom laughed at his own doubleheader of lame jokes, but Billy was not in a laughing mood. Sometimes Tom ratcheted up his crudeness to a level where it was no longer appealing, even to another seventeen-year-old boy.

"Instead of working on those zingers all day, how about you come to school one of the periods that surrounds lunch every once and a while? How 'bout that?"

"Hey, watch it," Tom said, poking his finger out and adding some weight to his voice. Always the bully, even if that bully happened to be your best buddy.

"No, you watch it. First you make me pay to rent a movie we aren't even going to be able to enjoy, no offense Darcy." Billy looked over at her, but she wasn't listening anyway. "Then you have me blow twenty dollars on god-knows-what-the-fuck kind of shit. And then after I offer to hold on to those drugs, you don't show up until the cafeteria puts out the tater tots."

"Wait," Darcy said, suddenly interested. "What kind of drugs? You have a score?"

"Thanks for spoiling the surprise," Tom said to Billy and then turned to Darcy. "No, baby, *we* have a score," Tom said, ticking his finger between himself and Billy. His tone was almost seductive, dragging her in with his words. Darcy might be part fiend, but she was no junkie; she just liked to look cool and tough in front of Tom. That meant that she would smoke, snort, or otherwise ingest anything to get his attention, even if he wasn't partaking. "We have a score that's exclusive to good girls who bring their hot friends to video night."

"You're a bastard," Darcy said, which came out in a faintly Boston accent, dropping the "r" and with heavy emphasis on the As in "bastard". Billy would have found this funny were he not completely tired of it. The novelty was gone from Darcy's Brando-esque command of several of the world's most abrasive dialects.

"Yes, I am a bastard. That's the main reason you're attracted to me, sweetcheeks," Tom said as he brushed back her bangs and kissed her on the forehead. Billy hated himself for being so quickly won over by his friend's palpable coolness. "How about going up and getting me some lunch?"

"Fucker," she said and stood up, pushing the table's plastic chair across the polished stone floor. "French fries or tater tots?"

Tom raised his thick but manicured eyebrows into an expression that said, *You know.*

"Taters it is, then." Darcy walked off toward the lunch line. As she walked she spit her chewing gum into a nearby garbage can and picked at a hot-pink neon spandex wedgie with one dignified motion.

"Is it really worth not jerking off and not having to get your own tater tots? Is it really?" Billy's joke was brazen, landing on one of the duo's very few taboo subjects. Billy wasn't supposed to talk trash about Darcy, no matter how much she asked for it.

"Knock it off. She's all right," Tom said. "What's with all this mopey stuff? Everything is going to be fine. Because what I just did there, is I cemented a very special video night guest."

"I'll believe it when I see it."

"Well, you'll see it all right. You'll see both of them. You'll see them in three-fucking-D."

"You're really eloquent when you want to be. And I assume that's a joke about Rachel, so now we're even," Billy said and quickly realized how silly it sounded.

"Now we're even? You say that like she's your girlfriend or

something. Like you and her are on a first-name basis or, ya know, talk to each other at all."

Billy scowled into his lunch. There was an uncomfortable, wounded silence before Tom sighed. "Come on, enough of this soap opera shit. What's new? Movie-wise," Tom said. It was as close to a sincere apology that Billy figured he was ever going to get.

Billy fought against the desire to keep up his temper tantrum and gave a smirk. "Sequels, what else is new? I hear Freddy's getting a new one next year."

"Well, the last one was pretty good. It was no *Dream Warriors* though," Tom said.

The third *Nightmare on Elm Street* movie was the only time Billy had ever skipped class, and one of the best moviegoing experiences of his life. It was the South Shore Mall's theater policy not to allow kids in during school hours. The boys had some trouble, but not much. Tom walked up to the counter and asked for two tickets. The cashier working the box office started to say something about their ages and looked like he was getting ready to ask for their IDs when Tom growled. His friend had actually growled. Made a deep feral noise from the bottom of his lungs and narrowed his eyes to slits. Billy had never seen, or heard, anything like it. The little man handed over the tickets very quickly.

Scrambled eggs, bacon and a tall glass of orange juice sat neatly arranged on the dining room table. Rhonda had started whisking the scrambled eggs when she heard her "father" turn off the water in the bathroom. Harold worked the night shift, so his breakfasts weren't usually eaten until Rachel and his wife had already left the house for the day. This morning, while Rhonda was taking a second hot shower, her sister must have come in to grab her schoolbooks, because she hadn't come home last night and wasn't around this morning. Rhonda would have heard her come in, as she was in her room, awake and listening.

Rhonda no longer needed to sleep. After talking with Harold and exploring the artifacts of Rhonda's past life (plaid button-down shirts in the dresser, black panties on the floor, Ozzy poster on the wall, an ashtray hidden under her bed and a stack of heavy metal CDs, under which sat U2's *Joshua Tree*, an album that Rhonda would have defended to her death) Rhonda had laid down on her bed to relax and plan. Lying there, watching the dawn break through her bedroom window, she would occasionally dip into the girl's memories and better acquaint herself with the family's complicated dynamics. Rachel rarely talked to her sister anymore, not since Rhonda had started dating Jake, smoking and listening to music in his van. Rachel claimed that Rhonda was becoming a "dirtbag", but before she had died alone out there in the woods, Rhonda had had suspicions that her sister was jealous.

Rhonda cooked the eggs until they were light and fluffy, allowed them to cool, and then dropped in a handful of small black seeds. She had become more comfortable in her host body and was able to produce an average of two pellets an hour. Grabbing the imitation Hummel salt and pepper shakers (a sad-looking little boy and girl holding black and white umbrellas), she garnished the dish and placed it on the table just as Harold entered the small dining room/kitchen.

"Will you look at this spread?" Harold said, clipping his suspenders down over his sleeveless undershirt. Harold was getting old and his hair was getting lighter, his voice gravellier and his belly more pronounced, but to the old Rhonda he was still a strong, proud, loving man. He had never once seemed unappreciative and never gave the slightest hint that he was disappointed with his oldest daughter, who had no job and minimal education. "Thank you, darling," he said and gave her a kiss on the cheek. He mussed her hair, then plopped himself down at his usual spot at the table.

Harold bowed his head in the briefest of prayers and dug into his meal, going for the bacon first. Rhonda had burned it to a cinder, just the way he liked it. Next he picked up a forkful of eggs, put it to his lips and stopped. "What did I do to deserve such a nice breakfast?"

"You..." Rhonda paused for a second, searching for words that sounded believable yet remained sincere. "You earned it." Rhonda held the spatula over the sink, rinsing it and placing it on the drying rack. "How is it?"

"It's great, sugar," Harold said after swallowing a mouthful of eggs. "I don't want to seem ungrateful, but do we have any instant coffee? I'm still beat."

"Of course." Rhonda scanned her memories, but soon realized that her former self had never known where her mother kept the Taster's Choice. The old Rhonda never would have helped with breakfast, and thus had no idea where to find the coffee. She began opening cabinets.

"What are these little black things? They're delicious." Harold audibly crunched down on a seed and sent blackish-green juice flying out of the corner of his mouth. Rhonda winced at the sound. The destruction of some of her children was inevitable, but he would not crush all of them.

Sweat stippled her father's skin, rolling down his scalp out of his receding hairline. He dabbed himself with his napkin and continued to eat.

"They're pimentos," she said as she laid her hands on the jar of coffee. "Found it." In the small kitchen, Rhonda's long arms and new dexterity allowed her to fill the teapot and turn on one of the stove's burners at the same time.

"I work hard at that place," Harold said, taking another mouthful of eggs. Her father worked as a mechanic and supervisor at the town's water treatment plant. Since he handled the night shift, not only was he understaffed, but he also had to double as the night watchman when local kids decided to try to piss in the reservoir tanks. "And I know your mother works hard too, raising you kids," he paused for effect, "and digging in the dirt." He giggled to himself; a fit of nostalgic indulgence was on him now and he would keep speaking for his own enjoyment. "But it makes it all worthwhile when I get to come home to my little girls. Well, one of them at least."

"Oh, I'm sure Rachel was just at a friend's studying or whatever," Rhonda said.

"Or 'whatever', what an odd new phrase. Nah, I'm just...I know she's a good girl," Harold said as he began to cough.

He reached for the juice, downing the small jelly-jar glass in two gulps. Unsuccessfully, he tried to clear his throat and pointed at the cup, signaling to Rhonda for a refill. By the time the teakettle started to whistle, a lump had begun to form in Harold's throat. Rhonda turned off the burner. The sound petered out and finally stopped as her father banged his fists on the table and started to convulse. Blood streamed from both corners of his mouth and a darker stream trickled steadily from his nose.

Tears mingled with blood as he wordlessly begged for his daughter to help him. It wasn't only his neck that had swollen; his already prominent belly was beginning to grow. Rhonda showed no malice. She remained impartial and did not smile, even though a dark, deep part of her wanted to.

Watching this same transformation just a day earlier, Rhonda had been sobbing, screaming and breaking down. Now, she merely watched as Harold bucked and swelled. His suspenders pushed farther apart and his shirt ripped down the center. He was dead now: the rapid expansion of the seeds had both crushed and skewered his internal organs. Even if he had only swallowed one or two seeds, his heart and lungs would have been punctured by the formation of the children's quills. Three or four seemed more likely. It appeared as if his torso was quite crowded.

Out of his mouth crawled the first infant, its spindly legs and spines glistening in the noontime sun that came through the kitchen window. It cracked Harold's jaws apart and fell onto the table, tripping on the plate of mostly-eaten eggs and clattering to the floor.

Rhonda gave a tiny giggle at its antics and it scuttled clumsily over to her, its many legs slipping and making clattering sounds on the kitchen's linoleum tiling. Its legs were rigid enough to support its weight, but they still carried the slight greenish translucence of insect larvae. The young creature's skeleton would darken into a dark brown and harden in a minute or two.

Two other creatures had finally found their way out of Harold's body through the hole in his head. They jumped out of his mouth with ease. Each one plopped to the table, their evacuation causing the body's broken lower jaw to bounce against Harold's neck like a grotesque, miniature diving board.

They stood before her, shaking themselves dry and raising the flaps below their spikes to test the kitchen air around them. The middle one made an alarmed series of noises and expelled its stinger when it heard the water heater click on in the basement directly below. Rhonda put her hand out and coughed as she produced a similar appendage from her own mouth. The changes had not fully taken over her physical form yet, but she was still able to communicate. She generated a few calming clicks to tell her children that everything was going to be fine.

Rachel took her seat at her sixth period chemistry lab table and contemplated the various definitions of the word "friends". As far as the public was concerned, Rachel Krieger and Darcy Roberts were good friends. In addition to being lab partners, they went to the same parties and talked on the telephone, and their mothers attended the same knitting circles and happy hours.

Rachel thought otherwise, but everyone at school *knew* that Rachel and Darcy were friends, possibly even best friends.

Darcy was vain, manipulative of other girls, vulgar, too eager to mess around with drugs, and too eager to mess around with boys. In summation, to put it mildly: Darcy was an asshole. At least to everyone but Rachel. To Rachel she was sweet, protective and only a little condescending. Why then did Rachel feel so terrible that everyone at Islip Terrace High lumped them together?

Rachel knew that the two friends had nothing in common. Darcy preferred her men to be tall, future ex-felons while Rachel *tried* to date nice boys. Rachel liked to listen to music for which the singers wrote their own material, while Darcy preferred that her idols didn't even sing their own songs. It wasn't that Darcy wasn't popular; she was. Invited to the best parties, hit on by the cutest boys and capable of pulling off the craziest of fashions, Darcy was the All-American girl for the modern age. She was Madonna, without the singing. An acceptably promiscuous gal with a fiery attitude and outspoken demeanor, who demanded your camaraderie, if not your respect. But just because everyone in America had heard of Madonna, it didn't mean that they were in the fan club.

The main reason Rachel felt she was saddled with the dubious honor of being Darcy's "go-to girl" was Rachel's physiology. She was the redheaded girl with big breasts and nice skin. In the excruciatingly long TV miniseries that was high school, how could she be cast as anything but the "popular bitchy girl's best friend?" People considered her "the quiet one" when in actuality she was an accomplished conversationalist. She only seemed shy and reserved when placed next to Darcy, who, when she had her volume cranked up, was a boombox in a halter top.

Puberty had hit Rachel late, but fast. It had seemed to fill out her chest overnight. In elementary school you didn't need to impress anyone—most girls were in the same large group of friends. Unless you were the one unlucky outcast who was chubby or smelled funny, in which case nobody could help you.

When you reached middle school, you began to need cultural cachet if you were going to make it. Rachel had ample cultural cachet because the moment she filled out, both the boys and girls took notice. The girls didn't notice in a sexual sense, but in what Rachel felt was a dirtier way: her breasts were their fortune. By having her on their side, girls would have an "in" with the boys, without having to suffer the boys' constant attention. In Sunday school Rachel had learned all about why someone would want to keep a "fatted calf" around, and in middle school she was it.

At the end of the scuffle to see who could claim Rachel as a best friend, Darcy Roberts stood victorious. A younger, stupider Rachel had been showered with sleepover invitations, friendship bracelets and the head of the table at bowling alley birthday parties, the kind where you received a pin with your name painted on it. Somewhere along the road to high school, she had sold her soul to Darcy and the two had become inextricably linked.

Rachel wiggled uncomfortably on her lab stool as Darcy stepped into the classroom and waved emphatically in her direction. Darcy skipped over to the table and half-whispered, half-screamed, "I hope you don't have anything planned for tomorrow night, because boy do I have a plan for us!"

Without hearing what it was, Rachel already knew that she didn't want to do it.

Chapter Six

Darl was tired of listening to the radio. Over the police band came the *second* request for a *second* ambulance for a *second* person choking on his food. This time the call came from Berg's Pizza on Main Street. He clicked off the radio and decided to talk to himself instead. "Some people on this rock are too dumb to live."

Darl himself was not a dumb man, and because he was not dumb he also knew that the Island wasn't technically a "rock". It was actually a clump of sediment that had formed a landmass because it was located at the precise place where a glacier had begun to recede millions of years ago. The Island was comprised of all the rocks and debris that the glacier had accumulated on its way down from the Arctic. A junk pile. A glacial turd. That's all it was. Combining this factual tidbit with his real-world experience, Todd Darl had come to this conclusion: Long Island was a junk pile with the world's capital city at one end, some nice rich-people houses on the other, and in the middle a whole mess of morons who couldn't chew their calzones properly.

He left one hand on the wheel and began to open and close the clasps on his belt with the other, starting all the way on his left with his handcuffs and ending with his gun holster on the right. Darl rarely had occasion to use the cuffs and his gun had remained holstered for a good six years, but undoing and redoing the metal snaps on his belt had become an unconscious habit. If questioned on the matter, Darl would have equated it with the way ball players and compulsive gamblers had their little superstitious tics. Why take only cold showers during the playoffs? Why stay at a slot machine when it's "hot", even when you know that the odds aren't changing? It's just something that people do.

Ominous dreams had started the superstition. During his first few years on the force, Darl had had the recurring nightmare that he needed to use his weapon but was unable to pull it out of his belt. Either the clasp had rusted shut or been glued in place. His adversary (the "perp") would change every night. At times it would be a random civilian; sometimes it would be a character from a movie he'd seen as a kid. Other times it would be a snarling monster, a malformed creature who laughed as it overpowered the defenseless deputy. The dreams had lessened with his time on the job, but the ritual of checking the clasps stayed with him.

Despite his superstitions, Darl wasn't much for religion. It might have gotten him struck by lightning, growing up in a Catholic household like he did, but he didn't give a damn. Still, occasionally he would have a lapse in his atheism, and driving to question Rhonda Krieger was one of those times. He drove and prayed.

Please let her be home. Jake went to the park without her. They had had a fight earlier in the week. Please don't let that fucking girl be kidnapped. Amen. Swearing was probably against the rules, but if God didn't like it, He knew where to find him.

Darl pulled up into the Kriegers' driveway and cut the engine. As he opened the car door, he began to doubt himself. By this time the sheriff's office had probably handed the case off to the police department, which was probably in the process of trying to get a higher government office involved. The Suffolk PD was well paid and professional, but whatever had happened to that boy was out of their league. Why was he troubling himself with this? It wasn't his problem anymore. The police might have even been here already this morning. Darl could not come up with a reasonable answer for his actions, but stepped out of the car anyway.

The lawns were well kept all the way down the block, nary a fallen leaf in sight, something Darl liked to take note of when entering a new neighborhood. Lawn-work was both his cruel master and secret lover: he grumbled about having to do it for the small lawn in front of his apartment door, but detested when his neighbors shirked their own responsibility. A well-kempt block put him in a good mood.

The street was quiet, no traffic and no one outside. The residents were either still at work, in school or watching daytime television. Darl walked up the three front steps, took a deep breath and knocked. While he waited he noticed the placard above the doorbell that read "Welcome" and the uncarved pumpkin on the top stair. It was his first reminder that Halloween was in a few weeks, as well as the fact that he should stock up on cleaning supplies for the front door.

After a few moments passed without an answer, he rang the bell. It was one of those newer ones with speakers that sounded like church bells. That noise probably got very old, very fast. Halfway through the ringing he heard something behind the door. A kind of scratching, then a shuffle. "Who is it?" The voice was female. A shadow formed behind the door's frosted window.

"Suffolk County Sheriff's Department, ma'am. May I have a minute of your time?" There was some more shuffling; the woman must have been pushing an especially rambunctious dog out of the way. Darl could hear it jumping up on the door, probably destroying the paint with its nails.

"May I ask what this is concerning?" the voice said. There were some clicking noises that Darl didn't recognize, like a combination of a loud inhale and a teletype machine. The dog stopped jumping and the sound of its paws got fainter and fainter as it click-clacked away from the door.

"I think you would rather speak to me face-to-face," Darl said. "Ma'am, is everything all right?" The door opened to reveal a pale girl in her late teens. She wore an old, ripped Joan Jett T-shirt and pajama bottoms. Her eyes looked heavy, as if she had just woken up after quite a bender. She was pretty though, and alive. Darl's excitement got the better of him and overrode protocol.

"Are you Rhonda Krieger?" he asked, pushing the words out quickly, sure of the answer. Jake Connolly's mother had said that the Kriegers had two daughters, a younger redhead named Rachel and an older brunette, Rhonda. The girl in front of him had tossed long hair so dark that it was almost black.

"Yes? What's the problem, Officer?" she asked. She still had not opened the door all the way and was blocking the entrance to the house with her body.

"Thank Christ...excuse me, I'm sorry. I'm just happy to see you're all right."

"Why wouldn't I be? What's happened, Officer—"

"Darl. Lieutenant Todd Darl. May I come in, Miss Krieger? I have some news you may want to sit down for."

"One second, please," she said and closed the door in his face. Her voice was strange; it didn't carry the aloofness of most young girls of her generation, but there was no weight to it either, just a detached, pitch-free tone. Behind the opaque glass of the door he heard movement as she walked down the hallway. She was either getting dressed or locking up the dogs. If he were not still riding on the high of finding the girl alive and relatively well, he would have said that something was wrong here, something about the way she had body-blocked him, and her tone. As it was he just shrugged, thankful that he was a cat person.

At Islip Terrace High School, Rachel's ninth-period classes ended fifteen minutes early to allow time for a school-wide announcement. The bulletin was delivered in Assistant Principal Dekker's nonthreatening monotone. "Students, faculty and staff. It is with a heavy heart that I inform you that former student and friend-to-everyone Jake Connolly has passed away. There are no further details at this time, but we must keep his family and friends in our prayers tonight. Jake was a fine athlete, a scholar and a constant reminder of the benefits of hard work and perseverance. He will be missed. Thank you."

There was stunned silence in the classroom. Mrs. Rutherford, Rachel's English teacher, held her hand up to her mouth in a motion that indicated a sadness bordering on nausea. If Mrs. Rutherford had ever had Jake in class, she was probably faking her distress. Rachel felt an empty semidisbelief, but traded it for genuine concern when she shook off her fog and realized that Rhonda must be devastated. She had never liked Jake—nobody had, really—but she loved her sister.

Ronny Emmerick turned around in his seat and motioned to another boy. "Friend to everyone," Ronny whispered with a roll of his eyes. The other boy mouthed "Bullshit" in response.

As inappropriate as the two boys were being, they were right. That wasn't Jake Connolly at all. Still, suddenly Rachel had a strong desire to see her sister, something she hadn't felt in years.

Rhonda returned to the door a minute later and was greeted with a question from the old sheriff. "Locking up Rover in the backyard?" he asked, leaning on the doorframe.

She blinked a few times, stalling. "Yes. We have a dog." It took Rhonda a few panicked fractions of a second to cross-reference the old Rhonda's memories and deduce that "Rover" was a common name for a pet dog. It was a close call. It was getting increasingly difficult to form connections in a brain that was rapidly being repurposed to keep up with her changing body. Synaptic tissue was decomposing and reforming, and the connections between her neurons were dulled before they could be strengthened into their final, new shape.

Rhonda stepped away from the door and pointed the way to the living room, trying to block Officer Darl's view of the hallway. As they entered the living room, she smiled and motioned for him to sit on the far end of the couch. That way, the kitchen would be out of his field of vision.

"I understand that you and Jake Connolly were, are...um, romantically involved. Is that correct?" Darl stammered. It was obvious that the old man was uncomfortable. He held his hat in his hands and looked as though he was trying his hardest not to fan himself. The house was filled with a balmy, soothing warmth after Rhonda had left the heat on all night. Beads of sweat rolled down his neck and mingled with the gray chest hair that nested above his undone top button.

"Yes, he's my boyfriend. Has something happened?" she asked. She was in a hurry, not giving the performance the nuance it deserved;

she just wanted this man out of her house. He was causing trouble and she hadn't even cleaned up Harold's remains yet, never mind the blood all over the kitchen.

"Jake's dead, Rhonda. I'm sorry." There was a loud thump in the hallway closet on the other side of the living room wall. Rhonda watched anxiously as the old man pretended not to hear it. His mustache remained stiff as he tried to maintain his tone of sincerity and give Rhonda a moment to process Jake's tragedy.

"My God, how did it happen?" she asked, even though she knew the answer.

"We don't exactly know yet. I came over here to make sure you were okay and to see if you could tell us anything," the officer said, having regained his composure. "I know this is a difficult time, but your cooperation is of the utmost importance."

Rhonda swallowed with deliberate force, trying to conjure an image of grief. "I understand," she said.

"Thank you. I don't mean to pry, miss, but if you could just tell me where you were last night so I can more fully form a picture of Jake's last hours."

"Well, we had gone to the movies, but we've been hot and cold all week, so I asked him to take me home afterward. I went to bed as soon as I got home and then woke up to cook my father breakfast. He works a late shift."

"I see. Now, could you tell me if Jake had any enemies, anyone who would want to hurt him?"

"None that I know of. He was a nice boy, Officer."

"I'm sure he was." Darl paused before his next question. He dropped the decorum he had possessed earlier and began to fan himself with his hat. "Rhonda, is it hot in here or am I just having a bad day as an old man?"

"No, it's quite warm. The thermostat's broken. I'm sorry." She looked down at her hands and then back at Darl.

"Where was I?" Darl sucked a gulp of air through the space between his two front teeth, exhaled through partly closed lips and continued. "I'm not looking to get you into trouble, but I need to know: was Jake involved with drugs? More specifically, was he selling drugs?"

"He was an occasional user; we all are. But my boyfriend was no drug dealer."

"Please, it's just procedure, no offense intended, miss." Darl took a deep breath through his nose, his nostrils expanding. His pores looked like pie plates to Rhonda. She took in every detail, every gesture the old man made, trying to discern how much of a threat he posed. She needed to know how much he knew, whether Jake's remains had been completely destroyed. Her set-it-and-forget-it method of disposal had been a mistake; if anything about Jake's corpse looked too strange, it could lead to trouble. Trouble not just for her, but trouble for the plan as a whole. Trouble for all involved, not just those in this sector.

"I don't mean to be rude, but is something wrong in the kitchen? I smell, hmmm, I smell something off. Meat maybe?" Officer Darl stood, touching his fingertips to the ends of his belt buckle. "You don't want to leave anything out in this heat. It'll go rancid."

There was more banging in the hallway closet and Rhonda jumped up from her seat. "That's just the dirty dishes from breakfast. Sorry the house is such a mess. As you can imagine, I wasn't expecting company."

"Well, I'm sorry for not calling first," he said, but his voice was distracted. The policeman's gaze was not meeting her own. Something in the doorway to the kitchen had caught his attention, and he took a step farther.

She shifted past him and no longer tried to stop his progress into the kitchen. Instead she doubled back into the hallway and wrapped her hand around the doorknob to the closet. It was time to release the hounds.

"Wow, he's really dead," Billy said. He and Tom were just outside of the high school, beginning their walk home.

"You are correct, sir," Tom replied, in a voice that was not mocking, but confused and deflated. Billy had never seen Tom openly sad, but during difficult times Billy had seen him become like he was now, as if someone had turned off his switch. He was still Tom, but he was too preoccupied with his own thoughts to have much of a personality. It was as if someone had tipped Tom's head to the side and poured out everything that made him unique. Jake's death would not weigh on Tom for long, but a few years ago he had been like this for weeks following the death of his aunt Trudy. Tom had been helping his uncle more and more with the store after that, but the work didn't take his mind off of things.

"I never really knew him. You did, though, right?" Billy made a habit of only asking questions that he knew the answer to. It was a tactic that carried over from the classroom to his social life.

"Yeah. He was a pretty nice guy. Bought some beer for me a few weeks ago. I wasn't good friends with him or anything; he was just nice to me. A lot of those older guys are real pricks, but he tried not to be, ya know?"

"Yeah." Billy didn't know what to say to his friend, so he decided on silence. In the mornings he got a ride with his mother, but in the afternoons he took the scenic route home. It was a twenty-minute walk if you hurried, but Billy didn't mind. The walk afforded him some personal time with Tom, who lived ten minutes from the school. The excess alone-time was also precious physical exercise, since Billy didn't get much activity outside of gym class. That was the excuse he gave himself for the extra walking, at least, but deep down he also knew that the extra travel time coincided exactly with how long it took Rachel to be done with her student council meeting. The two friends walked in silence for a couple blocks before the next words were spoken.

"If I were going to bet which one of those idiots would bite the bullet first, I would have bet Reggie Kline. Couldn't you just see that loony fucker flipping his shitty Corvette?"

With that joke Tom was back to his normal self. Billy laughed. The boys meant no disrespect to the dead, but depression just wasn't a good look on them.

The duo spent the rest of the walk to Tom's house hypothesizing grisly deaths for the burnouts who comprised the graduating class of 1986.

When they reached Tom's rusted chain-link fence, Tom changed the subject. "Hey, since your parents are leaving, do you think that I could come hang out tonight?"

"No problem," Billy said, and tried not to get caught staring at Tom's small, battered house.

The tiles of the kitchen floor must have been old or shoddily installed because the blood had flowed into large puddles and stayed there, nudging the thin vinyl tiles even further out of alignment. The bubbles formed small crimson pools that were now congealing in the early afternoon sun. Darl moved closer to the room, feeling his heartbeat inside of his ears. There was a man sitting at the table with his mouth stretched and contorted into the same inhuman expression that the Connolly boy had been wearing. The faces made the corpses look like they had died mid-yawn. Grotesque, toothless yawns. Or as if the victim's last moments had been so ghastly that they had screamed too hard and ripped the corners of their mouths apart in the process.

Darl stood in the doorway between the living room and kitchen, immobilized by shock. He was about to retch with disgust when he realized that the girl had to have been involved in this mess. With the speed of an officer ten years younger, he turned his back on the kitchen and instinctively put his hand to his holster. Sharp arthritic needles shot up his sides and back, his body's painful reminder that he was no longer a young man and could not move that quickly without paying the pain-piper.

He squinted through the pain and started into the living room, ready to confront Rhonda, but the girl had disappeared.

"Come on out," Darl yelled toward the hallway on the other side of the room. "We need to discuss this." *Understatement*, he thought as he began to cross the room with his hand still on his weapon.

Reaching the couch, he paused and listened. A hallway door was flung open, followed closely by the same clicking sounds he'd overheard while waiting for Rhonda to answer the door.

Misinterpreting the sounds as an attempt to escape, he started to deliver a warning to Rhonda before the two creatures burst through the doorway. "Don't run—" was all he could muster before he was struck silent. The two animals spilled around the corner, tripping over each other to get at him. Their small, jagged mouths clicked like wind-up chattering teeth, but the sound was less intimidating than their pointed, gore-streaked bodies. Darl stumbled backward over the glass end table set up next to the recliner, knocking a framed photo of Rhonda to the floor. The table fell, causing a domino effect and taking out a stand-up lamp in the corner, the room's only source of light. Luckily for Darl, the table was cushioned by the living room carpet and didn't shatter.

Body wrenched control away from brain. Years of muscle memory stood front and center as Darl sat up from the floor, drew his gun and fired all in one fluid motion. Between the dim light sneaking through the curtains and the frenzy of activity, he couldn't see if the shot was a kill, but he was encouraged by the scream of an injured animal. His eyes began to adjust at the very moment that one of the creatures lashed out with a long, sharp appendage. Rolling to the side, Darl caught the blow with his shoulder rather than in his chest, where the creature had been aiming.

Todd Darl had never been seriously injured in the line of duty, but there had been one instance where he had came into contact with "gang violence". A few years ago he had been exiting his local 7-Eleven, hot dog in hand, when he saw a junior high school kid waving a switchblade around on the corner. As he approached he listened to the crap the young boy was spewing to his larger friend. "In LA there aren't punk posers like there are on this fucking island. Those motherfuckers will cut you like that." The kid pushed the knife in front of his friend's nose and flicked it away to emphasize the word "that". A stubby white kid in an AC/DC shirt was no cause for alarm, even if he was carrying a knife. Darl walked over and put his hand on the boy's shoulder, but he must have surprised the boy, who spun around and left Darl with a scar on his right bicep. It had hurt like hell. He hadn't dropped the hot dog, though.

The pain from that knife was nothing compared to what he felt from the edge of the tentacle.

Darl let out a yelp. Gritting his teeth for strength, he lashed out and spun the thing around with a kick of his boot. It swiveled, dazed briefly, before trying to attack once more with renewed ferocity. Darl dug his elbows into the carpet to gain more leverage and kicked again. He caught the creature right in its smooth, spineless underbelly. High school football was several decades in the rearview, but old number seven could still score a field goal. The thing flew a short distance, crashing into the doorframe with a satisfying crunch and a pitiful squeal. His howling joints numbed by adrenaline, Darl propped himself to his knees. As he stood, he leveled the 9mm in front of him.

His eyes adjusted and he attempted to regain "situational awareness". The room was a mess of his own bloody footprints, broken lightbulbs and overturned furniture that was speckled with a blackish-green slime that he assumed came from the animals, or aliens or whateverthefuck they were. He now saw that his first shot had taken two of the six legs off of one of the creatures. It floundered, screeched and clicked as it tried to raise itself off the living room carpet. Darl assessed that its four remaining legs were not up to the task: *target incapacitated.* The critter that he'd kicked was floundering on its side, trying desperately to right itself, but its large bristles were stuck in the carpeting. Darl aimed the 9mm at the wounded creature. A metallic clang smacked the gun out of his hand in a flash of movement so quick he could barely see it. The third creature must've flanked him, entering the living room from the kitchen behind him. It stood a few feet away, lifting its front legs in challenge, waving around a long tentacle that extended from its mouth. The six-inch blade on the end of its tentacle bobbed up and down in the air, dripping blood on the carpet. Darl dove away from the clacking beast and was looking to retrieve his gun when he noticed that the blade had not just knocked away the gun. It had mutilated his hand.

He looked down at the stubs of his middle and ring fingers. The two fingers were severed completely while his pinky held on by a thin strip of flesh. The clean, round wounds produced surprisingly little blood, but he put them under his armpit and squeezed anyway. The blood would come soon enough, and he would have to stop the flow if he wanted to make it out of this house alive. He felt the room around him bubble and collapse. Darl suspected that this was the light-headed precursor to fainting. He fought against slipping into shock, shaking his head and biting his cheek. The wound on his shoulder continued to burn like dry ice, but there was oddly no sensation in his mutilated hand.

"Fight" was out of the question, so "flight" it was. If he could get to the street, someone would notice a bloody law enforcer being pursued by two octopi-cactus monsters.

Darl kicked the first injured, legless creature into the one that had finally freed itself from the carpeting. They collided, spoke some angry clacks and tangled themselves up further. Darl tried to ignore the little bastard that had taken his fingers and concentrated on escape. If it could get him before he could reach the door, it would.

Darl started to allow himself a small puff of hope when his hand touched the doorknob, but it was destroyed by the reappearance of Rhonda. One of her hands clenched down on his arm, just below the gash on his shoulder. Digging her nails into his tan uniform, she slammed her other hand down, keeping the door flush to its frame.

"Officer, we need to discuss what you've just witnessed," she said calmly into his ear. She controlled his two hundred pounds easily with her hundred. When she spun him around to face her, he could see that she was smiling. It was a wide, shit-sucking, "sell you toothpaste" smile.

"Fuck you, girly," Darl said, attempting to muster defiance despite the unbearable pain. He was beginning to sweat through his uniform, and with each drop that entered his wounds he was given a fresh, painful reminder of how bleak the situation had become. The stubs of his fingers came alive as the sweat from his armpit met his hand.

"It may be the other way around at first," Rhonda said. Below her coy Mona Lisa expression, something abnormal began to percolate in her throat. The skin there shivered and stretched.

Darl looked back into the living room; the two creatures had regained their faculties and stood in the doorway, clicking softly.

Rhonda never took her attention from Darl but gave the critters a few sounds in response, her neck vibrating wildly as she did.

"That's pretty good, but how's your Spanish?" Darl asked, but the joke just made him even more aware of his impending doom and he let out a single sob. The girl did not respond, just continued making a low choking sound. His eyes darted around the hallway, looking for a way out of this nightmare. She had his arms tight: knocking her down was his only option.

With all of his remaining strength, he lifted one leg behind him and kicked off the door. Rhonda was knocked back, but not down. She braced herself against the hallway wall. *I'm going to be killed by a teenage psycho with a hairball.*

Then it happened: her mouth opened and his world fell apart.

Her tongue split at the tip and then parted. There was little blood, but what little there was had turned inhumanly dark, a sickly brown color. The halves of the tongue pushed to the sides of her mouth. The bifurcating of the tongue heralded the appearance of a new appendage, which slithered from the back of her throat out between the newly formed, bloody pink flaps.

Her throat constricted behind this unnatural structure, her uvula lifted up by what looked like something trying to claw its way free from her esophagus. Sharp and skinny at the end, but bulbous toward the base, the glistening spike pushed out until it tore at the bottom of Rhonda's jaw.

It stretched a full foot beyond the girl's teeth. It was slimy and dripping like a long brown-green banana slug, but rippling and muscular under the thin membrane of its glistening outer skin. The needle at the end of Rhonda's new tongue dripped a clear liquid and then split again into a beak. Darl pissed himself a second before the beak burrowed five inches deep into the meat between his neck and shoulder.

"Hi, Mom," Billy yelled as he burst through the front door and ran up to his room, taking the stairs two at a time. It sounded like she asked "where's the fire" from downstairs, but he couldn't be sure—not that he much cared.

He threw his books down on the bed, then ran to the window and parted the blinds with two fingers. He could see Rachel turn the corner and start down the street toward her house. She walked alone, shouldering her Jansport book bag and large neon-pink purse. She had once spilled the contents of that book bag in the hallway at school, and Billy had been lucky enough to be nearby to help her clean it up. As she zipped up the bag she had said, "Thanks, Billy." No matter what Tom said, she *did* know that Billy existed.

Billy's eyes were good enough to see the puzzled, concerned look that blossomed on Rachel's face when she noticed the sheriff's department car parked in front of her house. *It's there for Jake*, Billy thought. *I wonder how he died.*

Rachel walked up to the door, but it swung open before she could even touch the knob.

Chapter Seven

Rhonda walked downstairs, pulling a new shirt down over her head as she did so. The last one was soaked in Darl's blood. When she reached the living room, she silently observed him for a moment.

Darl paced circles around the room. His marching had left an oval of crusty footprints in his own blood. Most of the blood ran down from the hole in his neck, soaking his shirt and dribbling down his pant leg. He paused at the shuttered living room window.

"Your sister is home," he said, clenching his teeth, looking like he had a serious case of lockjaw. The old man was resisting the change. Not successfully, but he was giving quite a try. Rhonda was impressed that one person could offer this much trouble.

"Thank you, dear," Rhonda said. She chattered to the two uninjured children, telling them to drag their wounded brother out of sight, farther into the room. She opened the door halfway just as Rachel reached it.

"They told us at school. I'm so sorry, Rhonda." Rachel put her hand on her sister's shoulder and tried to walk in, but her sister stood firm.

"Please, don't come in," Rhonda said, beginning to cry. It took a moment of cerebral exploration before the thing was able to streak Rhonda's face with tears. She was careful not to cry too much, but enough to look genuine. "The cop is still here. I... I'd like to talk to him some more. Alone."

"Is Mom home?"

"She's at Aunt Mary-Kaye's. I asked her for some privacy." Rhonda answered the question quickly, surprising herself by keeping to the same alibi. Consistency didn't matter now that Harold was dead.

"I understand. Is there anything I can do, something I can get you?" Rachel tried leaning on the door to push it open further. "Just let me run up to my room for a quick sec."

"No, you can't," Rhonda said in another attempt to keep the girl out, but then decided to let her in: the more the merrier. Turning her would be another strain on her not-yet-complete body, but so be it.

The moment she made that decision, Darcy Roberts drove up in front of the Krieger household in her father's car, radio blasting, and gave the horn two quick taps.

Darcy's radio was so loud that Billy could tell what song was playing from inside his second-floor bedroom. It was the upbeat second half of "Scenes from an Italian Restaurant."

Billy Joel was the patron saint of Long Island and every radio station served as his temple. Those bastards in New Jersey got The Boss, so the Island was stuck with the Piano Man.

Rachel took her hand off of her sister's shoulder. She then surprised Billy (and by the looks of it, Rhonda too) when she popped up on her toes and gave her older sister a kiss on the forehead before throwing her bag back over her shoulder and running to Darcy's passenger-side window. The two girls spoke for a moment, Darcy never lowering the volume on the radio, and Rachel got in.

The car pulled away, leaving Rhonda blocking the doorway. It was hard to pick out the details at this distance, but Rhonda looked terrible.

Was leaving Rhonda alone the best idea? Sure, the policeman was there right now, but if she went over to Darcy's for dinner, then Rhonda might be alone for a while before Mom got home. Would she do anything? Anything suicidal? Not likely. That was the kind of thing that other girls did, girls that the hard-as-nails Rhonda Krieger would not associate with. Besides, her father might be there to look after her. Rachel had forgotten to ask about him. He might have taken the night off, given the circumstances.

In the driver's seat Darcy bent over, fishing for something under the cushion, not looking at the road. Rachel was about to say something but stopped herself. Darcy was providing her an escape from the emotional terror going on in her house right now; it would be rude to criticize her driving. Darcy finally found what she was looking for and straightened up in her seat.

"My mom drives this car all the time. They both smoke in it, but she's the only one you can count on to leave a pack. My dad keeps them in his briefcase." Taking her hands off the wheel completely and steadying it with one knee, Darcy withdrew two Newports and undid the lighter that was rubber-banded around the package. "It's been a crappy day. Would you agree you need a cigarette?"

Rachel had smoked maybe three cigarettes in her life. They tasted awful and made her queasy, and she hated the smell that they left in her nostrils, but she took one from Darcy after zero deliberation.

Darcy smoked so often that her parents had to know it. She smoked every time she drove her friends around, leaving evidence of her "I don't give a shit" attitude all over the car. Like most Island girls, when she spoke, she gestured, so while talking and flinging her cigarette around she left a path of destruction. She melted divots into the plastic around the doorframe and the faux leather of the steering wheel and burned small holes into the upholstery.

"Tonight is pizza night, honey. I've also got a little over a half bottle of that vodka left. Let's get drunk, okay?" Darcy puffed on her own Newport and took one hand off the wheel to light Rachel's for her. "Honey", "sweetie"" "babe"—Darcy was always calling her the kind of pet names that should have remained reserved for Tom and Tom alone, but this afternoon it didn't annoy Rachel. In a way it was actually comforting.

"Sounds good to me," Rachel said, then took the lighter away from Darcy and lit her cig herself.

"I mean, we both know that your sister is a bitch sometimes, but this is really terrible."

It was a roller coaster of emotions when you were with Darcy; sometimes you could hug her but most of the time you just wanted to break her teeth in.

Billy Joel was finishing up and Darcy changed the station before digging for her second smoke. The first cigarette wasn't close to done yet, but she liked to squeeze in as many as she could on the short drive from Rachel's to her house. "There we are. That's the good stuff," Darcy said and took her hand off the radio. It was Whitesnake's "Here I Go Again." Darcy pounded on the dashboard with the lighter and looked over at Rachel. Rachel took a deep puff and then coughed.

Chapter Eight

Dinnertime at Billy Rile's house was a family affair. Sometimes that family extended to include Tommy Mathers, but not tonight. In a few hours his parents were leaving on their trip, and they wanted Billy to themselves.

"I know, you're going to be fine. But we still have to say it again, so indulge us," Billy's father said as he passed the instant mashed potatoes to his wife.

"We know Tom's a good kid at heart, honey," Gwen said. "But we also know that sometimes he hits—how to put it—life's speed bumps."

Andy interrupted, his wife clearly not hitting the nail as directly as he'd like. "We just want you to use your head. Don't let Tom do anything in the house that makes you feel uncomfortable," he said, sounding as parental as possible. "Also...don't share needles." He laughed. He couldn't help it; he was a funny guy.

Rachel followed as Darcy collected her two slices of pizza at the dinner table, balancing a second plate of slices for Rachel, and took them directly to her room. Darcy had taken it upon herself to invite Rachel over for dinner. Rachel could tell that Darcy's parents hated this practice, but if pressed they would probably both admit that a dinner table without Darcy was much less irritating.

Darcy set the plates down on the floor in her room, where Rachel was already sitting cross-legged. Darcy had her own private door to the bathroom, so she ducked in and grabbed two small Dixie cups (they were normally used for mouthwash, but they also made perfect shot glasses). She locked both doors to her room and sat down on the carpet across from Rachel.

"It's right by your hand there." Darcy pointed under her bed. Rachel turned, lifted up the pink bed skirt and reached in, bringing out a bottle of vodka. The lettering on the label was so Slavic she couldn't read it. The label was a shiny gold Russian crest: an inarguable indicator of quality. She undid the cap and poured, handing the cup to Darcy.

"How are things with you and Tom?" she asked while pouring her own cup. The liquid mushroomed at the brim of the Dixie cup, almost spilling over. It was two shots at the very least. She slapped the cap with one hand, spinning it back shut.

"Well, ya know, things are okay," Darcy said. Rachel took a long gulp, her eyes fixed on Darcy, anticipating the spiel to come. Darcy continued, as Rachel had known she would, "He's sweet, you know, a lot sweeter than you or anyone else gives him credit for. He's good for me and I'm good for him. We're good together."

"Better than Rhonda and Jake, I guess," Rachel said, and she felt herself begin to tear up.

"Don't let it hit you so hard. We don't even know what he died from. Jake was always kind of an idiot, never good enough for Rhonda. You remember her before she met that jerk?"

"It's not even that." Rachel wiped at her lightly freckled cheeks. "It's everything. Everything is too much sometimes. I'm fine, really." She turned her small paper cup over. Empty.

Darcy unscrewed the cap on the vodka. "I know the feeling. You drink some more and stay here tonight. We can watch MTV, talk about boys and fall asleep."

"Yeah, I think you're right. My mom can take care of Rhonda and I'll see her tomorrow. Your parents won't mind me sleeping over?" The last question was a joke; Rachel and Darcy slept over at each other's houses so frequently that parental consent was no longer even a formality.

"You really are a good friend," Rachel said. The tears on her cheeks were beginning to dry and she could feel her color turning into an alcohol blush. She wanted to take back all the awful things she had ever thought about Darcy.

"I know. You are too, babe." Darcy hugged her and Rachel felt hot, new tears soak into the shoulder of her old Minnie Mouse sweatshirt, the one that Darcy lent her. The one she used to wear during sleepovers.

Dinner at the Mathers household was served an hour later than Tom had ever seen other families do it and came conveniently wrapped in three microwavable single-serving containers. The family sat in the dining room, but the television was still on and visible in the adjacent room. Conversation was kept to a minimum while they ate. Between forkfuls of mushy turkey and Camel cigarettes, Tom's mother asked how school was going.

"Same old. A kid two years ahead of me died today. They announced it over the loudspeaker." Tom looked away from the television and stared at his mother. She called herself a sun worshipper, and forty-three years of faithful service had given her skin the color and texture of an old leather wallet. There was still one curler left in her hair. She must have overlooked it this morning. That, or it had been there yesterday as well. Tom couldn't remember. Her eyes remained on the television as she thought of a response.

Tom's father snorted in deep and hocked a glob of brown phlegm into the paper towel he used as a combination napkin/handkerchief. The sound caught his mother's attention and she focused on her husband with twitchy eyes. He was not being disgusting or rude; he couldn't help it. The mowers he worked with all day pumped out black smoke and flung tiny particles of dirt and grass clippings into the air.

His mother remembered what she was going to say next and finally looked at Tom. "I saw it on the news. Did you know him?" She put a new cig to her lips and paused before lighting it. "Poor dear. I'm sorry."

Tom thought "poor dear" was an odd choice of words, but his mother had been so fried for the past few years that some conversation was better than nothing. He looked back at the television.

It was a campaign commercial, the narrator listing taxes that Tom had never heard of while bills overflowed through a homeowner's mail slot. The narrator's voice went solemn and said, "Now Michael Dukakis wants to do for America what he's done for Massachusetts. America can't afford that risk."

"You're damn right." Tom's father spoke his first and only words of the night. His voice was filled with a gruff workingman's indignation. Tom didn't give a shit either way. Politics wasn't his thing.

The children were eating greedily. Children: that's what they were and now Darl could finally see it. They tore off tiny bites of Harold's flesh with their sideways insect mouths, chirping as they swallowed the raw meat.

Standing in the kitchen, waiting for the little ones to sate their hunger, Darl touched the hole at the base of his neck. He tentatively probed and found out that not only had the bleeding stopped, but it no longer hurt. It was difficult for him to remember a time when it did hurt. His memories of the attack were a jumble of white noise in his brain. The hole was less a wound than a new orifice; it just felt right.

No, not right at all. He could hear the voice at the back of his mind, sealed away, scared, angry, but still capable of fighting back and being heard. *It's not right, you stupid shit. You're drunk. Drunk on what she put in you. That's a big fucking hole in your neck and those aren't children. Fight back. Bash those creepy crawly little fuckers to death.*

Darl tightened the remaining fingers on his gnarled hand into a fist as Rhonda entered the kitchen. "They've had enough. We need to clean this place up, at least a little," she said.

She clicked at the children as she had before. It sounded smoother now; her throat was becoming better acclimated to the sounds. The children offered small clicks of their own and then backed away from Harold's body, retreating into the living room.

Thumb and forefinger a hand did not make, but at least both fingers were working. He wiggled them and inspected the stumps. The middle finger had been severed down to the knuckle and the ring finger had been taken completely with only a sliver of proximal phalanx remaining. The strip of flesh holding his pinky on must have given out during the struggle. All three fingers were gone; more food for the children. The wounds were clotted and the edges of the dead skin showed the beginnings of a green scab. It wasn't gangrene or necrosis, but new growth.

That is not healthy, not right at all. I should be dead by now, should have bled out. She did this. Pick up that chair and whack her in the head. Stuck deep in his mental cage, the real Darl tried to make sense of it all, while the new owner of his body chuckled at his efforts.

"What about what we are doing here is funny?" Rhonda asked, using a towel from the linen closet to sop up the partially coagulated blood.

"This isn't funny." Darl waved a hand at the kitchen. "He's the funny one." Darl pointed to the brim of his hat. "I can hear him talking in there. He's making a lot of noise."

"That's not how it's supposed to be. Don't worry. He should disappear in a few minutes. Try your best to block him out. You're in control now," she said, brushing the back of her hand against his forehead and running it down the side of his face. Her touch was calming. She looked down at the mess at her feet. "Now. Wrap him up with the tablecloth. There's a shed out back. Put him with his wife. Don't let anyone see you."

"It's dark. Nobody is going to see me."

"I don't care. Be cautious either way," Rhonda said. "We've got a plan and we're going to stick to it. We have to avoid detection for as long as we can. Revealing ourselves will soon become inevitable, but by then there will be nothing anyone can do about it."

It was fifteen minutes from the time Billy's parents' taillights disappeared around the corner of Irish Lane to the time Tom knocked on Billy's door.

"Red rover, red rover, can Tommy come over?" Tom yelled through the door and held up a partial six-pack of Coors Light cans (now, technically, a four-pack) to the peephole.

"Get in here before someone sees you, Jesus Christ." Billy reached for his friend's shoulder and pulled him inside. "You smell like a bar. And not a clean one."

"I've had two beers. What are you, my father?"

"No, but those are his." Billy pointed to the four-pack.

"He'll never miss them, and if he does..." Tom gave the finger and jerk-off signs concurrently. "So what's the plan, what do you want to do?"

"Want to watch a movie?" Billy didn't mean *Re-animator*. He didn't need to say what movie he meant. It was an established rule that the duo would never watch a scheduled film ahead of time. Billy owned very few movies. In fact, he owned exactly two: a retail copy of *The Adventures of Ichabod and Mr. Toad* that his grandmother had given him for Christmas two years prior (even though it must have been expensive, Billy had only watched it once) and an ex-rental copy of *The Evil Dead.* The latter had been a birthday present from Tom, who had stolen it from behind the front desk at VideoLux while Russ was helping a customer. Even Billy, not one to break rules, saw that it was a victimless crime. Russ had always bragged that he "backed up" his favorite tapes using the recording equipment in the back room of the store. Before that, Billy had rented the movie so many times that he probably could have bought the cassette six times over.

"I'm probably going to go crazy if I watch that movie one more time, but yeah, sounds good," Tom said, moving past Billy and leading the way downstairs into the converted basement/screening room.

By the time Billy reached the bottom step, Tom had the trunk freezer open and was placing two of the beers inside. He closed the lid and offered one of the two remaining beers to Billy.

"Keep an eye on those. If they freeze, they'll explode."

"How about keeping your bra on? It'll be fine. I'll drink them before they get the chance. Pop in the movie, will ya?" Tom raised his feet up onto the couch, occupying the rest of the available seating.

"Yes sir, right away, sir." Billy dug one of his nails down under the top of the can and broke the seal with a loud hiss and click, trying to look cool but also being careful enough not to spill foam on the carpet. He dropped to one knee in front of the television stand, selecting *The Evil Dead* from the shelf and loading it into the VCR.

Billy turned and looked at the couch. Tom had the Coors upended and was shaking the last drops onto his tongue. Billy looked at his feet. "What, the floor's not comfortable enough for you?" Tom said. "Don't put on that face. I'm only kidding. Jesus."

Tom stood, shook the can and looked at Billy. "Where do you want this?"

"Just put it next to the freezer, I'll clean them up later."

Tom took his seat again as Billy experimented with the tracking on the videotape, trying to reduce the lines and static as much as possible. The tape got frequent use so it was never going to have a perfect picture.

"Let me ask you a question. Why do we always come back to this one?" Tom opened another beer and swished a swig between his teeth, like someone attending a trailer park wine tasting.

"Well, it's the only tape I own." Billy sat down, keeping his eyes on the television. Needless to say he had never told Tom about *The Adventures of Ichabod and Mr. Toad*.

"It's the only tape you own because it's the one we would rent the most. You know what I mean. Why this one?" Tom pointed at the screen, then sipped his beer and prepared to listen to Billy philosophize. He'd listened to Billy speak on the subject of *The Evil Dead* before; Billy knew his friend found it both entertaining and informative.

"I don't think it's just the gore, I don't think it's the pacing, I think it's a lot of different things all coming together at once." Billy took the first sip of his beer. Tom was almost done with his fourth of the night already. "There's also a sense that this movie is a rite of passage. You remember how proud Russ was when he got this in? Remember how he told us about how it's banned in a bunch of places, and to this day in Britain you can't get the uncensored cut? This is the movie that changed things: a movie made by kids. Kids a bit older than us, but just like us. They made it with pure blood, sweat and tears. That, to me, is really cool."

"It also has a girl getting fucked by a tree."

"That too," Billy said and smiled. They watched the film until the beer made their eyes heavy and they fell asleep on the couch.

"Is he still in there?" Rhonda asked. She was standing on her tiptoes to look Darl directly in the eyes. After the cleanup she had changed a third time and was now wearing one of Rhonda's long nightshirts over her black underwear.

Yes, you mangy slag. I'm right here and I'm ready to take your goddamn head off.

"Yes, and he wants me to say hello for him," Darl said, laughing. "He's very...persistent." In the first few hours in its new host body, the thing had tried every way it could think of to suppress and destroy Lieutenant Todd Darl, but it had only succeeded in segregating him to a small area of the mind, present but locked away. Rhonda was surprised, said that it was highly unusual for a host to stay conscious for this long. The thing that had taken hold of his body was less surprised: Darl was one tough motherfucker.

"Well, let's give him something to watch, shall we?" Rhonda took his left hand (the intact one) and brought it up to her mouth. She gently kissed the bruised knuckles, kneading the callused skin of his palm with her fingers. Darl could see that her hands must have sustained some kind of injury but had now healed almost entirely. Small specks of green scabs still pimpled the backs of them.

What the hell is this now? Rhonda looked up from his hand and smiled. It was the kind of smile that a lover gives to answer such a question.

Keeping a light grasp on his hand, Rhonda led him to the couch. Darl sat down and she followed, lifting one leg high and straddling him.

"How do you feel? Has the change taken hold?" Rhonda said.

79

"I feel." Darl cleared his throat. He felt something twitch against the inside of his jaw. "New."

The hippies would have called it an "out of body experience". That was the closest thing Darl could think of to describe it. But it wasn't "out of body"—that was the problem. He was still plugged into his body. He had to see, hear, feel and smell everything that was happening to him.

Rhonda stood up, took off her fresh T-shirt and folded it, placing it on her mother's recliner. She then slipped off her panties and bra and placed them on top of the shirt. The hole in her chest looked like an off-center third nipple. She had the milky-white skin of a girl who spent too much time inside. Although it wasn't white, not completely: there were spots where the skin looked more translucent and other places (the cracks of her arms, behind her ears) where it appeared mossy.

"Are you ready for this?" she asked and took a step toward the couch where he sat.

"I think so," Darl said. He peeled off his own blood-caked undershirt and began to rub the area where his neck connected to his chest, curling the graying hairs on his chest into tiny fuzzballs. The real Darl could feel the pinch, but couldn't do anything about it.

When he started coughing and grunting, the day went from weird to worse.

He could feel it, slithering up behind his tongue and finally poking its way through. Splitting the tissue of his Adam's apple and crawling its way up, getting thicker as it went. It felt like he was puking up a small chainsaw. Not only could he feel the damage it did on its way up, out of his mouth, but he could feel sensation in the appendage itself. As if he were growing a new arm, only it was pushing through his lips and out of his mouth. It was similar to Rhonda's, but with a smaller, ridged beak on the tip.

The pain was excruciating, but passing out was impossible because Darl was no longer in control of his own mind.

The tentacle ran itself along Rhonda's body, leaving spots of blood and greasy brown slime where it touched against her near-white skin. Rhonda began to moan, a sensual human sound that trailed off into a series of alien clicks that came from deep in her chest.

"Is he still watching? Does he like this?" Rhonda giggled and ran her fingers up between her breasts as she asked. It was a rhetorical question: in its current state, Darl's mouth could not possibly form words.

I don't swing this freaky deaky way, you monster whore. The projection of Darl's voice took on a strained hiss. The pain was that strong.

Darl's new growth started to work its way between her legs as her own tentacle poked beyond her teeth. Eventually the agony of the physical transformation subsided and a brute sexual pleasure blossomed. It was better than the pain, but not by much.

The imprisoned Darl screamed in terror and disgust.

If the two lovers heard him, they gave no indication. They continued for what seemed like hours.

Chapter Nine

Friday

"Wake up, fuckface, it's time for school." Billy dropped something heavy onto Tom's stomach, knocking the wind out of him but waking him very quickly out of his deep sleep. There was a large spot of drool on the cushion he'd fallen asleep against.

"What did I do to deserve this?" Tom asked, removing the bag from his chest. He squinted, still visibly sleep-addled. "What is this?"

"It's your backpack. You left it here Monday when you came over."

"Oh yeah. To tell you the truth, I thought I lost it. Why's it so cold?" Tom didn't wait for a response. He put his hand in the large unzipped pocket and pulled out a Coors Light can. The aluminum had swollen and the top and bottom were misshapen into bubbles by its frozen contents.

"You're so lucky it didn't explode. We would have had to rinse beer- flavored Slurpee off of everything in the freezer."

"7-Eleven should start to carry those. I'd buy 'em."

"Get up, we're going to be late." Billy was dressed in fresh clothes and brushing his teeth. He talked out of the side of his mouth and looked like he was trying very hard to keep toothpaste foam off the carpet.

"I don't have first period class today, it's a study hall." Tom rubbed his eyes. "You go on ahead and I'll catch ya at lunch."

Billy put a finger up to indicate "one second" and then spit his toothpaste into an empty Coors can. He wiped his mouth with the back of his hand and continued. "That's bullshit. Today is a B day. You have math first period. It's remedial math, with Howitzer."

"That Kraut is going to fail me anyway."

"He will if you never show up to his class. Come on. You're already up. Let's just go."

"Up? Who's up? Not me." Tom closed his eyes and crossed his arms.

Billy paced in frustration, tossing the beer can into a plastic garbage bag he must have brought downstairs while Tom was still sleeping. "Don't you get this? It's been four fucking years. Why don't you understand how school works? Don't you get that you'll be able to graduate if you just show up? I mean, you'll get a D, but you'll still pass."

"Someone woke up on the wrong side of the couch this morning," Tom said, and began investigating the pockets of his rediscovered Jansport. He looked disinterestedly at slips of paper and unused academic paraphernalia, trying hard to ignore the war brewing with his friend.

"I know you're not going to college, but the least you could do is graduate high school. If fucking Jake Connolly could do it, so can you!"

"And look at him now!" Tom threw the backpack down at his feet. "A real fucking pull-himself-up-by-the-bootstraps achiever. Dead at twenty-whatever."

"That doesn't have anything to do with what we're talking about and you know it. This is about you being a lazy bastard who can't wait to say 'paper or plastic with your handle of Jack Daniels'?"

"Oh, well, I'm sorry I don't have three televisions. You spoiled fucking brat."

"Brat? Just because I'm not *poor* doesn't mean that I'm rich." There was a pause as both boys processed the insult. Billy's face told the whole story: *I shouldn't have said that.* He shouldn't have, but it was too late for that.

Tom was on his feet before Billy could take a step out of arm's length.

Tom gave Billy a swift punch in the stomach, knocking the entitlement out of him, and started to mount the stairs. "Have a nice day at school and a fun video night. Alone." When he reached the last step, he slammed the basement door after adding, "Fucker."

It was horrible. These things never slept. There were a few moments after the two monsters finished screwing that Darl felt his eyes close, basking in the afterglow, but after the strange, painful thrill dissipated his body was up and at 'em, with a refreshed monstrous host in the driver's seat.

Night had turned back into day again as Darl watched his body clean a stranger's house, completely against his own will. If his will had its own way, he would be four fingers into a pint glass of bourbon and passed out on his floor again.

Around dawn he reached out and tried talking to himself. *What are you? Why are you doing this?*

There was silence for a few minutes as the creature went about its business. It checked the thermostat again, something it did every fifteen minutes, regardless of the fact that it was turned as hot as it could go. They seemed to be more active the warmer they got, but the creatures were still slow as frozen molasses when they had nothing better to do.

He raised his hand and tried turning the knob. Darl inspected the new growth that had formed on his right hand in the last few hours. His fingers were growing back, or something's fingers were growing back. The nubs lacked the sinewy features of human flesh, and instead resembled the chitin shell of an insect. They were already the size of his missing fingers, pointed at the end, and their growth showed no signs of slowing. If he didn't know better he'd think he had some virulent strain of gangrene, focusing strictly on the color of the wound and not the science-fiction-alien claw growing on top of it.

What is that? Darl continued, returning to his questions. *Why are you doing this?* The thing in control of his body would not answer him. It seemed able to read his thoughts, but he could not do the same.

Rhonda was in the room with him, inspecting one of the children, the broken one that Darl had shot the legs off of. She clicked to it and it clicked back, trying to stand and then toppling over onto the coffee table. Her clicks became softer and she looked up at Darl, giving him a small frown.

"You have to take care of this," she said, not clicking but speaking English so as not to alarm the child.

He nodded and offered a few clicks of his own, picking up the injured creature and bringing it with him to the kitchen. The thing felt around in Darl's brain, looking for something that would help him. When it found what it was looking for, it placed the creature down on the countertop and took a steak knife from the drawer next to the sink.

Darl placed the knife gently between the creature's spines, right below its head. He clicked to it in a whisper and pushed the knife quickly and firmly into its back.

That's the way I always kill a lobster before I toss it into the boiling water. It's nicer for the animal that way. You took that from me, didn't you? You poked around in my brain, found that and used it. What the fuck are you?

The monster piloting his body didn't answer him, but Darl could feel it thinking. It was trying harder to ignore him. It put the knife into the sink and began wrapping the small corpse in a plastic bag.

I think I have it figured out now: you guys aren't all that smart, are ya? You need our big fleshy human brains. You need to know what we know.

If he was locked in here with nobody to talk to, he might as well get some entertainment out of yanking this bastard's chain and figuring out what the hell was going on in the process.

The creature tied off the plastic bag and opened the refrigerator. Darl assumed he was trying to keep the little bastard from rotting and stinking up the place.

Y'all are not going to eat that, are you? Have yourselves a little celebratory seafood cookout? I don't think it would make the best meal, ya know, with me shooting it and all. You might contract, uh, lead poisoning on account of the bullet. Plus, I mean, cannibalism. That's a bit unsavory.

He was almost there. He could feel it.

Boy, did you hear that ugly little piggy squeal when I shot it? Suweeee.

"Shut up! Shut up, shut up!" His screams startled Rhonda and he motioned to indicate that he was talking to himself. "You annoying fucking cracker. Die already. Let go of your pitiful, bothersome hold!"

Darl was quiet for a moment, pausing to allow the thing to regain a bit of composure. Then, *If you aren't cannibals, what are you then? Why are you doing this?*

"You want to know why? It is just what we do. You're weaker, stupider, fleshier, and we are here to take advantage of that. We're going to take everything you love and tear it down. Then when we're done, we're going to rebuild everything the way we want it. I hope you stay around long enough to see it. I hope you see what we do to this place!"

"We are here?" So you and your Queen Bitch in there are aliens, little green men? I figured as much. So do you have a spaceship or did you crash as part of a meteorite?

"You have no idea what you are babbling about. I've said all I'm going to. I hope you enjoyed our talk because it was probably the last conversation you will ever have. Now do yourself a favor and shut up."

Whatever you say, Hoss. But Darl didn't stop. He kept asking the things he wanted to know in the most foul-mouthed manner possible. Considering the circumstances, it was a pretty enjoyable way to spend his time.

Rachel was awakened by a histrionic groan from Darcy.

"Ugh, we're going to be late," Darcy said, holding onto the "a" in late, fashioning it into an earsplitting yelp. Not the most pleasant way to wake up, Rachel noted.

"Shit, what time is it?" Rachel threw off the top layer of the sleeping bag and boosted herself up off Darcy's bedroom floor. Darcy didn't answer her question and instead pulled the bedspread over her face, muffling her continued whining.

Rachel looked at the clock. "Is that the right time?"

"It's fifteen minutes behind."

"School started three minutes ago." Frustrated, Rachel grabbed her backpack, knocking over her plate from last night, sprinkling crumbs on the floor and the sleeping bag. Normally she would be mortified to make a mess in someone else's home, but right now she was in too much of a rush and too annoyed with Darcy to care.

"What happened to your alarm clock?" Rachel asked, shimmying out of her borrowed pajamas and into yesterday's jeans.

"I'm, like, really really good at turning it off. I'm sorry, hon, I thought you heard it."

"No, I didn't hear it, or else I would be in homeroom right now."

"Ugh, I'm sorry."

"Look. It's fine. Sorry I snapped. Can you get up and give me a ride?"

"My dad's probably got his car out, work and all. Plus I need to shower anyway."

"Goddamn it, Darcy. I have to run." Rachel said, grabbing her bag and running for the stairs.

"I'll catch up with you later, girl. Sorry," Darcy said to an empty hallway before falling back to sleep.

At half past noon the mailman walked up the stairs to the Krieger residence, holding a handful of letters and a small parcel.

Rhonda was sitting in the living room, looking through family photo albums, when the mailman knocked. She looked up at Darl, who was seated opposite her in the recliner. He was using an empty egg carton and cotton balls to construct a mini-nursery for the seeds she had been expelling, roughly two every hour. He packed the black pellets three to a chamber and watched as they occasionally wriggled in the warm air of the room.

Rhonda met his gaze and smiled. "Get him to come inside," she said, motioning with her head to the front door.

Darl put down his project on the coffee table and rose. "How am I supposed to do that?"

"Any way you can."

Darl let out a small, evil giggle in response.

You laugh like a sissy. I would never titter like that. I'm a grown fucking man.

"You're going to love this," Darl said in a low voice, indicating to Rhonda that he was speaking to his inner self.

There was a third knock on the front door and Darl ripped it open, startling the short older man on the other side.

"Good afternoon. Mr. Krieger? I need you to sign for this." The mailman looked up at him, returning to business as usual.

Darl felt his facial muscles contract into a large, exaggerated frown. "I'm afraid I'm not Mr. Krieger, sir. I'm also afraid that I'm going to have to ask you to step inside for a moment." Darl held up his badge.

"What's this all about?"

"Sir, I assure you it's only a formality, but there's been a crime perpetrated in the area and I really need you to step in off of the stoop and help me with an ongoing investigation."

Perplexed, the mailman stepped inside. He was short and skinny, with a tangle of oily gray hair combed from the back of his head and stretched over the top. He had a thick beard and tiny mole eyes that blinked as they adjusted to the darkness of the house.

The thing smiled and closed the door behind him, making sure to keep his right hand hidden inside his pocket. The creature could feel the real Darl squirming around his cage, preparing a tirade.

What the hell is wrong with you, pal? This guy with a bandage on his neck and an unbuttoned plaid shirt over a wife-beater shows you a badge and you step inside. Jesus, you're going to get yourself killed.

Darl led the little mailman into the living room. He was still clutching the package, as if the mail, along with his government-issue navy shorts and knee-high socks, were somehow protecting him from indictment.

You aren't in legal trouble, idiot, you're in mortal danger.

"I'm Lieutenant Todd Darl, Suffolk County Sheriff's Department. What's your name?" Darl said and put out his left hand.

With hesitation the mailman put out his own left hand and traded an awkward shake. Darl couldn't tell if the poor old fogy was normally this bewildered or whether it was just the circumstances. "I'm Leonard. United States Postal Service."

"Do you have any ID on you, Leonard?"

Leonard began digging into his back pocket.

"I'm just kidding with you, Leonard. I believe that you're really a mail carrier," Darl said. Rhonda laughed, still sitting on the couch, watching the proceedings. "Leonard, this is my associate Rhonda."

The creature was warmed up, both physically and conversationally. Darl hadn't heard him take this tone before. Whatever they were planning for poor Leonard, this sick bastard was getting off on it.

Leave him alone.

"I think I'm going to hand this over to Rhonda now. She has a few questions for you, Lay." Darl had even picked up the aggravating Long Island habit of abbreviating names in a way they *weren't* meant to go.

Look at him. He's old. Listen to him talk: it doesn't even sound like he's playing with a full deck. Pick on someone your own size. Or better yet, your own species. Why don't you cross the room and deck that irritating broad right in the mouth?

"I'm not going to do that," Darl whispered.

It was worth a try.

"Do what?" Leonard asked, wincing. "What's going on here?"

"Just talking to myself; no need for alarm. Isn't that right, Rhonda?"

"None whatsoever. Now Leonard, before we begin, how old are you?" Rhonda entered character without missing a beat. Darl hadn't been sure she would be able to. She had seemed like the more serious-minded of the two murderous aliens.

"I'm sixty-five years of age." Leonard mopped his brow with the back of one wrinkled hand. "Boy, it's hot in here."

"Excited for retirement?" Darl said, ignoring the comment about the heat and cutting off Rhonda's next question before she could start. *You're sick. You're prolonging this, whatever this is. Make sure you don't pop a big ol' boner; might give the old man a heart attack from seeing your octopus mouth-dick.*

"I think I have a few more years left in me," Leonard said. Darl scoffed and motioned for Rhonda to continue. Leonard's face had gone from uncomfortable and sweaty to scared.

"Do you have any preexisting heart conditions, Len?" She was good. The creature had probably learned how to be such a high-caliber wiseass from picking through the old Rhonda's memories. Though not a father himself, Darl knew that some teenage girls had a limitless capacity for cruelty.

"No, I don't. What does that have to do with anything?" Leonard had apparently mustered some courage. "You two are trying to pull one over on me right now and I don't like it. I'm leaving. I'm a government employee and what you're doing is illegal."

I hope he's the kind of mailman who carries a .45 in his mailbag. Pull a Dirty Harry *on you clowns.* Darl knew that Leonard probably wasn't, but he could dream.

"Please don't be alarmed, Len. There's just one more thing," Rhonda said, motioning to Darl. Darl bent down, picking up the egg carton. "For your own safety, we need you to take these pills, Leonard."

"I'm not swallowing those. You people are crazy. Some kind of cult, that's what you are. What happened to his neck?" Leonard pointed at Darl. "And why are you dressed like that? It's the middle of the day. Shouldn't you be at work or school? Jesus."

"Leonard, please. It's just vitamins and minerals. We believe that something has been released into the air in the neighborhood. Possibly of Russian origin," Rhonda said. She had four seeds in her hand now and was pushing them toward him.

"You're full of horseshit, missy, and I ain't putting those in my mouth." He swatted her hand away, scattering the pills to the carpet, and made for the door.

Attaboy, Leonard, run! You can make it!

Despite Darl's cheering, his arms were out and on Leonard's shoulders in a second. Darl grappled with the mailman, who offered some fierce resistance for such an old man. While they struggled, Rhonda was picking up the seeds, clicking in frustration.

"Open up," she said. Darl had Leonard's hands pinned behind his back. His grip was solid and it felt like Leonard was straining so hard that he was liable to dislocate his own shoulder.

Fucking pissant bastards, roughing up an old man.

Leonard held his mouth firmly clenched shut as Rhonda tried slipping a nail between his lips and prying them apart. This tactic only resulted in a bloody lip for Leonard.

"The lady said open up," Darl yelled into Leonard's ear, his face close enough to see the wispy hair on the back of the older man's neck go stiff. Darl felt the remaining fingers of his right hand (he had no feeling in the new growth) let go of the mailman and work their way up to pinch the mailman's nose. Darl was now holding both of the old man's wrists with only his left hand. It was a feat of strength he would never have been able to manage before, regardless of how feeble his captive.

There was no way of telling whether it was lack of oxygen or the shock of seeing Darl's new green-brown insect claws that made Leonard open his mouth, gasping and trying to scream before Rhonda shoved a handful of seeds under his wagging tongue.

Rhonda pushed up under his jaw and clapped his mouth shut, his teeth colliding with an audible snap. She then kept her hand over his lips, the way you make a fussy dog swallow a pill from the veterinarian's office.

Darl unclenched his right hand, releasing Leonard's arms. The small man dropped to his hands and knees, retching.

You sons of bitches.

"Pick him up, bring him to the upstairs bathroom and put him in the tub," Rhonda said. "Do it quickly and we might be able to avoid making a mess."

Chapter Ten

Down at the mall.

That's where Darcy was, and she didn't feel the slightest tug of remorse for ditching school and her friend. If Rachel wanted to be a prissy bitch when it came to getting to school on time, then Darcy had no choice but to go in the opposite direction and skip the whole day.

By the time she woke up for good, it was already after lunch. She walked downstairs, grabbed a bowl of Special K (no milk) and found her mother's car keys on the kitchen counter. Without leaving a note or checking if it was okay, she grabbed the keys and hit the road.

The cereal helped to sop up some of the nausea that last night's vodka caused and the drive on the wide-open midday highway had her feeling good. She'd barely begun to enjoy the ride before the mall appeared beyond the trees on the horizon.

As she approached the eastern end of the Sunrise Mall, she began to smell the ducks. The mall thought it would be cute to keep live, shitting, molting ducks in a pond at one end of the building. It was probably great for business—the kids loved them (and Darcy had too once upon a time), but all they did now was stink up the place and wreak havoc on her allergies. Normally she would avoid this end of the mall entirely. The stores in the "duck wing" consisted of a Waldenbooks, the arcade, and Macy's (her mother shopped at Macy's, for crying out loud). Nothing that she would miss.

Today she was walking for the sake of walking and, her protestations aside, the mall staff did a good job of keeping the ducks clean, so she decided to walk the eastern wing.

Paying attention to no store in particular, she let her eyes wander over Sunrise Mall's unique architecture. It was one of the few two-story malls on the Island, with elevators in the middle and escalators peppered throughout. Letting her mind free-associate, Darcy's thoughts turned to Tom. During one of the boys' video nights they had sat her down and forced her to watch *Dawn of the Dead*.

This had been early in her and Tom's relationship, back when Billy thought it was cool to have a girl around. He wanted to share his nerdy little hobby with her, be her buddy. "Educate" her or something.

She thought the movie itself was pretty crummy, but had enjoyed looking at the old-time shopping mall, an aspect that kept her paying half attention to the television set.

"It's not even that old!" Billy had said, to which Darcy replied, "It's old enough for the blood to look like paint, and not even the right color paint." This was a comment which sent Billy into what looked like a geek seizure. She was pretty sure that she loved Tom, but he had some shitty taste in friends.

She dropped the memory as easily as it had come as she reached the edge of the duck pond. She peered over the edge, craning her neck to look inside the ducks' shit-covered duck house.

"Where are the ducks?" she asked aloud. Where were the people for that matter? There were never that many during school hours anyway, but you always had groups of moms and grandmothers in tracksuits doing a few laps of the mall. What few shoppers she did see looked dazed and confused: pacing slowly along the shops, staring into the fountain, riding the escalators. *Just one of those days.* Everyone was bummed out now that the weather was cooling off.

Maybe they had finally gotten rid of the feathered disease pots. *No big loss.* Before she could fully finish the thought, a window display featuring a mannequin wearing a cute little two-piece caught her eye. She thought no more about how strange it was that most of the people and all of the ducks were gone from the Sunrise Mall, and started thinking how crazy that bikini would drive Tom (and any other boys who happened to see her in it). It would probably even be on sale, it being so far after the end of the season.

Darcy entered the shop and found the bikini. She nodded to the clerk, who appeared to be the only person to show up for work that day. "I'm just going to try this on," Darcy said and then added, "Cute sweater. Looks warm."

The woman behind the counter gave a slight nod.

Bitch, would it kill you to crack a smile? Darcy thought as she slid back the curtain to one of the changing rooms. The Police's "Can't Stand Losing You" played softly on the store's sound system, and Darcy gave a combination dance/jiggle as she shimmied out of her jeans and panties and slipped on the bikini bottoms.

The Police, in Darcy's estimation, were the perfect band to feel sexy to. After taking off her shirt, she unhooked her bra and had begun tying off the bikini top behind her back when she spotted a large, dark shape move past her feet and out of the dressing room. It darted from under the mesh screen out into the store. She could hear its feet scurry across the store's cheap acrylic carpeting.

"Are you fucking kidding me?" Darcy yelped the words and had her jeans refitted over the bikini bottoms in less than five seconds. She ripped open the curtain before she could fully pull her shirt down over her head. Then she snapped herself into character and was set on full-tilt, raving city-bitch mode by the time she was halfway out of the store.

"Hey, lady," Darcy said, pointing at the woman who hadn't moved from her post behind the counter. "You've got rats. Huge fuckin' things. You're lucky I don't call the health department and have them shut your ass down." Darcy ran out the front of the store, pulling her shirt down and tucking it into her jeans, making sure to hide that she was still wearing her new bikini as she flew past the register and the dazed clerk.

This mall trip was over. At least she had picked up something cute. She needed to find a pay phone, give Tom a call. There was a much better chance that he was at home instead of at school.

Stupid little Terry Manfred: *not so stupid now, not so little either.* Terry could now lift the heaviest weights in his brother's dumbbell set.

The set of weights that was in the basement, the set next to the poster of a half-naked woman that his mother hated. His brother was at work now, and Terry felt like he could lift the biggest barbell all day long. He would have, too, if his mom hadn't yelled downstairs and reminded him that he had to go to school.

Normally he hated school. He hated having to listen to the teachers ramble on about nothing, having to tell Dr. Deloris what he was feeling today, having to apologize for bumping into weaklings like Billy Rile.

Billy might be taller, but Terry was a lot stronger, even stronger now. At least today was a B day, meaning that Terry wasn't scheduled to go in until after lunch.

Terry "The Sped" Manfred. That's what they were calling him behind his back. At least, he was fairly certain of it. Sure, he was in "special ed", but he wasn't like the rest of those retards: no pushed-in face, no fits, no crying. Terry could read and write and everything like that. He just didn't give a shit about his stupid classes. Dr. Deloris had even told him that his IQ was slightly above average. He just had "impulse control" issues. That and he had punched a few of the other kids one too many times, and now was paying the price.

That morning, before Terry's brother went to work, and before Terry was able to sneak downstairs and begin his morning workout, Terry had gone outside to give Bailey a snack. No one was up yet, not even the sun, but Terry was awake. The pills he took for his mood always did that to him, made it difficult to sleep (*may cause mild insomnia*).

He had used the crank-opener to pry open a can of Cesar Savory Beef Brisket, then plopped it into Bailey's dog bowl. Because the can hardly made a dent in the big doggie dish, and because Bailey was a big dog (and Terry liked using the can opener, ripping open the metal so easily, like it was paper), he also opened a second and third can and put the contents in the bowl as well.

He carried the heaping bowl of Savory Beef Brisket (it didn't look like much, but it smelled pretty good) outside to Bailey's doghouse.

"Breakfast," he had said into the doghouse. It was still dark outside and the doorway to Bailey's house was a wall of shadow. "Come and get your breakfast, stupid."

Terry knocked on the roof of the house. He was growing impatient. Terry had made sure that he pushed the empty cans of Cesar to the bottom of the trash bag, but if Bailey didn't start eating the excess dog food and hiding the evidence of Terry's overfeeding, then his mother would catch him for sure.

"Bailey, I'm serious." Terry dropped his voice to a growl in an attempt to intimidate the dog the way he tried intimidating kids on the lunch line. His anger was greeted with a low click-clack sound. Terry went to his knees and put his hand on the door to steady himself. His hand had come back feeling wet. Not wet with water though...it was stickier than the morning dew that sprinkled the lawn and wet his jeans.

There was blood on his fingers, and Terry was sure it wasn't his own. "Bailey?"

A rope with something sharp tied to the end; it was something like that. It shot out of the darkness of Bailey's doghouse and dug into his stomach. Right below his belly button. If he hadn't been in such terrible pain, he probably would have thanked his lucky stars that it didn't hit him in the schlong. As bad as the pain was in his stomach, being schlongless definitely would have been even worse.

Once, in second grade, back before he was known as Manfred the Sped, Terry had sharpened a pencil for upwards of three minutes and then jabbed it into the meat of Barry Schultz's arm. Barry carried on like Terry had hacked his arm off: crying, bleeding and screaming. Terry hadn't imagined something that small could have hurt that much, but now he realized that he was a real asshole for having done that.

His screams didn't wake anyone. Last summer he had helped his father and brother redo the insulation and install new windows; they did a very good job of keeping the sounds of the neighborhood out.

The bastard had killed Bailey. When it walked out of the doghouse, he could see that it was matted in blood and strips of beagle fur. He wanted to fight back against the creature, which looked like a real-life scary movie, but between the pain and the inexplicable impulse to leave it alone, he decided to focus on gripping his bleeding belly. There was the sensation that his tummy was filling up like a balloon; he felt like he couldn't take it anymore, and then everything went black.

When he woke up, his brain seemed fuzzier than usual, but he kind of liked it. He went inside, switched into his workout clothes and started pumping some iron. Boy was he strong now. Smarter too—less impulsive, he was sure of it.

Terry hated when he was called "special". The way he saw it, he was normal, a normal kid who lifted weights, got in fights with his brother, took out the garbage, jacked off, listened to music. Now he was *special* though. Now he was strong and smart and he could make babies. There weren't too many boys his age who could claim that.

There wasn't much for Tom to do at home, but it beat sitting in school. His father's car was in the driveway, meaning he either had an early day or hadn't even bothered going into work. Dad was a hard worker, when he was sober. But he had also taken measures, should the occasion arise that he couldn't make it in, to ensure that the landscaping business could run itself for a day or two without suffering complete economic implosion.

His father's second-in-command, Ricky Tobin, would look over the schedule, gas up the machines and send out the labor. Ricky would cover for Mathers, no questions asked, and some nights, when his dad was feeling spiteful, he would joke that Ricky was moving in on his territory and trying to hustle him out of his top-dog spot. His father's favorite movie was *The Godfather Part II* and his favorite actor was James Cagney. This probably contributed to his paranoia about his small business.

Assuming his father was asleep, Tom would still have to hope his mother did not hear or see him if he came in through the front door. So he opted for climbing through his bedroom window when returning from Billy's house.

On his bed he tried to remain motionless while he listened to his mother and father shuffle around the quiet house. Alone in his small room, Tom began to wonder if he'd made the right decision in skipping school. He could have put his senses on the back burner, sat in the rear of his classes and imagined what the girls around him looked like naked. This was a hobby of his, and after Darcy had matched up to his estimation (more or less), he'd liked to believe he had become quite good at it. Not only the pretty girls, but the homely ones as well. He was an equal opportunity pervert. It wasn't so much a sexual thing as much as it was a...creative curiosity.

A thump echoed through the empty house, rousing Tom from his reverie. *What the hell was that?* There was more shifting coming from the adjacent room, his parents' bedroom. Tom held his breath and listened. *Oh, gross me out! Mom and dad afternoon delight, Jesus Christ.* After a few unsuccessful attempts to drown out the sounds with low music and a few swigs from his flask, Tom decided it was best to crawl back out his window and take a walk around the block.

"What do we do now?" Darl asked. He was perched at the edge of the toilet, hunched over the tub, scooping up bits of flesh with his fingers and flinging them into the bucket that he'd set down on the floor. Each handful landed with a satisfying wet smack.

"Now, we wait until dark." Rhonda said, "but after you finish that, of course."

"Can I ask a question?" He turned the knobs and ran the spout, cupping his hands and throwing water up onto the sides of the bathtub.

Leonard had left one hell of a mess. The children had grown too quickly and couldn't find their way out of his mouth in time. His stomach had popped like an overfilled water balloon. It left quite a mark, but it had very quickly shut up the real Darl, who now cowered deeper in his own mind, not daring to speak up since it happened. Since Leonard the Mailman had popped.

"What's the question?" Rhonda said, not indicating whether she would answer it.

"Why the extensive cleanup? Why the secrecy?" Darl hooked his finger inside the drain and pulled out a long strip of wrinkled flesh, allowing the red water to drain from the tub much faster. "Isn't it too late by now? Can't we just walk outside?"

"Procedure," Rhonda said, offering no other explanation. "Finish this up and then come into the master bedroom. I'm going to go check on the little ones." She walked out, leaving him to his work.

Her brood, their brood, was expanding. Four seeds had been successfully sown, resulting in four glistening, clattering new infants. There were now six healthy children, four newcomers to make up for the unfortunate euthanasia of their brother.

"On second thought," Rhonda said, poking her head back into the bathroom, "run a load of laundry. Try and get the stains out of your uniform. They won't come out all the way, but it doesn't have to be perfect. We will be able to use it later."

"Is that so?" Darl asked, allowing himself a small smile, the kind of expression that Rhonda had already warned him against once today.

"Yes. It's all part of the plan." She smiled back before leaving the room a second time.

Chapter Eleven

Billy Rile never had to study, never had to take a makeup test or stay after class for extra help. Billy Rile would now have to pay for that. Terry Manfred sat through his mandatory ten minutes with Dr. Deloris, answering her yes or no questions and fixating on how he was going to get Billy Rile to have one of his babies.

No, not like that. That's not what I mean. Not "make babies" in some homo way. A different kind of baby in a different kind of way. In a meaner way.

Dr. Deloris scribbled down her final notes and placed them in his file. He had seen that file once. It wasn't a secret file or anything. The teacher and the principal and some other people he didn't know had shown it to him during a meeting a few years ago. His mother had been called into school and then they opened the tan manila folder for him.

Terry had just turned fourteen, and they told him that it was his legal right to see inside his folder. There were lots of words that drew the eye's attention. First and foremost, in the upper right corner of the page were the words "Emotionally Disturbed." Halfway down the line, "unpredictably violent behavior: mild to moderate" also stood out. That day had made Terry feel small, had made him feel useless, but Dr. Deloris had been there. Terry liked Dr. Deloris because she didn't speak down to him like he was an idiot.

"You see, Terry," she had said in that meeting three years ago. "The human brain is like a computer, only it is the most complicated computer ever made. All the smartest scientists and best doctors in the world still don't really know how it works. The reason for that is that everyone's brain is a little bit different. In young people, teenagers around your age, the brain is still developing, still growing." She had placed a hand over his then, ignoring the rest of the people gathered in the room. "It says here that you're impulsive, that you are quick to become violent before you can think about the consequences. It's not that there is something wrong with you, Terry; it's that your brain works differently from everyone else's. And I want to help you learn to control it." Terry couldn't remember anything from this week in science class, but he remembered everything that Dr. Deloris had said that day.

"Sorry, Terry. Looks like we've run over our allotted time. I'll have to write you a pass," Dr. Deloris had large dimples and wore glasses that made her eyes look like she was constantly smiling. It was fucking obnoxious. "Where are you supposed to be right now, Terry? What class?"

"My next class is, uh." Terry tried hard to focus, but his mind was moving around too quickly, like there was something else rolling around inside of there, pushing all his memories around and making it impossible to find the one he was looking for. He pressed his hands into his coat pockets. Under his coat he was wearing his Metallica sweatshirt. It was cold in here, which made it harder to think. Under the sweatshirt he was wearing a T-shirt, and under that he had rolled gauze around a bunch of paper napkins, covering the wound on his stomach so his blood and guts wouldn't get everywhere if it started to leak again. He especially didn't want to lose any of his seeds if one should pop out without him feeling it. "My um, first class...on a B day. Is..."

"All right Mr. Comedian, that was a trick question. I know that you have home economics with Mrs. Delta. I helped you fit it into your schedule, remember?"

"Oh yeah." Terry paid her little attention. He took one hand out of his pocket and held it to his temple. He was trying to silently communicate with his new friend, telling it to quiet down in there. It was speaking to him. Most of the things it said were in a language that Terry could not understand, so he decided that it was best to ignore the instructions he could understand.

"Are you all right? You aren't feeling feverish, are you?" She reached out, intending to place the back of her wrist against his forehead, but he recoiled before she could touch him.

"I feel great." Terry made a big show of snapping himself out of it even though he was far from with it. "I've got to go. I'll be late to class." He grabbed his backpack from under his seat and stood up.

"Make sure you wash your hands. There's a wicked bug going around. Lots of kids are out sick today." Terry Manfred was out the door of her office before she could finish.

Even during this time of lush economic prosperity, public schooling was what it was. So instead of a properly furnished home-ec classroom with sinks and stoves, Mrs. Delta's class was taught in a science laboratory during an off-period. The classroom's emergency faucets were used as the sink and hot plates were plugged into the sockets on lab tables that were usually home to microscopes.

"I know we are missing a lot of students today, but that doesn't mean we can't be productive," Mrs. Delta said. Her announcement was greeted with silence by the small crowd of students. Class was at one-third attendance. Was it "senior skip day" and Billy had missed the memo? Every year the majority of the senior class played hooky on the same day, and (school solidarity being so strong) so did most of the other grades.

Mrs. Delta's cheer was far from infectious. The students had no desire to be productive. Billy in particular had had enough of this shitty day, and learning how to bake a Bundt cake on a hot plate was low on his list of priorities.

He didn't need the credits to graduate, he wasn't learning much (he knew how to boil water, for Christ's sake) and he didn't hold any particular love for Mrs. Delta. She was a blubbery old woman with a manic "happy homemaker" disposition. He had chosen to take her home economics class only because Rachel Krieger was taking it too. It might seem trite, following his crush as she went about her day, but he was not about to go and pad his schedule with three study halls in a row, so why not see Rachel for one more period instead?

103

The six students were spread around the room, all missing their deskmates except for Roger Kline and Sue Murphy, who were staring deeply and lovingly into each other's eyes at the lab table behind Billy's. Roger and Sue were bopping, and so were Roger and Deb Donnelly, and Roger and Stacy Mogan. Sue Murphy did not know any of this. She was blissfully ignorant. (Some would say stupid.)

Billy sat at the same table he used for biology, because it offered both a small creature-of-habit comfort and was a seat directly behind Rachel's table.

"Since Danny isn't here, why don't you work with Beth today, Samuel?" Mrs. Delta said. Beth gathered her book bag and moved one table back. Billy saw where this could be going and his heart jumped.

"And Billy, since Tommy isn't here—" The door swung open and she paused.

Rachel! Rachel! "Billy, since Tommy isn't here, you should work with Rachel." *Say it. Say it, goddamnit!*

In walked Manfred the Sped. Billy was always reluctant to call him by his nickname, but everyone else did, so Billy wasn't going to make waves. Manfred looked haggard. A few locks of his greasy hair were matted to his forehead. He moved sluggishly, but he smiled big and wide as he handed his hall pass to Mrs. Delta.

"Terry, glad you could join us. Why don't you go on and work with Billy?"

Figures, Billy thought.

"That's probably not entirely sanitary," Billy Rile said, offering nervous laughter when Terry scowled back at him. Terry ignored him and continued petting the science lab's rabbit, Bilbo Baggins. "I'm just saying that Bilbo's kind of a shit-machine and we are going to be handling food in a minute." Rile's high-pitched voice squeaked its way into Terry's ears and poked holes into his thoughts. Jesus, had this pussy's voice even dropped yet?

Bilbo, although he had a faggy name, was very soft and let you pet him without too much squirming around. Most importantly the small, furry creature was warm to the touch. Terry kept both hands on him, trying to warm up his fingers. The rabbit's tiny heart beat much faster than that of larger animals, warming his blood, pumping it around inside his little bunny veins that were encased in thick fur to keep in the heat.

"Be careful there, Lenny. Don't squish him," Billy said.

"My name's Terry. Terry Manfred. We've been in lots of classes together."

"I know that, Terry. Sorry, it was a dumb joke. Never mind."

"Joke, yeah. Sure." Terry looked up at the teacher, then around the class at the other people he hated. Why couldn't they just disappear for ten minutes, leave him alone with Billy?

"All right, now that everyone has their supplies, let's—" Mrs. Delta was interrupted by the classroom phone. The ringing phone was somehow more high-pitched and annoying than Billy Rile's voice, and Terry was thankful when Mrs. Delta squeezed herself out from between the teacher's desk and the blackboard to answer it.

Terry couldn't even follow her side of the conversation. To him it was just noise, the clucking of a wound-up old bag. "I'll be right down," she finished and clicked the phone back against the wall.

"I have to go down to the nurse's office. Somebody please read the directions aloud. Do not attempt to add the eggs until I get back," the teacher said in a frantic tone, then jogged out the door. Terry imagined her footsteps cracking the floor tiles as she ran.

Nobody in the classroom was elected to read the recipe aloud. Instead, the students waited until Mrs. Delta was down the hall and then talked among themselves. All except for Rachel, who had no partner, no one to talk to, and instead doodled in her notebook.

"You joke around a lot, don't you, Billy?" Terry asked, standing up and placing Bilbo back into his cage. Billy looked in his direction, tearing his eyes away from Rachel Krieger. It was obvious that the twerp liked her. *Dream on, pal.*

"What do you mean?"

"I mean." Terry put his hands back into his jacket pockets, fingering his two seeds. One he had made while he walked to school and the other had just popped out in the bathroom before Terry came to class. "I mean that when you see somebody, ya know, who's dumber than you are, that you like to make a quick joke. Somebody who's, say, maybe shorter than you are, doesn't wear those fancy clothes that you do."

Billy looked down at his own clothes. "This sweatshirt was my dad's when he went to school, and these jeans are ancient. They don't even fit right."

"See what I mean? You've got a smart-mouth answer for everything," Terry said.

"No, I don't," Billy said, seeming like he was trying to prove a point. He was already scared. Terry could tell that he was. It felt like he could smell the fear, too, bubbling off of Billy's skin like wicked BO. It was time to crank it up.

"Why did you make up that name for me? You know the one: 'Manfred the Sped'. I don't appreciate it. Frankly, I don't think that's a very nice thing to call somebody. Somebody you hardly know, even though we've been in classes together since second grade." He didn't know why, but Terry loved using the word "frankly". It wasn't a big word, but it carried a certain weight, made him sound both serious and smart.

Everyone was watching them now, trying to figure out how the situation would develop. Everyone except for Sue and Roger, who were more interested in cleaning each other's tonsils with their tongues.

"I didn't make that up," Billy said. "I think you've gotten some bad information about me somewhere, Terry. I'm more of a geek. I'm not the class clown, believe me."

"Don't bullshit me, Billy. I see how you laugh when I've got to be taken out of class." Terry took a step toward Billy's seat. With the other boy sitting down on the lab stool, the two were eye to eye.

"Look, Terry." Billy put his hands out, smiling.

"Shut up!" It was the first time Terry raised his voice. "You're gonna get it now. Because I've had enough. Enough of your shitty shit-

106

eating mouth." This gave Terry an idea. He palmed one of the seeds. This was called "sleight of hand". When Terry was little his brother had shown him a few magic tricks, but he could never get his small fingers to remember the complicated movements needed to make a coin disappear and reappear. He pinched the seed in the palm of his hand, reached into the cage and dug around until he had a handful of Bilbo Baggins's rabbit turds.

"Terry, listen. I've got no problem with you. I haven't been making fun of you. This is crazy," Billy said. He sounded so sincere that Terry almost believed him.

This was unbelievable. It was the kind of bullying that happened in the movies, not in real life. Terry Manfred wasn't even one of Billy's normal harassers. On the contrary, Billy had thought, up until this point, that the two had been almost friendly. They exchanged nods in the hallway, had a few classes together and were both outcasts. Sure, Terry would occasionally bump into him, but the guy was supposed to be a few raisins shy of bread pudding. There had never been any harm done before now.

"I want you to eat these," Terry said, flattening his lips into a thin line against his small, off-yellow, Chiclet-looking teeth. He held out the pile of rabbit pellets. The skin of his face had gone white, so pale that the large veins on his forehead and neck were a prominent blue. He was having some kind of mental breakdown, had lost control in some violent, radical way. *Just like Cujo.*

Billy took a quick glance at the rest of the class. Even Roger and Sue were interested now, although Roger still had his hand on Sue's thigh. Billy felt he had to look tough for Rachel; if he couldn't be overtly macho, at least he could try resisting the urge to be a total pushover.

"No, Terry, I will not eat the bunny poop." He made sure his statement was firm, but still tried to lighten the mood. Making a quick mental note to keep saying Terry's name, form a connection, Billy tried to talk him down like a police negotiator. "Terry, I think you're just having a bad day. Either that or you just have a really weird sense of humor. And I can appreciate that."

"I'm not your buddy, Rile, so stop acting like I am. Not your fucking loser butt-buddy like Tom Mathers." Okay, so the friendly approach could use work. "Tom ain't here to save you either, so now you are going to open your goddamn mouth!"

"Leave him alone," Rachel said, standing up from her lab stool. This was an unexpected turn of events. Billy was quick to stand up as well, not wanting to be the only seated party in this negotiation.

"Wow, this must be a real dream come true for you, Rile. Your big-titted sweetheart comes to the rescue. You must be so proud," Terry said, keeping his eyes locked with Billy's before turning to address Rachel. "Sit your prick-teasing ass down!"

Rachel remained standing, trying to knit her brow in resolve but weakening around the eyes. *He better not make her cry.*

"Don't talk to her like that," Billy said. Where the hell was Mrs. Delta? This kid needed a rubber room and two or three burly orderlies. *"Put the ball in the hole, Chief."* That would straighten his cuckoo ass right out.

Terry ignored him, still focused on Rachel. "Why are you always hiding those things?" Terry asked, motioning to his own chest. "Sweaters, always with the sweaters. I don't think I've ever seen you show a single...uh, inch of tit."

"That's enough, Terry," Billy said, then looked around the room at the other four students. They all looked like they were rooting for him and Rachel, but none of them were running down the hall to get help either. If nobody was going to help, Billy was going to have to do something to stop this besides asking nicely. He reached out and put his hand on Terry's shoulder.

"You a tough guy now? Genius, funny man and a tough guy? You're the fuckin' triple threat, Rile," Terry said, turning and catching Billy's hand just as Billy started pulling away. His grip was strong, and his arms must have been even stronger because he pulled Billy in and had him in a headlock with minimal effort. "This one right here is a real catch, Rachel."

"Fucker," Billy tried to yell but it came out as a muffled cough. The blood was pooling in his head and he could feel pins and needles prickling his cheeks as Terry flexed his arm muscles, tightening his hold. *This idiot is going to kill me. He's not going to mean to, but I'm still gonna choke to death.*

Terry kept talking to Rachel. "By the way, did you know that my brother once finger-banged your sister? Before she started dating Jake Connolly, of course, a bunch of years ago. He told me all about it."

"Let him go, you're hurting him." Billy couldn't see Rachel, but he could hear her. All he could see were his and Terry's sneakers. Were there drops of blood on Terry's shoelaces? Maybe he hadn't snapped just now. Maybe this was an all-day event and he just came to school after ax-murdering his entire family.

"Oh yeah, forgot about your snack, Rile." Terry put the rabbit feces up to Billy's nose, letting Billy appreciate the delicate bouquet of aromas before moving them to right in front of his closed mouth. Billy's vision spotted and wobbled, a VCR in bad need of tracking.

"You're going to eat this or I'm going to break your neck." Terry's muscles tightened. This kid had been working out, and Billy had no doubt at that moment that Terry could do it.

Rachel wanted to stop Terry from killing Billy, but after all those things he said about her, it had taken a backseat and become her secondary objective. She wrapped her fingers around one of the science room's many glass beakers. Terry had made the mistake of turning his back to her, and she took a step toward him. Billy grunted and squirmed in the headlock. His face was red and veiny and a snot bubble had formed in one nostril. He kept his mouth cemented shut as Terry tried mashing the poop into his face.

Rachel gave one last look around the classroom, making eye contact with everyone she could. She was letting them know that she meant business: she was going to break the glass over Terry's head. If they had a problem with that, they could try to stop her. She remembered every bitchy joke that had ever been directed at her, every guy who'd ever snickered as he gestured to his friends to check her out, and her knuckles went white. *This asshole is going to hit the floor.*

"What the hell is going on in here?" Mrs. Delta stepped into the classroom, wearing a new coat over the blouse and skirt she had left in. "Terry Manfred, what do you think you are doing?"

Her voice was far too calm for the situation she was witnessing.

Terry looked at her for a moment, trying to recognize what was different about her. It was hard to think, hard to reconstruct all the details that his twitching eyes were taking in. Drunk with power and the thrill of revenge, his thoughts and senses were a jumbled mess.

He put it all together when he spotted the blood dribbling down Mrs. Delta's sleeve: she was playing on his team now.

He let Billy go. The putz collapsed to the floor, gagging and coughing. Terry put his hands back into his pockets, rabbit shit and all.

"Class is dismissed. Please collect your belongings and leave." The students glanced around at each other, Billy gasping for air and Rachel still looking on edge, sweaty and red in the face, a weapon in her hand. Terry would remember that. They packed up their book bags and left. Rachel didn't even bother packing, just pressed her Trapper Keeper to her ample breasts and stormed into the hallway.

Terry made a show of packing his bag and closing the door at the top of Bilbo's cage.

"Not you, Mr. Manfred," Mrs. Delta said with a smile. "We have to discuss your unsatisfactory behavior and decide what to do about it."

The big woman gathered up the short teen in her arms, laughing and clicking. Terry had never thought of her in a sexual way before—at least, never in a way that wasn't intended to gross himself out. Now as she enfolded him in her large, soft breasts, he caught a whiff of her mature scent and felt a tug in his pants, as well as one beneath his tongue.

Tom hated to crumble a perfectly good fight so quickly, but walking around the empty neighborhood had softened his resolve. There was nothing else to do tonight, so he might as well watch *Reanimator* at Billy's. There would always be plenty of opportunities to give Billy the silent treatment. Plus the gut punch had been a bit much; he would admit that.

But school wasn't going to let out for a few more hours, and Billy would stay to the bitter end, so adventure would have to be scrounged up around town.

The streets were quiet. When he played hooky he was used to the roads being half-populated by mothers running errands and the occasional delivery truck, but today he spotted only one car every few minutes. It was as if the entirety of Islip (East, West, Central and Terrace, maybe Bayshore as well) was conspiring to keep his day as boring as possible.

If I had my bike, I could ride out to the mall, he thought. Tom was three blocks away from his house before realizing that he should have taken his bike out of the garage if he was going to do anything interesting, but he was not walking back for it.

Tom's mouth was dry and his stomach felt ready to collapse in on itself. He was ten minutes from the school when he decided to check out 7-Eleven for some refreshments. While he was there, he could see if any of his fellow losers/dropouts were hanging outside. There were normally two or three, standing on their skateboards and smoking cigarettes. Tom didn't really like any of those kids (a few could be called men—"super seniors" or dropouts who were years older than Tom), but it was better than sitting in the parking lot of the school. At school he risked harassment from Jerry, Islip Terrace High's seventy-year-old, one-man security detail.

Tom turned the corner and approached the convenience store from behind. There was no one out back by the loading dock. Turning again toward the storefront, he found it deserted as well. "Shit," he said to himself. He usually didn't like coming here when the dropouts were around, unless one of them owed him money or he was looking for one of them to buy him beer, but now he wanted the conversation, shitty as it would have been.

I can still get a Big Gulp, he thought and peered in the front window, past a poster advertising "Savings So Good, It's Scary!" Tom was checking to make sure the coast was clear; he had recently been caught trying to boost a twelve-pack of Bud Light while the clerk was in the storeroom. It was the fat white guy who'd caught him and threatened to call the cops after beating the shit out of him. Tom hadn't stayed to hear the rest. He had just walked out the door and not looked back.

Good; it was a different guy behind the counter, the Indian guy with the mustache. Tom liked that guy. Not only was the guy friendly, but he was pretty much clueless when you paid for a sixty-nine-cent Snickers bar while holding fifteen bucks' worth of merchandise under your jacket. Tom undid the snaps on his leather jacket, unzipped his pockets and entered the store.

"Hey, how's it going, buddy?" Tom waved to the Indian dude, who gave a single nod back. That was weird. Most days the guy was all smiles, adding "my friend" to the end of all his sentences. Now he just stood behind the soft pretzel carousel with the door open, his eyes focused on nothing specific, looking like he were trying to warm the pretzels with his heat vision.

Tom walked over to the soda fountain, debating between the large Big Gulp and the Fuckin' Huge one. He settled on the large, popped in some ice and then mixed Dr. Pepper and Coke, waiting for the carbonation to subside and then filling it to the brim. Tom liked to get the maximum soda for his buck, especially when he was actually paying.

With his drink full, he moved over to the candy aisle. He touched one of the short black leather tassels on his zippers, considered the candies for a moment, and then zipped up his pockets. He wasn't going to steal anything today. He didn't feel like being a punk this afternoon. It wasn't that he was morally opposed to the idea; he just didn't want to give the Indian guy any trouble. The guy had it bad enough working this crappy job and dealing with shitty people twelve hours a day. He didn't need to catch heat from his boss because he couldn't stop shoplifters.

Tom picked up Sno-Caps and put them back down, opting instead for Razzles ("First it's candy, then it's gum!"). In an attempt to kill time, he browsed the rest of the aisles. Entenmann's crumb cake, Little Debbie's, TV dinners in the freezer, Bic lighters, and he was done.

The Indian guy looked at him from behind the counter. His mustache wasn't as neatly kept today. They stared at each other in silence for longer than was customary. "Uh, I think I'm ready to go now," Tom said, sounding like more of a jerk than he wanted to.

"Sure, my friend." The Indian guy roused somewhat and began ringing up Tom's soda and candy. There were some beeps from the cash register as the man pecked one button at a time, a look of solemn concentration in his eyes. There was a ding and the man spoke.

"Ten sixty-six, please."

"I think you made a mistake. This is, like, two bucks' worth of stuff," Tom said.

"I'm sorry." The man rubbed his hands together. He looked sick.

"You all right, dude? You don't look so hot."

"Hot?" the man said. The guy was obviously loopy, although he didn't look like the drug-ingesting type.

Before Tom could ask if he could call the guy a doctor or an ambulance, the front door swung open. It was the short, fat, white guy, the one who had caught Tom stealing. He had his standard-issue 7-Eleven shirt under his arm and the cap already covering his bald head, obviously arriving for work.

"You! I know you, kid." The fat guy was already red in the face. After Tom had run off, the guy must have been hungry to catch him in the store again. The fat guy put down his shirt on the stack of *Newsday*s by the door and readjusted his cap, creasing the brim. "Barun, call the cops," he yelled to the Indian guy. "This is the fucking kid I was telling you about."

"I don't know what you're talking about, pal." Tom dug into his back pocket and brought out his wallet, pulling out a fiver and slapping it on the counter. It was his only money, and leaving it stung.

"You got sticky fingers, kid. Think I don't know you? Looking like Fonzie in that fucking jacket." The fat man approached, clenching his fists and squatting down. With his neck and body language and hairy arms, he clearly was trying to look as Neanderthal-level imposing as possible.

"I didn't steal anything," Tom said, and for this visit it was true. He tried a quick pivot to get around the guy, but it didn't work. Already heaving with exertion, the short guy spread out his arms and backed up, blocking the exit.

"Barun? What the fuck are you doing just standing there?" the fat man said and coughed. "Call the cops."

"Look, Barun over there is acting screwy. I think he's sick. Now get out of my way." Tom pushed past him with the hand holding the Big Gulp. The cup bent and the cap loosened, spilling his combination Dr. Pepper/Coca-Cola down the guy's neck and shoulder. The shock from the cold liquid knocked the fat guy into an end-cap of Doritos and almost put him on his ass.

Tom wasted no time, making a beeline for the exit. As he ran out he heard Tubby yelling at Barun, and hoped the Indian was so delirious that Barun punched the bastard and then sought medical attention for himself.

Tom walked down the street toward school. Grumbling, he shook off his wet, soon-to-be sticky hand. Not only did he overpay, but that fucker had made him spill half of his drink.

This day could not possibly get any worse.

"Are you okay? Do you need me to walk you down to the nurse's office?" Rachel asked. She rubbed Billy's shoulder as they walked the empty hall. He shook his head to indicate that he was okay.

"Then let's get the hell out of here," she said, even though they still had twenty minutes before the bell for ninth period. "I've had about all the education I can stand."

"Okay," Billy coughed, trying to speak at a normal volume when his throat was far from up to the task. "Let's go," he said, whispering this time.

They walked a few steps before either spoke again. Billy's heart rate had begun to level off after Terry Manfred let go of his neck, but now that he was walking side by side with Rachel, he felt on the brink of cardiac arrest.

"Thanks for helping." He stopped midsentence, not for emphasis but out of necessity. He swallowed hard, getting rid of some of the excess spit that seemed to be pooling in his mouth. The motion hurt his throat. He wondered if the surplus saliva was because of the attack or a side effect of Rachel Krieger talking to him.

"I didn't do much," she said.

"No, you were awesome." He studied her expression. The attack and Terry's harassment must have shaken her as much as it did him. "How are you doing?"

"I would be doing worse if I was the one who was just put into a headlock by a crazy person."

"Good point." Billy tried to laugh, tried to point out that he was kidding, but it sent him into another heaving fit. What was it about this girl? Out of all of the many other unattainable, good-looking classmates and neighborhood girls, why was it Rachel who made him feel like an even bigger asshole? It wasn't the physical attraction—though that was part of it—but something else with her.

Billy did not consider himself a romantic, but over the years he'd gleaned certain information about Rachel, and with each new snippet he'd fallen deeper into hopeless, stupid love with her. Occasionally Darcy would mention a band Rachel liked or he would eavesdrop on their conversations about their weekends, and Billy would spackle another piece onto the mosaic of Rachel he'd constructed in his mind. Creepy? Yes, he would admit that. But it was also genuine. He'd watched the way she was with Darcy, polite but also separate, her own person with her own opinions that usually didn't mesh with her friend's. In a way he even doubted if Rachel considered herself Darcy's friend. She was too nice.

Now, standing there and actually talking to her, all of that meant nothing and he realized how insane and unproductive his fixation had been. If he wanted to know more about her, he should have just been asking. So why couldn't he? Aside from the physical pain of conversation, why couldn't he ask Rachel one of the million questions he had always wanted answers to?

Tom tossed the last two Razzles into his mouth and balled up the bag. They were most tasty when they were candy, but he didn't spit out the gum. Instead he had an entire bag's worth of Razzle-gum packed into his cheek. He was a block away from school now and the last bell wouldn't ring for another half hour. Chewing his gum, he walked and brainstormed excuses for rejoining video night. A straightforward apology would work, of course, but he would lose face.

I'll have to play up the "I have nothing better to do" angle, he thought. *After getting my apology, obviously.*

The school soon came into view, and his scheming ended when he spotted Rachel and Billy exit out of the side door and into the parking lot. "There's gotta be a fire drill or something," he said to himself and waited. No one else came out of the door. Not the double doors at the front of the building either. "You've got to be shitting me," Tom said.

Billy and Rachel Krieger are skipping class together. Tom smiled so wide that the corners of his mouth hurt at the place where his stubble cut into his deep dimples.

They hadn't spotted him yet, and probably wouldn't if they turned left out of the parking lot, toward their houses. Tom was possessed by the sudden urge to drop out of sight. Inexplicably, he wanted to follow the two lovebirds in secret and see how things developed. The desire was quashed almost as soon as it arrived. Billy talking to a girl was news, but not something Tom wanted to waste a huge part of his day investigating.

Making sure that neither of them saw him, he walked back the way he had come, trying to remember where the nearest pay phone was. Tom wondered if Darcy had skipped ninth period as well. If he could get hold of her, it would be better than any show Billy and

Rachel could offer him.

He's blowing it big time, Rachel thought, *but he is cute. In a squirmy, stammering, not really attractive way.*

Why was she such a cruel person? The idea came unbeckoned into her mind, but it had a ring of truth to it. Why lead this kid on for so long without acknowledging him? It was so obvious that he liked her. Not in the way that the football team liked her, either. Not because of her red hair and big breasts. "Hey, do you think the rug matches the drapes?" Each one said it within earshot of her, like she'd never heard that one before.

Her hair wasn't even *that* red; if anything it was a light brown with a hint of scarlet.

Billy seemed to like her for who she was, not just how she was built. Just as she thought this she saw his eyes fall to her chest and then shoot right back up to her face. *He's only human,* she thought and giggled out loud.

"What's that?" Billy asked. His eyes were darting around, before hovering on her for a second and then pointing down the block. The poor guy was going to have a heart attack if she didn't take over the conversation soon. He'd been both strangled and had some one-on-one time with his crush in the same hour. She had to make it easier on him.

"Oh, nothing," she said. She stopped walking, placed her hand on his shoulder. "We've lived next to each other for a very long time, but I don't think we've ever had a conversation longer than 'hi' or 'good morning'."

"Well," Billy said. She resumed walking and he had to step double time to catch up. Suddenly she really wanted him to know about the beaker, about how she had almost assaulted Terry Manfred to save him, but there was no way to go about it without looking like she was boasting. Besides, Billy probably didn't want to think anymore about the incident.

"I guess we'll get a chance to talk tonight, then. You know, since Darcy asked me if I wanted to come to your movie night."

"Video night," Billy corrected her abruptly, then looked like he regretted it the second that the words left his mouth, staring down at his shoes and trying to downplay the excitement with which he had said it.

"You say that like a 'movie night' is different from a 'video night'." Rachel smiled. She poked her tongue up against the back of her teeth. Rhonda had gotten braces as a kid, but the dentist said that Rachel would probably never need them. The teeth were all straight except for one of the bottom incisors, which butted in at an odd angle and gave her what Darcy called an "adorable and acceptably crooked smile".

"Well, that's just what we call it," he said. "Tom and I, we call it video night. It's silly."

"It's not silly, but I do sense that there's something else going on there."

Billy had gone total deer-in-the-headlights. She felt the back of her teeth again, smiling wide but with her mouth closed. Just so he didn't think she was coming on to him.

"Something else? No, there's no reason. That's just what we call it. Kid's stuff, old habits die hard, and more clichés like that."

"Well, the way I understand it is that a movie is a movie and a video is a video. There is supposedly a big difference. Not only in the size of the screen but in the kind of light."

Billy's jaw looked like it was about to hit the ground. She had him now and was giving him a warmer, fuzzier variety of heart attack. She wasn't just being nice because he'd almost had his head popped off; she wanted to prove she was different from most of the girls who'd probably snubbed him in the past. She didn't want to date him, but she did want to be nice, and indulging his interests was a good way to do it.

"It's the difference in the way our eyes tell our brain to perceive the light. The difference between reflected light—the kind you get in a movie theater when the light bounces off the screen—and projected light—the kind you get from a TV as it shoots the light directly into your eyes. Am I getting this right?" Rachel asked him, playing innocent.

Billy nodded, smiling like a little kid. "Yeah, that's exactly right. I tell that to Tom all the time, but I don't think he actually gives a shit. That guy never listens. Excuse my language."

"I give a shit," Rachel said, ignoring his apology and tossing him her best Mona Lisa smile, no teeth. "Kind of."

Rachel was now glad that she at least half-listened to the things that Darcy told her, even though most of it was just stuff Tom Mathers told Darcy parroted back. Rachel had found some use for it.

Maybe Manfred the Sped had succeeded in choking him to death. Maybe this was heaven; was it possible that there was a heaven and it was just a projection of Billy's own greatest and most secret dreams? Or maybe he had passed out and this was the delirious, drug-induced hallucination on the way to the hospital, pouring his heart out to a very confused EMT.

When he knew that Rachel was cool, and that she was coming over tonight, he should have felt less inhibited. But he didn't.

Be funny, dickhead. Now's your chance to "wow" her.

"So, you like movies then?"

"Yes, sometimes. I used to go all the time. My dad's big into them. He used to bring me. When I was really young he would even let me skip school and go with him. He'd say that 'nothing before high school counts anyways' and then take me out of class."

"You don't get to go as much now?"

"With him? Jeez, I can't remember the last one we saw together."

She's opening up. Hurry up, we're almost home and this may be your last chance to talk with her without Tom and Darcy around.

"So, uh, do you like music?"

Rachel gave him a look like he'd missed an opportunity. "Yes. I think everyone likes music now and then."

Music? How fucking stupid are you? You completely change subjects

119

now?

"That was abrupt. I didn't mean to cut you off about your father," he said. His head was swimming: trying to do the backstroke and the butterfly at the same time before finally settling on the doggie paddle.

"Your color really hasn't gotten any better since we left school. If anything it's worse. I mean, you're still all red in the face." She smiled. Her bottom row of teeth was slightly off alignment. It was endearing and Billy had noticed it before, but he'd never gotten such a good look. It was beautiful.

That's a joke, it's got to be. The girl made a joke: laugh at it, you fuck.

Billy laughed. Almost too hard, but it still served to let some of the tension out of his stomach muscles.

"I must seem like a real mess, but I promise I'm usually much more boring," he said. He found his footing and was now exploiting what he saw to be his niche: the goofy, moderately funny guy with the mediocre face (at least he hoped it was mediocre). It may have been too little too late, because they were approaching their block. At least he would go out swinging, conversationally speaking.

"Well, don't be boring, never that. Boring is so much worse." She was an angel, being so nice to him. "Just try not to be so much of a basket case next time we hang out."

"That's a good movie," he said. *You dick, it's an expression. She did not mean the Frank Henenlotter movie* Basket Case. He couldn't help it. Maybe it was an incurable psychological problem, like dyslexia or Tourette's.

"What is?"

"Nothing." He looked over at his empty house; his parents were in the city, a world away.. "Well, this is me." He pointed, even though she knew where he lived. It was a lame attempt at a joke.

"Yeah well, thata 'un over there is my homestead." She put on a cowboy accent and put his crappy joke to good use.

"So I'll see you tonight, like in a few hours?"

"Yeah, I'm just going to shower. I'm horrendous amounts of grody."

"Cool," he said.

"Cool that I'm showering or cool that I'm dirty?" she asked. She was kidding him but it still brought the blush roaring back to his face. "Jesus, please don't have a stroke, Billy. I promise I will stop making you do that." She reached out and put a finger to his cheek. "Your best impression of a fire hydrant."

She's way funnier than you, he thought as he watched her run up the path to her house, trying not to get caught staring slack-jawed as she took the front steps. *She's way funnier and she just touched your cheek.*

The house was dark, hot and humid. The blinds in the living room were shut, blocking the light of the cloudy day.

Despite the heat, which instantly made Rachel uncomfortable, the house smelled cleaner than it had in years. Mr. Clean and bleach burned their antiseptic scents into her nostrils. Had the shock of losing Jake sent Rhonda on a grief-fueled cleaning spree? It might have been the first time the girl had cleaned. Ever.

Rachel kicked off her shoes and left them beside the front door. In the days since she'd been home to change them, her socks had gone from white to brownish gray. *Should have taken a pair from Darcy's,* she thought and then remembered the hurry in which she had left.

"Rhonda?" she said into the still house. There was no answer.

Her feet clung to the carpeting as she walked upstairs, toward the bathroom and salvation from her own grime. She hadn't showered since Wednesday night, and her sweat was mixing with two days' worth of grungy buildup.

She reached the top of the stairs and called again, "Anyone home?" At the end of the hall Rhonda's door was closed, and Rachel inferred that she was probably sleeping it off.

Rest up, sis. It was a thought that made her feel dirty. *Sure, now you start calling her sis. Only after she's suffered a...*

"Hey." The voice startled Rachel, and she turned around to see

Rhonda closing the door to their parents' bedroom.

"How are you?" Rachel asked. Rhonda looked up at her, but Rachel couldn't make out her expression in the darkness. She reached for the hallway light switch and flicked it on. The bulb was dim. It was more of a night-light that kept the family from stubbing their toes than anything else, but it allowed her to see her sister's face.

"I'm fine," Rhonda said and motioned behind her at the door. Rachel could hear movement inside her parents' room. "You just missed him. Dad's going back to sleep. He says he's going to have a really busy shift tonight."

"You should rest too," Rachel said. Rhonda looked terrible. Bloodshot eyes, blotchy skin. The smell was the worst part; it eclipsed Rachel's own sweaty body odor with a fog of putrefied sadness. How had she gotten this bad in only one day? "Have you eaten recently?"

"I had some eggs this morning," Rhonda said. She looked Rachel in the eyes and attempted to soften her expression. "Don't worry about me. I'll be fine. I just need to rest."

"You should. I'm going to shower and then go to this thing across the street. Need me to make you a bite to eat?"

"No, thanks. Across the street?" There was an inordinate amount of interest in Rhonda's voice. The poor girl was out on her feet, a sleepwalker. She'd probably sleep until tomorrow afternoon.

"Yeah, I don't know if you know Billy Rile? Our neighbor? I don't think he has any older siblings; you may not know him. He's my age."

"I've seen him, but we've never talked. He's having a party?"

"Not a party, just a couple people watching a video. It's nothing, really. I can stay here if you need me to."

"You go. I'll be okay." Rhonda offered a weak smile; it was the first time in a long while that Rachel could remember seeing her sister smile. She hadn't seen much of Rhonda at all in the past few years, and when she had, Rhonda had been scowling or Rachel would see only the back of her head as she walked out the front door.

"Are you sure there isn't anything I can get for you before I hop into the shower?"

"No. I'm just going to sleep." Rhonda started down the hallway and Rachel searched for something else to say to her. She wanted something to make her feel like she had a sister again, however briefly.

"Rhonda, wait." Her sister stopped and looked over her shoulder and Rachel struggled for a way to keep the talk going. She grabbed the first idea that entered her head. "This is a weird question, but it came up today. Did you used to go out with Andy Manfred?"

Rhonda paused, standing in the hallway looking like she had forgotten why she was there, and then spoke. "Back in early high school, freshman or sophomore year, maybe. It was nothing serious. Why?"

"He's got a younger brother named Terry. I, uh, talked to him today," Rachel said.

"That's nice. Why did I come up?"

"Yeah, he says that Andy really liked you back then." Rachel had no idea why she was making this up. She knew nothing about the situation: that could have been a dangerous thing to say. She hadn't even known that her sister and Andy had ever had anything, not before Terry had said what he said. *By the way, did you know that my brother once finger-banged your sister?* She hoped this wasn't a painful subject for Rhonda, but she guessed that it wasn't.

"That's sweet. I liked him too." Rhonda stood zombified, but smiling, for another moment. "This boy. The one across the street. Do you like him?"

"Maybe. We'll see. First I have to shower." It was the first real conversation the girls had shared since Rachel had entered high school.

"Why not turn her?" Darl had his thumbs tucked into his waistband, a gesture of impatience that he had mined from his earlier self. "Just let one of the kids into the bathroom with her and it'll do the rest."

"No," Rhonda said.

"Why not?"

"Because I say so." Rhonda made an annoyed click and waved one of the children off of the bed. Its spikes were tearing into the sheets, and it would hurt itself if it got its legs tangled up inside the plush fabric of the comforter.

"Well, that's not a very compelling argument," Darl said. Sarcasm was something else he had picked up the more the annoying lieutenant droned on inside of his skull.

"Keep your voice down," Rhonda said. The shower was going strong in the opposite room. The girl would never be able to hear him. She continued in a harsh whisper. "You want one? Here's a good reason: if we send one of the children in, not only is there a chance that my sister might hurt it, but even if it worked out perfectly, there's the fact that a child can't just turn someone and be ready go turn another person in a few minutes. We need them ready. We're sticking to my plan." Rhonda was growing exasperated. Feeling was entering her voice, Darl noted, for the first time.

Looks like your girlfriend's got some anger issues.

Darl ignored himself (it was becoming easier) and kept talking to Rhonda. "All right, then, if that's the problem. If we need more kids, I'll go on in there and shove this down her throat." He held up a black seed and could feel its subtle undulation between pinched fingers.

"We're not taking the time to clean up another body."

"What body? If we get rid of her, then that'll be it for the entire family."

"What about this Aunt Mary-Kaye? What if she comes over to check on her sister or her nieces? Did you think of that? She finds a bloody crime scene."

"In a day or two it's not going to matter." Darl was tired of this.

"Procedure. This is the way it is. If you don't like it..."

Darl cut her off. "Forget it. Whatever you say is fine." They both heard the shower shut off and Rhonda put a finger to her lips, signaling for quiet.

"She leaves and we start the plan, got it?"

"Yes, ma'am."

"Maybe, if everything goes smoothly, you can pay her and her friends a visit tonight."

"To quote Lieutenant Todd Darl of the Suffolk County Sheriff's Department: *That's more like it*," he said, smiling, getting Darl's Mayberry tough-guy drawl just right.

Chapter Twelve

Rhonda picked up the remote from the nightstand and flicked on the television. It was the five o'clock news, a New York station. Despite their argument earlier and Darl's emerging lack of faith in her command, she snuggled closer to him for warmth. He put his hand on her chest below the neck, squeezing her gently. They watched together.

The newscaster's speech was not as confident as usual. Her non-region-specific accent was fraying along the edges, breaking occasionally into a harsh Queens tone. Her left eye was far redder than her right. She blinked hard and begged the viewers' apology: she must have caught a case of what was going around.

"Look how far we've come," Darl said.

Rhonda peeled herself off of Darl, got out of bed and went to the window, stepping over the children lying on the ground, their six legs folded under them. "It looks like it will be getting dark soon. You should go get your uniform out of the dryer. There is an iron and board in the downstairs hall closet. You should use it."

"Don't be an idiot. Take the fucking hat off." Tom was sitting on the bed, playing Nintendo while Billy changed clothes in preparation for the night.

"It's the coolest item of clothing I own." Billy tugged on the flaps of the hunting cap, dragging them down over his ears. He looked himself over in the mirror and then tried it with the flaps up. The hat had looked better on the family ski trip three years ago.

"It's a winter hat and we're inside. You're going to look like a mental case. Put the hat back in the closet."

"Then what do I wear?"

"Clothes—you wear your regular clothes. Either the ones you're wearing right now or the twelve other sets you just tried on," Tom said, tossing the controller down on the bed and turning to Billy. "If you don't cool it, you're going to scare the girl. I mean, scare her even worse than your ugly fucking face does already."

"Come on, man. I'm not that ugly," Billy said, looking at the end of his nose up close in the mirror. He appraised himself while tipping his head back. His nostrils were large, but not comically so. His features were just strong.

Tom shook his head and continued playing.

After a closer inspection, Billy spoke again: "Am I ugly? I can't really tell what ugly is for guys."

"Jesus, man, I'm kidding. No, you're not ugly."

"Really?" This was getting uncomfortable, but Billy needed to know.

"Yeah, you're not, like, a mutant." Tom sighed. "Look, that whole deal about 'it's only what's on the inside that counts' is bullshit. But as long as you don't have any serious deformities and don't fall to your knees and try to make out with her feet, I think you'll be fine. Just act natural, like you do around me."

"Okay, like I do around you."

"On second thought, maybe not exactly like you act around me. Try for a middle ground: be slightly more normal than you are around me, but not as shy as you are around her right now."

"Thanks, good talk," Billy said, but Tom was back into the game, so it seemed that the sarcasm had passed unnoticed.

"Rhonda?" Rachel called down the dim hallway toward her sister's room. Her call was intended to be soft enough not to wake Rhonda if she had gone to sleep, but loud enough for her to hear if she was awake. There was no answer but a soft scratching sound coming from down the hallway.

"I think I'm going out," she continued. "I'm going to go hang out with Darcy and then go over to Billy's." The stillness of the house was making her uneasy, and she felt guilty for wanting to get out so badly. Also for her freshly applied makeup and the sweet smell of her perfume. "If you need anything I'll be right across the street." There was no reply except the same small shuffling. Except for this tiny sound, the house was warm and silent. This early in the night, the house was never so quiet. A death could do that, even one as removed from the family as Rhonda's boyfriend. Rachel thought about it for a moment, but she couldn't remember Jake ever visiting their house. He was that much of a noncharacter in her life. His absence, or maybe it was just Rhonda's sadness, was still felt.

Leaving the dying house, Rachel was unhappy to find that the streets were spooky as well. Not because of the dark and chill, but because of the lack of activity. At this hour on a typical Friday night, the younger neighborhood kids would be either riding their bikes around or hiding in bushes and playing a game of "manhunt" (which was just "hide and seek" with a cooler name). The older kids would usually be gathering in someone's garage and drinking or getting a carload of friends together to go to the movies. Tonight there was no one. Rachel quickened her steps and blamed her excitability on the bizarre week she'd been having.

Dead boyfriends, absent parents, nutzo sisters, homicidal school bullies: it was little wonder that she was headed to hang out with Darcy. Her pseudofriend's unflagging bitchiness and predictable conversation topics (Tom and crappy music) provided normalcy at the end of a very unnormal week.

Rachel didn't consider herself a feminist (she'd heard conflicting reports on what that even meant), but she knew that she was a lot more of one than Darcy Roberts would ever be. Darcy's level of male dependence was almost as frightening as her penchant for risky substance abuse. It was a rare occurrence when Darcy was able to bait Rachel into participating in boy-talk, but maybe just for tonight, just because it felt like the normal "girly-girly" thing to do, she would talk about Billy Rile. She'd tell Darcy about his goofy humor, his awkward half smile and his genuine personality.

Darcy would probably laugh. But that was okay.

Geraldine Dobson, sitting comfortably at the dining room table, touched the tip of the pencil to her tongue and then completed another word. Twenty-seven down, the hint was, "Tom's Slave Driver."

She thought for a moment and then spoke aloud. "Simon Legree," she said and filled in the puzzle.

"Could you please not do that?" Kenny said and looked up at her from over his thick glasses.

"Well, I'm sorry, honey. I just plain forget that I do it sometimes. I get so caught up in the crossword, finally find a word, and I've just got to share it with the world," she said, but that was a lie. She announced every single word, because it annoyed Kenny. Kenneth Dobson who had his Budweiser perched on the edge of his Barcalounger and the television turned up just loud enough to be a distraction.

When you've been married for thirty-one years, you have to figure out novel ways to annoy your partner just to keep your own sanity: that was Geraldine's policy. If she, the wife, was expected to cook his meals and clean up his mess, she'd make damn sure that he couldn't fully enjoy drinking himself to sleep.

"Oh, would you come on!" Kenny yelled at the Jets and pointed to the fuzzy screen with the top of his beer can. "I can go round up the neighborhood winos, buy them some jerseys and have them in better shape by Monday. Unbelievable. The fans aren't even into them anymore. Look, the stands aren't even a quarter full. Buncha stiffs."

This was part of Kenny's new routine, ever since buying the video recorder: professional football every night of the week. Most nights he was asleep before the fourth quarter, so the majority of the week's games were still fresh.

Geraldine did not look, and tried ignoring him to no avail. "Lout," she said. "L. O. U. T," she repeated and then scribbled in the margin of her crossword puzzle.

"Funny, very goddamn funny." Kenny took a glance over his shoulder at his wife.

"What's so funny, dear? It's really one of my words. You want to see?"

"Yeah, sure it is." Kenny waved her off and went back to watching the game. It was only the first quarter, and it was going to be a long night.

To retrieve the pruning shears, Darl had to open up the tool shed. Throwing open the door to the cramped shed invited gawking stares from Harold and Deborah's dead faces. The faces didn't unnerve him and they didn't amuse him—they just were.

It wasn't only Darl's body that refused to react to the two bloated, pale corpses, but deep inside his mind even the original Darl had grown desensitized to the gore. He was still present, still watching, but his voice had devolved into a low, deflated whisper. He was muttering curses, but Darl no longer cared to decipher exact words and phrases.

Hopefully he will be gone soon, Darl thought, and for the first time the thought seemed wholly his own. Maybe the old Darl was finally dying.

It was getting chilly and he pulled his jackets closed with his good hand (under his department issue vinyl squad coat he had a flannel hunting jacket, on permanent loan from Harold Krieger). Using the two remaining human fingers on his right hand, he carried the shears.

As he walked back to the fence, he glanced down at the triangle of his uniform left exposed at the necks of the jackets: his shirt was stained all to hell. By the time his shirt was in the wash, the blood from his neck wound, along with the smaller blotch from the cut on his left arm, had dried into a consistent shade of burnt umber. The washing machine had taken some of the intensity out of the stain, but his right side was still considerably darker than his left and nobody was going to confuse it for a coffee stain. Viewed outside, under a darkening sky, his upper half resembled a black-and-white cookie. He'd stapled the cut on the left sleeve closed, but if it weren't for the squad jacket there would be little to add to the impression that he was, in actuality, a law enforcement officer.

"Good. Now we cut a hole." Rhonda said, tracing an imaginary half circle on the chain-link. She was wearing thin, black fall gloves that the old Rhonda had cut the tips of the fingers off of. Mutilating the gloves was no doubt a cutting-edge fashion statement at the time but of little utility to her now in the cold night air.

Darl knew that there would be no "we" involved in this work. He would be the one cutting the hole. He wanted to complain about this stage in the plan one more time, but Rhonda had a point. Simply tossing the children over the fence was an unnecessary risk. They'd seen how clumsy the creatures were on unsure ground, and how easily their spindly legs could snap. Darl would cut two lines in the bottom of the fence and then pry the flap open, allowing the children to run easily under it. Just like a doggie door.

The process took only a few minutes, but by the time he was done and Rhonda had gone back inside to fetch the children, it had gotten much darker. The effort it took to clip the chain-link made his good hand ache in the cold.

"All right," she said, motioning slightly with her chin. "Open it up."

Darl dropped the shears onto the dead grass and gripped the bottom of the fence with his good hand. It was difficult to even curl his fingers, much less pry the half-rusted metal fence apart, so he resorted to testing out his newly augmented right hand.

The new digits had stopped growing an hour or so ago, and had since begun to harden, solidifying themselves into their final, rough, thorny shape. His middle finger was easily double the length it had been before being severed. The finger now had three points of articulation instead of the customary two, and at the tip it curved into a sharp brown point. His ring finger was roughly the same size, with a dark red thorn growing out of the first knuckle. The new pinky finger had almost zero mobility, but its sharp point still looked "nasty as hell", as Darl would say. He had grown three weapons to replace his fingers.

Before placing it through the chain-link, he made his first attempt to flex the hand. The new growth was so incongruous with his old flesh that he would wind up hurting himself if he made a fist. If he did, the tips of his new fingers could reach all the way up to his wrists. He could slice himself right down the veins. That would be messy even if his blood didn't seem to be pumping as powerfully as usual. Outside, his heartbeat had slowed to an irregular thud, pushing what felt like icy sludge through his arteries.

After the creatures shimmied under the fence, Darl started the slow, frozen trudge back to the house before she caught his arm to stop him. "One last thing," she said. "Would you be a dear and please climb over there and cut the Dobsons' phone line?"

Geraldine Dobson wanted a cigarette. Badly.

The Jets were losing (not atypical) and Kenny's spectatorship was becoming more animated (also not atypical). Walking outside for a smoke would allow her not only the cool, mentholated nicotine rush she desired, but also a muffling of Kenneth Dobson's vitriolic rant about the Dolphins' offensive line. *They aren't even playing the Dolphins*, Geraldine mentally noted.

She grabbed her lighter from the end table and shrugged on her coat: fall was in full swing and winter was knocking on the window for early admittance.

"Make sure you close the door. Don't stink up the hallway with your goddamn cancer gas." Kenny didn't take his eyes from the television to yell at her and resumed sipping his beer after he added, "Plus, it's gettin' cold and heat ain't free!" What a walking, farting cliché.

Despite Geraldine's great strides in busting down her consumption (in this year alone she had gone from two packs of Marlboros a day to a scant one and a quarter of Virginia Slims), Kenny had begun insisting that she smoke outside. The announcement had sounded something like, "It is a filthy goddamn habit anyway and the brand-new couch

132

already smells like an ashtray."

So she put on her jacket, checked her pocket for Slims, stepped into her heavy rain boots and walked out the back door. She kept the door open just enough that some smoke could waft inside and be absorbed into the decades-old wallpaper. *It's all about finding ways to drive your opponent,* in this case a spouse of thirty-one years, *fucking nuts.*

She had a cig between her lips before she was out the door. These days she only wore lipstick on special occasions, but she still missed the way that it would cling to the paper of the cigarette, sometimes gluing it to her upper lip and allowing her to hold and light it without the need of puckering up. Tonight in the cold and the dark it took some effort to pucker. She squinted against the flash of the Bic lighter and was rewarded with a long drag of velveteen smoke. She let out short puffs with her mouth and sucked the smoke back up her nostrils. She held it at the back of her throat until finally letting it out into the autumn night.

Smoking so luxuriously was tempting fate: she knew that. But if she was going to have cancer in her lungs, she might as well have it in her neck, nose and tonsils as well. It was a terrible way to think, she knew that too, but with two parents dead from "the cancer", she felt that she was entitled to indulge in a little gallows humor now and again.

Broken twigs and a rustle set the end of her cigarette up in the night air.

"Who's that?" she asked into the night, the tip of her extra long cigarette bobbing along with her words ("You've come a long way, baby!" as the advertisements used to say). There was something skittering along the leaves piled against the side of the house. Although she'd never once broken down and fed them, she did enjoy the company of the neighborhood cats on nights like these.

"Spartacus?" she asked, knowing it was probably the one mangy tabby that had taken to visiting her regularly. He'd earned the name with his war-beaten whiskers and scarred left ear, and the fact that Kirk Douglas had been on television the night they first met.

The cat approached with uncharacteristic hesitancy. He was listing to one side, and before he reached the back steps had looked like he would lose his footing on more than one occasion.

"You all right, fella?" she asked. "Rough day at work? High on the catnip?" She giggled at her own jokes and sent two separate pillars of smoke out of her nose. Spartacus stepped into full view. She could tell that he wasn't all right, not at all.

"Jesus Christ," she said under the same breath that carried out the last of her precious smoke. She stubbed out the cigarette on the concrete steps and stayed bent over as she approached the cat, hands outstretched. She spoke the same way you would to a young accident victim in a crisis situation. "It's okay, Spart. It's gonna be okay. Don't run away now. Please just let me see you."

Instead of hissing and backing up, Spartacus seemed to regard her with a complicit understanding. The cat needed help and he knew it. Getting closer she could see that the fur on his one side (the side behind his adorably tough-looking nicked ear) was covered in blood. There was a small hole at the center of the splotch that was probably still oozing; she couldn't tell. Once she caught sight of the wound Geraldine began brainstorming theories of its origin. *Goddamn sadistic fucking kids, shooting a tabby cat with their slingshots or BBs or, or...* But the hole was bigger than that. She shuddered at the thought of what kind of neighborhood kid was sick enough to do this, and with what.

There was more rustling among the leaves again; it made both Geraldine and the cat jump. Without further hesitation she scooped the injured animal into her arms. As she'd predicted, Spartacus did not lash out, but instead placed his front paws gently over her shoulder. He was clinging to her for protection, but careful not to use his claws. "Let's get you inside," she said into his half ear.

"Kenny," she yelled as she stepped over the threshold, not bothering to take off her boots. "Kenneth!" she said, straining her lungs to compete with the television and impress upon her husband a sense of urgency. She had to call a third time before he would answer, so to spite him she left the back door ajar.

"What?" he yelled back, sounding concerned, but not concerned enough to leave the living room.

"Get the phone book out and find the number for the closest vet."

"The closest what?" Kenny asked as he walked out of the living room to get a look at his wife, smeared with cat blood and holding a tabby. "What's all this now? Jesus, Geraldine."

Both were so busy that they didn't see the three small visitors sneak through the open back door.

"Can you see anything?" Rhonda asked, pushing her face up against the glass of the laundry room window. The lights in the room were off, rendering her and Darl invisible to their prey. They both squinted out the window, watching as the Dobsons argued next door, Geraldine holding what looked like an injured cat.

"Maybe they couldn't get in? Maybe they're freezing to death as we sit here," Darl said. She didn't like his tone. He'd been looking to find fault with her plan since she had explained the way it was going to be. She would have to keep an eye on that: there was a point at which a lackey's helpfulness was overridden by the grief they gave, and Darl was reaching it.

"They'll get in, believe me." She paused, considered the situation and then elaborated. "They'll find a way, or they'll break a basement window, crawl toward the sound of those two jabbering idiots. What you don't understand is they aren't reasoning like you or I are." She paused again, unsure if a lecture was what Darl needed right this minute, but bored with the lack of progress next door. "A man of your age," she continued. "I'll assume that you are familiar with the ant."

"The ant?" Darl asked in response, just as she had planned him to.

"The ant and the rubber tree plant."

"Yes. High hopes. Todd Darl was familiar with that one. I get it, hilarious." He rolled his eyes and Rhonda glanced back out the window. Kenneth Dobson had the phone in his hand, from the looks of it trying to get help for the cat. His wife yelled at him with even more

135

ferocity. It wasn't his fault that there was no dial tone.

"Well, these children. Our children," she continued. "They aren't biding their time or waiting for the right opportunity. Every cell in their bodies wants to get at those people. That's not just determination, but biological determination. Do you know why we had to lock the door on them when Rachel was here? Because no matter what I said to them, no matter how much their mother begged, they would have ignored me the first chance they got and stuck her." She looked Darl in the eyes and reached a hand to his waist, neither watching the neighbors. She could tell from his expression that he didn't like her bringing up how she let Rachel go to her party. Tough. She was in charge. "It's their nature," she continued, forcing him to make eye contact. "An urge they can't outgrow. They only give themselves a temporary release." She ran the tips of her fingers along the front of his pants to accentuate the word release and was cut short by a scream. "Oops. There goes another rubber tree plant."

The first scream was not Geraldine's, but Kenny's. It eventually petered off into a mannish yelp, but the initial sound was a pure scream. He dropped the receiver to the living room phone and it hit the carpet with a thud. Its cord dragged the whole unit off the end table and to the ground. "What the hell is..." Were the only words he could finish before Geraldine caught sight of the thing standing on the dining room table and began screaming herself. Pointed crystalline spines, a soft belly glistening with slime, a small mouth lined with an abundance of sharp, carnivorous teeth, and long delicate-looking legs: the creature was a clicking mass of incongruent parts. The excitement startled Spartacus, who clawed at her shoulder and stomach until she was forced to break her hold and let the cat drop. Spartacus ran off between Kenny's legs and into the living room.

The creature on the table wavered for a moment, regarding husband and wife and then taking a few wobbly steps toward them. Slipping on Geraldine's place setting, it sent her crossword puzzle and pen gliding to the floor.

"Kenny," Geraldine said, imploring her husband's advice. "Kenny?" Her voice was low, but not the way she'd been talking to Spartacus. This time she didn't want the animal's attention at all.

The creature had no eyes that she could see, but waved around a couple of thin membranes in the area that she assumed was its face. It flapped first at her and then her husband. Kenny locked eyes with her and made a small motion with his hand. *Come to me. Carefully*, his body language said.

Geraldine took a timid step toward Kenny and the creature followed suit, taking one step to the edge of the rectangular table.

"Don't move. Stay right there, Ger." Kenny reached one shaky hand behind the doorway that separated the living room and the dining room. The creature sensed his movement and made a few nervous clicks, alternately picking up its two front legs as if unsure what to do.

"Ken. Don't do it," Geraldine heard herself saying. She knew he was grabbing for something on the end table, ready to be the hero.

As if on cue, it appeared in his hand: an old crystal ashtray, a sparkling relic of the bygone days when Geraldine was allowed to smoke inside the house.

The creature must have sensed danger because from below its teeth slithered a long tentacle, the tip glinting like the edge of a knife. There was no way Kenny could close the distance fast enough. His gut had grown considerably since his younger days and it weighed him down. It was written all over his knit brow and she saw what his plan of attack was going to be before he pulled his arm back. Thirty-one years married and you have a pretty good idea of what someone will do, even in the most unfathomable of situations.

The sudden movement of Kenny's windup spurred the creature to action. It lashed out at Geraldine: the spiked tentacle cut through the air in front of her eyes so fiercely that she could hear it. There was a flash as the crystal flew across the room. Kenny put enough force behind the throw that it would have broken through the drywall if he missed. But he didn't miss.

The animal was propelled from the table, the glass projectile not shattering but instead imbedding itself deep within its spiked carapace.

He may as well have shot it, for all the force with which it was swept off its feet and into the dining room wall. It stuck there for a moment, pinned in the air by two shattered legs until the weight crumbled the drywall and the creature toppled to the floor.

Before running to see to her, Kenny crossed the room, picked up a chair and smashed the dead creature (it *had* to be dead) to pieces, puffing with exertion as lumps of blackish-brown goo pelted his swinging belly.

"What," Geraldine started to ask and then heaved. The excitement of the moment had made the room spin and her stomach drop.

"I don't know," Kenny said. Now he came to her. Folding his big hairy arms around her, he hugged her close.

"That thing was, it was going to..." Her words trailed off and she put her forehead against her husband's. When she was a young girl she had always imagined marrying a man who was taller than her, but they were both five eight. Their similar heights precluded her from burying her face in his chest, but it didn't matter. They were together and for tonight—for the first time in a long time—Kenneth Dobson was her knight in shining armor.

"It's okay, it's dead," he whispered. Kenny rubbed his hands on her back. He used to have such masculine hands, but over the past decade they'd grown softer and the fingers plumper. The moment was there and gone. Gone at the exact second he dug his nails into the fabric of her sweatshirt and screamed into her ear.

"No!" Geraldine yelled as Kenny planted both hands on her shoulders and pushed her away. As he turned to face his attacker, she could see the bloody spot begin to blossom wider and wider on the back of his shirt. From the center of the wound dribbled a viscous green fluid. Below him on their dining room floor stood another creature, brandishing its spiked tentacle at waist level.

The animal clicked, making wild, triumphant sounds at Kenny. It was avenging its fallen brother, who was now in several greasy chunks soaking into the hardwood floor, dripping between the slats into the basement below.

Kenny grabbed at the back of the nearest chair, trying to steady himself but visibly wavering. He was fading fast. Blood shot out from below his left shoulder blade and painted the wall; the blade must have hit an artery. The animal clacked with palpable anger and Kenny collapsed. The animal slipped on the hardwood floor but couldn't get away fast enough. It was crushed under her husband's two hundred and fifty pounds and she heard him impale himself on the spikes with a light crunch and a squish.

"Kenneth," Geraldine said and stepped toward him. From under his gut the creature wriggled, not dead, but hurt badly. From between Kenny's legs came the tentacle, the creature stabbing at the flesh of his sides, desperate for release. Blood began to pool under his body and she heard the creature surrender to death with a gurgle.

"My God," Geraldine whispered to herself. Kenneth had said the phone wasn't working, but she had to try it anyway. He needed an ambulance. She scooped the phone off the living room floor and held it to her ear. There was nothing on the other end. She reentered the dining room and heard the now-familiar clicking begin behind her.

Another one! God! The thought was both exasperated and accusatory. She wasn't asking God for help but instead calling him to task. What were these things and what possible reason could there be for their existence in the universe?

She ran for the kitchen, away from the creature behind her and toward a hopefully functioning telephone. Without turning she heard the marching clack of clumsy footsteps as it began pursuit. *I'm going to kill you, you little bastard. If Kenny could do it, I certainly can.* She felt a pang of remorse that she'd reverted so quickly to trying to one-up her husband, but there was no time for second thoughts. Her knees burned. She hadn't moved this quickly since she was a child, and in the last few decades Kenny wasn't the only person who had put on a few pounds. It was anger that kept her upright and moving.

There was no time to place a call. She passed the kitchen phone and went straight for the sink. In the sink, under the leftover plates and silverware from this morning's breakfast, was the frying pan. She silently thanked her own lazy self for not doing the dishes this afternoon and grabbed hold of the pan. The skillet was flecked with fleshy globules of bacon fat that had crusted to the nonstick surface, and she wriggled her nose as she raised it high.

She whirled about-face just in time to level the pan to her chest, inadvertently blocking the creature's tentacle as it hurtled straight for her solar plexus. There was a satisfying metallic *tink* and the critter staggered backward in either shock or pain.

"You better back up," Geraldine said. She hefted the pan above her shoulder with both hands, mimicking the stance of a baseball player or very aggressive golfer. The creature clicked and lunged a second time, with much less ferocity than the first time. It was a tepid warning swing, nowhere near her, but frightening nonetheless. From behind the creature came not a click, but a hiss. Spartacus limped out from where he'd been hiding between the refrigerator and counter.

The cat provided the distraction she had needed. Geraldine dropped to her knees as she swung the frying pan downward. The blow shattered some of the creature's spines, impaling it with its own pointed body. Greenish-white blood flew up, splashing Geraldine's arms and face and sending Spartacus jumping back behind the fridge for cover.

When she delivered the second smack, she allowed herself a satisfied war grunt, a multipurpose sound of anguish and victory. After the third blow it was completely dead, not much left but a twitching mound. Its guts squeezed out of its flattened body like a tube of toothpaste, but she gave it a fourth crack for good measure. And a fifth for luck. Reluctant to lose her faithful weapon, she held tight to the skillet as she approached the back of the fridge.

"Com'ere, big guy," she said, and Spartacus jumped to her arms. Rising, she shouldered the cat and weapon with the same arm and reached for the telephone on the wall with her free hand. There was no dial tone: she would have to run to the neighbors for help, maybe ask Deborah Krieger to call 911. As she planned her next move, Spartacus began to cough, and her sudden concern for the pathetic animal finally caused tears to gather at the corners of her eyes.

"It'll be all right, pal," she said, assuming that the cat had chosen a poor time to start bringing up a hairball. That was her final thought before Spartacus's miniature tentacle shot from his mouth and impaled her under the chin.

Chapter Thirteen

Terry didn't leave the school until it was dark outside. Even on days when he had extra help or detention (sometimes he had both), he never got out this late. But Mrs. Delta wasn't offering him his normal after-school help. *Well, sex education class, maybe,* he thought and snickered to himself. The pain behind his temples got worse as he laughed.

Now that Terry Manfred had "made friends" with Mrs. Delta, he felt even stronger. He was still just as angry at Billy Rile though; maybe even more so.

Terry had never done it with a girl before. The closest he had ever come to a sexual experience was feeling up one of his brother's dates once when she had passed out on their couch. It had changed something inside him, just like he had heard that it would. Before, he may have postured like a man. Puffed out his chest, bumped into weaklings. But it was only now—after suckling and cradling Mrs. Delta's abundant flesh, probing and being probed—that he felt like a real man. He remembered the sickly sweet release of wrapping tentacles and smiled.

The change was immediate and profound. Colors were now brighter, crisper, and sounds were sharper. The streetlights looked positively neon, and the taillights of the few passing cars were dazzling crimson beams that zigzagged across his retinas. But the night air was still cold, and Terry pushed his hands deeper into his pockets after zipping his jacket up as far as it could go. He was walking home, but every time he came to an intersection he had to stop and think about where home was. The drop in temperature that had accompanied nightfall seemed to be slowing down his brain. It was hard to think.

Maybe I shouldn't go home. Maybe I should go get me a drink, warm myself up. Snatch and grabs were easy: his brother had shown him how once. The trick was to look innocent, grab what you wanted quickly and run like hell. *Once I'm warm, maybe I'll also go pay a visit to Billy Rile's house.*

Despite the cold, walking out the front door felt good. Darl hated all this sneaking around, and even though it was quite dark, he felt as though he was reclaiming his freedom by crossing the Kriegers' front lawn and walking up to the Dobsons' house.

Watching from the laundry room had only gotten them so far. They had seen Kenny get stuck and Geraldine being chased out of the living room, but that was the extent of the action. Darl assumed everything had gone according to plan, but Rhonda—ever the perfectionist—insisted that he go next door and check.

Darl secured his right hand (and newly formed claw) inside of his jacket, resting the tips of his human fingers on the butt of his gun. He wouldn't need the pistol, but his body still had some remnant of muscle memory that pulled his fingers to the gun as if it were a talisman bringing strength and luck.

Just training so that I can use it on you and your lady friend. Blow you away. A familiar voice sounded in his head. *Fucker.*

"Fat chance," Darl whispered. "Why aren't you gone yet?" It was the first time his mental tenant had spoken to him in hours. Shrugging off the old Darl's empty threat, he knocked on the Dobsons' door.

It took a moment, but when Geraldine finally answered, he recognized the knowing look in her eyes and spotted the wound under her neck immediately. "Ma'am," he said, touching his left hand to the brim of his Stetson and moving toward the threshold. "Do you know who I am?"

"Yes," she said, all humanity shorn from her voice. That was good.

"May I come in, see my children?"

"You may, but I'm afraid..." She paused, finding her words. "I'm afraid that there have been several casualties."

Darl nodded and pushed passed her, down the hall and into the kitchen. "Shit," he said, looking at the two crushed children: one beaten beyond recognition and the other pressed against the ground until its organs had begun to squirt out of its rectum.

"Kenneth, we have a guest." Geraldine had followed Darl into the room, and out from the shadows of the living room walked Kenny Dobson. The front of his shirt was bloody and dotted with quarter-sized holes. Kenny looked like he'd been peppered with buckshot but was still standing and looked strong, all things considered. It was easy to see what had happened to the child: the fat bastard had fallen on it. The poor thing never stood a chance and was crushed under his weight.

"Where's the other one?" Darl asked. "We sent over three."

"It's in the kitchen. Dead also," Geraldine said, bending down to pick up her cat. Darl couldn't take his eyes off of Kenny.

"Go take a shower and change your shirt. You look like hell," Darl said to him. "The wounds should scab over in an hour or so."

"And what about me?" Geraldine held the cat to her breasts. The bond with the animal must have been residual feelings from her human life.

"You—you should cover this up." Darl pointed to the small hole under her chin. "That cut is really tiny. Which one did that?" He motioned to the dead children.

"Not them. Him," she said and turned the cat around so that Darl could see the side of blood-matted fur and the familiar circular wound.

"Well now," Darl said. "I didn't even think that was possible. You learn something new every day."

"I am sorry. What do you mean?" she asked. Darl's human-tinged dialect was too much for her to follow. She would learn to speak more colloquially in time, but right now she only had a basic grasp of the people and their language. She was sifting through her memories, learning from them rapidly like the reference section of a library.

"I meant to say that I did not know that a host that small could support us."

It may have been in response to Darl stepping closer, or it may have been that the creature perceived an insult, but either way the orange cat looked him directly in the eyes and hissed, its eyes flattened into an angry squint. The hiss petered out into a series of small clicks and then a purr. Geraldine smiled at him.

While Darl was out of the house checking in with the neighbors, Rhonda was slipping into something a little more comfortable.

She stood naked in front of the bathroom mirror. Wednesday morning, when she had first woken up in Heckscher Park, she had admired the novelty of her nude body. Now the flesh sickened her.

Her breasts were lumps of sagging fat. After three days of being obsolete they had begun to droop, the fat curdling around the edges of her nipples. Not only her breasts, but all of her weak flesh had begun to rot against her body, turning a greenish gray. It weighed her down both physically and aesthetically. She was through using the excess meat; she had taken and reconfigured the cells she needed, and now it was rotting against her. It was time to slim down and shape up.

A straight razor would have been preferable, but Harold Krieger wasn't nearly old-fashioned enough to use one. Instead Rhonda had rummaged through the kitchen and found a paring knife: great for both her purpose and for de-boning the flounder that Harold had caught out of the Long Island Sound during summers. From the bathroom cabinet she had procured one of Rhonda's plastic disposable razors, cracked it open against the sink and taken out the blade. It was slightly bent, but still usable for the fine detail work.

Rhonda looked into the mirror and did not like what stared back at her.

"What are you looking at?" Rhonda spoke to her reflection. "You whore." She made a large, deliberate smile, then a scowl, and then let her face go slack. Her thin lips and her fatty cheeks jiggled and then slid into place. She picked up the paring knife and put the tip up to the top of her forehead, where the skin became scalp.

She drew a deep, fine line with the knife until she reached the top of her nose. She then turned the tip of the blade on its side and continued cutting above her left eyebrow. After cutting the area above her left eye, she began on the right. Then she grabbed hold of the flaps she had formed and lifted the skin away.

There was very little blood. The remaining liquid was dark, sludgy and discolored.

It should have hurt, but it didn't. Most of the nerves were dead, and Rhonda didn't mind agitating the few that maintained their connection to her ever-changing brain.

"No pain, no gain," she said as she raised one gooey hand and began to use the razor blade to scrape away the congealed blood and gore that clung to her new forehead. One of Rhonda's old memories came unbidden into her mind: scraping the seeds and stringy pulp out of the inside of a pumpkin before carving it into a jack o' lantern.

Over the past three days her body had undergone a lot of change, but no area was as extreme as her bones. Her skull (and the rest of her skeleton) had been repurposed and improved. The microscopic elements of life had been broken down, reconfigured and reinforced. As she scraped across her cranium with the razor blade, she did not expose off-white bone, but instead her new green-brown exoskeleton. It was lighter but tougher, a stark contrast to the waste that was her softer tissue.

The skin ripped like crepe paper, and in a few minutes most of the flesh on her head was cleared off.

Her new face looked much like her old one, only better. She ran hot water over a washcloth and cleaned the area so she could get a better look. Gone was the old Rhonda's useless fur, the protuberant nose and the fatty cheeks (that up until a day ago had helped to keep her warm but had begun to slough off this afternoon, such that they made chill of the cold air worse). Everything about her new face was streamlined.

The human teeth were there to stay, but her gums had hardened and the thin skin had shed to reveal more chitin. Her gums were now a shade closer to jade than the rest of her face.

When she was done inspecting her newly drawn cheekbones, she looked down at the rest of her flesh.

Digging deep around her thighs, she was able to work her thumbs under the dead flesh and roll the skin of her legs down like nylon stockings. Both legs peeled off easily, and she wiggled her legs at the knee. She was amazed how much lighter she felt, how much quicker she could move without the bloated fat of her calves weighing her down.

Her new form was taking shape, but there was still a lot more cutting to be done. She looked one more time at her face. Soon there would be many like her, but for now she was a beautiful rarity.

Now the real work begins, she thought and started slicing off her left breast with the paring knife. It did not hurt, but the sensation was...interesting.

"Billy? Rile? You like him? Man alive, that's unbelievable," Darcy said, pressing her finger to the doorbell. Rachel was already regretting her lapse into girl-talk mode. Darcy had been saying variations of "Billy? I can't believe it!" the entire walk over, as if the initial shock was replaying over and over in her mind. It was annoying, but it helped to take Rachel's thoughts off of the chill she had gotten earlier from the empty streets. Now that they were on Billy's front step, Darcy had to stop.

"Oh shut up," Rachel said, trying to sound friendly but actually wanting Darcy to shut her Long Island Princess face. Telling her had been a bad idea. Hell, coming here might even have been a bad idea; all she needed was Darcy blabbing to Tom and then Tom giving the high sign to Billy. What a debacle.

A shadow appeared behind the small, frosted window and stood for a moment. It was Billy. Rachel was sure that she could see him smoothing out his shirt.

"We can see you," Darcy said and gave Rachel a very deliberate smile and wink as the door sprung open.

"Hey there, guys. Come on in," Billy said, ushering them over the threshold. "You can put your coats right up here." He indicated the family's coatrack. Rachel suppressed her initial *Who the hell uses coatracks?* reaction. "Let me help you." Billy approached Darcy and tried taking her coat.

Darcy gently fought to keep her neon pink/purple rayon jacket. "No thanks, Billy."

"I'll hang mine up." Rachel gave him the coat and felt the small jump she elicited by brushing her hand with the back of his.

Darcy didn't wait for Billy to show them in. She grabbed on to Rachel's arm and dragged her along to the basement. As they passed through the house, Rachel tried to take in the feel of it. Despite the cream carpeting and muted salmon and white paint on the walls, it was a pretty nice place. Billy's mother had taste. It was nothing like Deborah Krieger's cluttered ticky-tack palace. It was only a hunch, but Rachel was willing to bet that there would be no "Jesus Loves This Garden" placard out in the backyard.

"Carpeted basement stairs! Swanky, eh?" Darcy said. She didn't have to make a crack about *marrying Billy for his money*. It was implied, and Rachel heard it. These times when she so readily picked up on Darcy's intonations were the instances when she knew that she was spending too much time with her.

Tom was on the couch, six-pack between his legs.

"Ladies, so nice you could make it," Tom said. Before standing, he tossed a can to Darcy, who caught it and gave him a look. He walked to Rachel and placed her beer in her hands. The message that the gesture delivered was clear: Tom was supposed to be on his best behavior and, for now, he was holding it together. The conspiracy was transparent. Tonight Rachel was the guest of honor.

I may not give Billy a green light, I may not enjoy the movie, but watching these two screw-ups implode by the end of the night will be entertainment enough. There it was again, the same bad-girl attitude she'd indulged in on the walk home from school. Where did it come from? Maybe she was picking up the slack, now that Rhonda had been forced to be the sober, serious sibling. Rachel didn't like it—it didn't feel like the "real" her—but she didn't hate it, either.

"How are you tonight, Rachel?" Tom asked after putting his arm around Darcy (resting his hand on her ass). It was an uncharacteristically courteous statement. Kids like Tom Mathers didn't ask you how your day was going. In fact, it may have been the first question Tom had ever asked Rachel besides once drunkenly inquiring if, in case of emergency, she could be used as a flotation device. Billy walked downstairs, staring at Tom with a softly pleading expression the whole way.

"I'm fine, Tom. How are you? You missed home ec today; are you feeling all right?" She knew damn well that he felt fine. She remembered home ec, the violent fury she had felt.

Tom chuckled before answering. "Yeah, I'm fine. I took a personal day. I am sorry, though, that I missed all the excitement with Manfred the Sped."

"It was pretty scary, actually," Rachel said, looking at Billy. "And I wouldn't advise calling Terry that anymore. I don't think he likes it."

"That kid's a fucking animal," Darcy said, her beer already open and sounding quite empty as the liquid sloshed around inside of the can. "You're lucky he didn't pop your head off, Billy. You're also lucky that Rachel was there to pry him off of you."

If only you knew, Darcy, she thought. Before either Rachel or Billy could speak up, Tom took issue with Darcy's comment.

"Well, honey, I'm sure that Billy could take care of himself. Probably had him right where he wanted him," Tom said. Rachel couldn't tell if he was joking—it sounded as though he was actually trying to defend his friend—but his word choice was unfortunate. Tom was out of practice when it came to giving compliments.

"Actually, I would have been," Billy began, but Darcy cut him off and continued arguing with Tom.

"That's not the way I heard it," she said, realized how insulting it sounded, remembered she and her boyfriend were supposed to be behaving, and then backtracked. "No offense to you, Billy. I mean, anybody would have been in trouble. Those kids are supposed to have, like, super strength. Ya know?"

The profundity of Darcy's statement was allowed to sink in. Rachel broke the short, uncomfortable silence before it could turn into a long one. "So, what movie are we watching?"

Tom looked at Billy and cocked his thick eyebrows as if to say, "Let's send it over to Billy for the weather!"

"Uh, well, it's stupid, really. It's a horror movie. It's called *Re-Animator*. It's kind of funny and very gross. It's about a doctor who can raise the dead. We really don't even have to watch it if anyone doesn't want to. Like I said, it's stupid." Billy was drowning.

"Sounds stupid," Darcy parroted, smiling all the way up to her teased-out sideburns.

"No, it doesn't," Tom shot back, giving Darcy a squeeze, not on her bottom but around the small pudge of fat that flipped up over her jeans.

This isn't fun at all, Tom thought while popping open his third, and last, beer. He had been under the impression, when he saw Billy and Rachel walking together earlier in the day, that their courtship would be a positive thing. Now not only did he have to keep an eye on Darcy's mouth (and his own), but he also didn't get to enjoy video night with his friend. Well, a video hadn't yet been put in, so technically this wasn't even video night.

"Is anyone else hungry?" Darcy said. Tom immediately knew that she was angling for free pizza. Billy always picked up the tab, and tonight, with Rachel here, that was doubly assured. "Can I have a sip of that, hon?" she asked and pointed down at Tom's beer. She'd already had two, and Tom had only opened a third to keep her from sucking up the last one. Not only did he not want to have to look after a drunken Darcy, he didn't want to go through this night sober himself.

"Actually, I think I'm getting a cold," he said and sniffed in deep. He tried to sound congested, although he wasn't in the slightest. He shifted on the couch and brought her closer. It was a three-person couch. Rachel sat on the far end with Darcy in the middle; Billy was still standing, looking panicked. "But you're right, I am hungry," Tom said, looking for a way to get Billy moving. Tom might as well give him some legwork if he wasn't going to sit down.

"Pizza anyone?" Billy said, now pacing slightly. They had to get pizza just to give the poor kid something to do. He looked mental. "What kind do you like?" He looked right at Rachel.

"Is pepperoni okay with everyone?" Rachel asked, polite to the nth degree but also, Tom sensed, putting on her own little act. *Who is the one getting played here, sister?*

Darcy started shaking her head no to pepperoni, but Tom gave her another squeeze.

"Yup, fine with me," Tom said. "You can just pick it off," he whispered to Darcy. "Don't be difficult tonight."

He shouldn't have added that last part, but the beer had begun to soak his judgment. It had fully saturated the "be nice to Darcy" quadrant of his brain. Barbs like this were quite common in their relationship; small, nasty remarks that would have sounded more natural coming out of one of their parents' mouths. Tom wasn't proud of them, but Darcy did not take them to heart...usually. He didn't want to hurt her. It just felt good to occasionally feed the bastard who lived inside himself.

Billy picked up the phone and dialed. He placed the order, repeating his address and order several times, each time increasing the volume of his voice until he was finally screaming "PEPPERONI!" into the receiver.

While Billy was ordering, Darcy caught Tom's attention. He could see the wheels turning behind her eyes. When Darcy took the effort to think so intently about something, it was never going to be a random act of kindness. She had a mad-genius glint in her eye. She waited until Billy hung up so she could have the group's undivided attention before speaking. "Hey, I just remembered something. I thought you said you guys said you had a score." Darcy bunched up her nose and the rest of her face followed. "Where is it? Didintja say that, Tom?" she asked, revving up the old fake Brooklyn accent.

She hadn't forgotten about it; she was just hamming it up. Tom hadn't either, but he had been hoping that she would have the good sense to let it go until tomorrow, considering that they had a special guest. Tonight was not the night for experimenting with new drugs, especially when he had no idea what they were or what they would do. They could be uppers, downers, or hallucinogens (which is what Russ had said they were). The goddamn things could be poison for all he knew. Russ could have sat one-too-many hours behind the desk at VideoLux and started selling cyanide capsules to the neighborhood kids, just for kicks.

"I don't think tonight is the night for that, baby," Tom said. The word "baby" came out like audible punctuation. It was the period at the end of a sentence that was meant to be imbued by its speaker with the power to stop a conversation.

Darcy ignored him. "What do ya say, Rachel?"

"I think you should talk to your boyfriend and see if *he* thinks it's a good idea," Rachel said. Tom had to admit: the girl had cojones. She stood up to Darcy routinely. It reminded him of the way Billy would sometimes get uppity.

"Oh, no. It's fine. Tom and I actually had already come to an understanding," Darcy said, locking her beady little overly made-up eyes with his. "We made kind of a deal."

Billy glared at him and Tom tried motioning to his friend with his eyebrows. It wasn't much, but at least after all their years together, Tom hoped that Billy could read the sign for "get lost".

"Actually I think we might have some snacks upstairs. I'm starving," Billy said. "And we all know how long the pizza guy can take," he added, trying to lighten the mood.

"I think I'll come with you, give these two some alone time," Rachel said and jumped up from her end of the couch.

Tom waited until he heard the door at the top of the stairs close before he allowed himself so much as a hiss. "A deal? What deal?"

"Rachel is here, isn't she? That didn't happen by magic, Tom. And by the way, what's with all this pinching shit? I'm not a little kid, ya know. You can't keep pinching me when I get out of line. You asshole."

"I'm sorry about the pinching, but I also know that you're full of shit. You never asked Rachel to come over; Billy did that all by himself. I saw them talking, then he told me all about it." Tom paused for emphasis. "Every fucking detail. Meaning you're lying."

Darcy was overcome with a blush. "No, no, no. He may have asked her himself, but I asked her last night. I got her to go," Darcy said. "I, like, convinced her."

"Bullshit. She told him that she was coming. You had nothing to do with it."

"All right, smart-ass, fuckin' Sherlock Holmes here. I may not have gotten her to give me a definite yes, but I can sure as hell tear this whole thing down."

"You would do that?" Tom asked, letting a modicum of sensitivity bleed into his tone. Darcy wasn't dropping the tough broad act.

"Hell yes, I would. Now you've already drank all the beer and pissed me off so that I don't even want to make out with you. You're at least going to give me something so I can entertain myself through this geek's shitty movie."

She had a point. She could send Billy's love life right back into the shitter, but Tom wasn't going to admit that she had that kind of power over him. "Fine. We can have some, but only because I want some too," he said, thinking that was a pretty good cover-up job.

"All right then." Darcy couldn't stifle her smile near well enough.

"Oh, one more thing," Tom clarified. "This movie isn't shitty. It's a fucking modern classic." He gave her a big, wet kiss and was happy that she was finally happy.

Terry slipped but quickly caught himself after stepping off the sidewalk to cross the street. Not only did it seem extra dark outside, he also he couldn't see out of his left eye. He figured that it was probably on account of the booze. *Blind drunk, I am.*

The grab and run hadn't been much of a "run" but more of a "grab and saunter." There was nobody in the 7-Eleven, not even a clerk. That wasn't half as weird as the fact that most of the lights in the store

Adam Cesare

weren't switched on and that he'd had to step over broken glass to grab a forty-ounce.

The world was going crazy, but he barely had the desire or inclination to take notice. He was good and drunk now and feeling really strong, despite the fact that his eye didn't work so hot anymore and his mind was still doing somersaults.

Revenge was as sweet as high-alcohol-content malt liquor. It was the kind that his brother used to drink by jamming two bendy straws together end to end so he could reach the bottom of the oversized bottle. It actually wasn't sweet at all, it tasted really rancid, but Terry sucked on the bottle anyway. Good thing he had taken a bag of Doritos on the way out of the store. He could wash this shit down with some delicious artificial nacho cheese flavor.

He put the cap back on the forty and wedged the bottle into his armpit. He tossed three chips into his mouth as soon as he could tear the bag open. Once the taste of the chips won out against the lingering stink of the booze, he was sent to his knees by the shock.

The chips tasted worse than the alcohol. A lot worse. They tasted like rotten eggs soaked in spoiled milk and then marinated in old-man farts. He retched on the sidewalk but didn't succeed in bringing anything up, not even a drop of the forty. Screaming in frustration, he threw down the bottle, smashing it on the sidewalk, and crumpled the Doritos bag with both hands.

"I can't eat! I can't see! I can't think!" Yelling in the streets made him, for the first time all day, completely aware of himself as he looked around to see if there were any witnesses to his tantrum. There weren't any that he could see, but he decided to hurry along anyway. He wanted to get off this block, wanted to find Billy Rile and beat him until the pain went away.

"This," Rachel said. "I don't quite know what this is." She cocked her eyebrow and peered down at the serving tray sitting on the kitchen counter between her and Billy.

"Well, I can tell you what Tom will call it," he said and looked up

154

from the tray, laying down a hunk of goat cheese. "He'll call it sorta gay."

Rachel laughed. It was a genuine laugh and it made Billy feel good and comfortable.

"Your parents like all this stuff?" she asked, gazing around at his mother and father's strange and pricey kitchen appliances and knickknacks. "More importantly, won't they be pissed that we're eating their expensive cheeses?"

"It's really not as expensive as Tom would like to think it is. My parents are just kind of crazy. They like to think that they appreciate the finer things, and they do. I guess," Billy said and then saw the opportunity for a compliment present itself. "Plus, there's a *real* guest here tonight. It's not like I'm serving this stuff up to just Darcy and Tom. That would be like throwing it away."

Rachel smiled, but not enough that he could tell whether picking on her friend was an okay thing to do.

She looked like she was getting ready to say something, but before she could speak, the basement door opened and Tom walked into the kitchen.

"Sorry to interrupt," he said to Rachel. "Can I talk to you for a second, Billy?"

"Not at all. I'll put the rest of these back in the fridge," she said and gave Billy a nod.

"You don't have to worry about it. I'll get it," he said, but Rachel was already ignoring him and packaging up the rest of the cheeses and snack meats. Tom touched his shoulder and reacquired his attention.

Great, Billy thought. *Here it goes.*

He followed Tom around the corner into the living room.

"I'm sorry about this, but can you get me the pills? Please?"

"Shit," was all Billy could say. He could already feel the familiar flutter he got in his stomach when he began to overanalyze uncomfortable situations. It was the same feeling he'd had in second grade when Tom said they should climb out the window while the teacher wasn't looking. The same feeling he'd gotten in sixth grade when Tom popped the lid on a Budweiser he'd taken from his father's cooler during a Fourth of July party. The same feeling he'd had as a freshman when Billy and Tom had gone into the woods behind one of their older friends' houses to shoot BB guns and smoke cigarettes. Billy hated that feeling.

"Look," Tom said, adding a rare note of sympathy to his voice. "I know it sucks and makes you get all weird, but look at it this way: you and Rachel don't have to do it. Also, it'll help me keep Darcy quiet during the movie."

"Okay, well, just so we're clear that I'm not doing it."

"Nobody said you had to. Now where are they?"

"We'll start slow, okay?" Tom looked up at Darcy. She was practically licking her chops. "We'll have a little bit now, watch some of the movie, and if we're feeling okay, we can have some more."

"Fine. Sounds good," Darcy said.

"You're sure you don't want any?" Tom said to Rachel and Billy. Billy was finally seated on the couch, remote control in hand. Tom had sat down on the floor, Indian-style, when they'd come back down the stairs. He knew the answer to his question, but he thought he'd ask it anyway.

"No; that's okay. Maybe later when we see whether or not Darcy can handle it," Rachel said.

"*Excelente!*" Tom said, using one of his three Spanish words, and dug out his pocket knife from his jeans. He flicked open the blade with a quick wrist snap. It was a bad-boy flourish that he had practiced to perfection. Only Billy knew that he compulsively rehearsed the motion. "We'll start with half and see where the night takes us."

Tom gripped one pill between his thumb and forefinger, placed it down on the coffee table in front of the couch, and pushed down on the back of his blade to cut the pill in half. He brushed the two halves into his palm. Upon further inspection, he made a quick gasp of disgust, surprising everyone, himself included.

"They're leaking." The halved pill was oozing a viscous slime onto his open hand. He lifted up a half and pushed it into Darcy's face, a long brown string of fluid stuck to his palm: "Quick, take it before all the goop falls out."

"Quit being such a baby." Darcy pinched, tossed and swallowed her half. "Don't act like it's the first time you've ever had gooey hands." She made a rude motion and Tom gave her the finger as he popped the other half in his mouth.

"Are we ready now? Is everyone sufficiently medicated?" Billy glared at Darcy, who sucked on the two fingers she'd used to pick up the pill.

She held up a moist finger in the one-second motion, walked over to the trunk freezer and shoveled a few more wedges of cheese into her mouth from the plate. "To wash it down," she said, white cheese globs glistening in her teeth as she smiled. "All set. Let the show begin." Darcy blew Billy a kiss. It made him squirm.

"Could you hit that light?" Billy pressed Play and Tom reached up from his position on the floor to turn off the nearest lamp.

The room was silent, with the exception of the low, mechanical hum of the VCR as it revved up. *Billy must be happy,* Tom thought. *Video night has officially begun.*

"Am I high already or is that a ringing sound?" Darcy said.

It was the doorbell.

"The pizza," Tom said, jumping up from the carpeted floor. "Don't get up. I got it." He realized that if Billy gave up his seat, he may never take it back.

"Well, let me at least give you some cash."

"No, it's okay. Really, my treat," Tom said, and Billy ruffled his brow into the picture of incredulity. Tom never treated. Tom patted his own ass theatrically. "Shit, must have forgotten my wallet at home. I'll get ya next time."

Billy sighed and pulled a crumpled twenty out of his front pocket. Tom could tell he was getting annoyed at all the delays, but what was he in a rush for? It wasn't every night he got to sit next to Rachel

Krieger. Might as well make it last.

"Make sure you tip the guy," Billy said before letting go of the bill.

"I will," Tom said. He wouldn't.

Chapter Fourteen

Tom opened the door, took one look at Terry Manfred and immediately transformed his face into his best "I'm gonna beat your ass" expression. Then he remembered that causing a fuss and fighting would ruin the night for sure. At the very least, knocking Manfred the Sped's teeth out on Billy's front lawn would make Billy look like a big pussy who couldn't fight his own battles.

"You ain't the pizza boy," Tom said, taking down a mental note to work on his growl. "Now get lost and be happy I'm being so nice."

"I'd like to see Billy. Is he home?" Terry said. Even in the low porch light, Tom could tell that the kid was pale as hell with dark circles under his eyes and a generally haggard countenance. "I would like to apologize," he added, and then shivered slightly.

Manfred didn't look like a threat. Maybe if Tom called everyone up from the basement, Billy could take on Terry in a fight and impress Rachel in the process. Tom caught himself before he called for Billy, remembering the gym class that the two friends had shared last year. For Billy the class had been one long string of botched catches, no chin-ups and other mild-to-moderate embarrassments.

"I'll give him the message. Now beat feet." Tom closed the door, taking care that he was not slamming it enough to arouse suspicion from the group downstairs.

Tom stepped back from the glass so the kid couldn't see him. Terry didn't move for a moment. Then Tom switched off the porch light, as if "beat it" had not been a strong enough hint.

Terry knocked and rang the doorbell at the same time. "What's the hold-up?" Darcy yelled from downstairs. Her fucking voice could burrow through concrete and steel, so the walls of Billy's house didn't stand a chance. Tom threw the door open.

"Look, now's not a good time." Tom looked at Terry's face, took in his slack-jawed, dumbfuck expression and decided he was being too polite. He added, "So go fuck yourself."

"Do you blow your father with that mouth?" Terry asked him with deadpan amusement. Tom was out the door tackling before Terry could start laughing. The kid was clammy, sick-looking, mentally enfeebled, but Tom didn't care: Terry was going to get a beating.

The first punch was dead on in the stomach, and it surprised Tom how fast Terry was able to prepare himself. He was also shocked to find that his hand stung way more than he anticipated it would. *Rock-hard belly shielded by layers of clothing. This spaz must be working out*, he thought, pressing his knees into Terry's waist and pinning him to the ground. Terry may have been built, but he was slow as hell. Tom was able to catch him with another hook before Terry could push him off.

"I'll give you one thing: you're well padded," Tom huffed and shook out his sore hand. "You came prepared. Got a pillow in there?" Tom pointed down at Terry's stomach as he rose to his feet. Terry also picked himself off the grass but with a slow, deliberate pace, as if he were worried he was going to fall down. He was drunk maybe?

"I didn't even hit you in the head yet. Pull yourself together," Tom said, Terry remained quiet. He clenched his fists though, and that was all the head start Tom was intending to give him. Tom tackled him, sweeping his legs out from under him, and began to pummel his face.

"What's that you were saying about my dad?" Tom's breath got heavy, rage mixing with exertion. He clipped Terry in the nose and stopped himself when he heard the crunch.

Terry just stared at him and smiled. A small cut had opened between his eyebrows, and it would look bad in a moment once the blood started to flow. "Okay, we're done here," Tom said. *Oh shit, I might have given this idiot a hematoma.*

"Look, I'm sorry if I hurt you too badly. But you have to admit you had it coming, assaulting my buddy and insulting me in the same day," Tom said, the fear that he could be in real trouble for hurting the kid caused him to backpedal. He was coming down from adrenaline, but a new kind of rush was taking its place: the fear that something stupid like this probably constituted assault. "I didn't mean to get you that bad." He pointed to the tear at the top of Terry's nose. The kid might not have even noticed it yet.

The streetlights were not bright, but on Billy's block did turn everything a pleasant hue of amber. Visibility was low and shadows were deep, so it was hard to tell, but it looked to Tom like Terry hadn't begun to bleed at all. Terry still hadn't spoken since the insult. Tom was wondering if he had really hurt the kid when Terry began to make a deep noise in his throat. It was a sound like passing phlegm, and Tom eased his weight off of Terry's chest.

"Hey, man, are you okay?"

That was when the cop grabbed him by the back of the shirt and lifted Tom off of Terry Manfred.

Darcy had called out a few times from the doorway, not that it mattered. Tom wouldn't have noticed her if she smacked him in the back of the head with a rock. He was too intent on beating the Manfred kid into the ground.

She'd decided to give Billy and Rachel some alone time and come upstairs to use the bathroom. She caught a glimpse of Tom as he leaped out the door, tackling Terry Manfred and rolling to the middle of the lawn.

The fight only held her attention for a few seconds (she'd seen better), and the appearance of the cop was both unexpected and cause for concern. From the doorway, she watched the Suffolk County Sheriff's officer walk out of Rachel's neighbor's house. Darcy knew that he didn't live there. That was the Dobson house. Darcy's mother was friendly with Geraldine. The guy turned down the driveway and made a beeline across the lawn to break up the fight.

It was hard to tell he was a cop at first. His uniform was covered up by a flannel jacket, but his hat and the glint of his badge gave him away before he had even started crossing the street. The cop was wearing a cowboy hat, which was different from most of the cops around here, but that wasn't the oddest thing about him. He walked slowly and with a slight limp, keeping one hand inside of his jacket, looking like a country-western Napoleon. The hand-in-jacket thing was the only thing Darcy remembered about Napoleon.

Is this crazy old fucker going for his gun? The thought made the hairs on her arms jump.

"Tommy!" But Tom didn't seem to hear her. Tommy was saying something to the Manfred kid, looking awfully concerned for someone who'd been pummeling away in a blind rage a moment ago. She was ready to yell for him a second time when the cop locked eyes with Darcy and motioned for her to go back inside. The cop didn't look angry or frightened, just busy. She hoped he wouldn't kill her boyfriend, or throw him in jail for battery.

In his previous life, Davis Mitchell had loved his job. He was paid to smoke dope, listen to loud music and drive very fast. Well, he was only paid to drive very fast, but he did those other things anyway. Tonight he wasn't feeling into it though. He wasn't feeling much of anything. Davis Mitchell was dead from a punctured throat and broken jaw, his body folded up in the trunk of his own pizza delivery vehicle (his father's 1984 Buick Grand National).

Behind the wheel of the Buick sat Earl Danby, night manager at Gino's Pizzeria and, more recently, their newest delivery boy. Earl took one hand off of the wheel and scratched underneath the green and red baseball cap that exclaimed, "Gino's Pizza: A Taste of Sicily Right Next Door!" He could barely see the numbers on the houses, and it was made even worse by the fact that he couldn't get the Buick's heat to go any higher. His fingers already felt numb, and he was growing frustrated that he could not find the house.

Earl had spent the entire night delivering pizzas. He wanted to deliver the pizzas himself after the realization that anyone calling Gino's and ordering a pizza was not a member of the club. Turning Davis would have taken up valuable time and resources, so Earl had fired Davis by opening up his throat with a pizza roller and stuffing him into the trunk of his car. Everyone had to do their service for the cause, and Earl's was delivering pizzas to the survivors.

With his eyes still aimed out the window searching for a house number, he tried the heat again. He must have hit the button for the tape deck by mistake and jerked the wheel in surprise when Motörhead's "We Are the Road Crew" blasted against his eardrums. Instead of turning it off, Earl simply turned it down. The old him would have hated the music. Earl Danby had been more of a Hall and Oates kind of guy, but the creature he'd become found comfort in the pulsing metal. He tried to rationalize it by telling himself the music bumped up his heart rate, which in turn might help to warm him. That may not have been true, but he relished the idea that somewhere deep in his brain, the old Earl Danby could hear the music and still be grievously offended by it.

"Sixty-six...sixty-eight." Earl pulled the car up the driveway, his eyes on the shadow behind the front door, not noticing the altercation underway on the front lawn until he was out of the car, pizza box in hand.

It took a fair amount of effort to pry the bigger boy off of the injured one. The kid was wearing only jeans and a T-shirt, so before Darl even got across the street, he knew that the kid had not been turned yet. He had nothing to protect against the cold.

"Calm down, now, calm down," Darl said as the bigger boy twisted and squirmed in his grasp, stretching out the back of his T-shirt until he finally realized that he was being held on to by a member of the sheriff's department.

"Sorry, Officer," the tall kid said, wiping a fleck of spittle from his upper lip. Darl looked up at the house. The shape of the girl was still there; she was watching. If this kid wasn't turned yet, there was a good chance that the girl wasn't either. The kid on the ground, though, looked pale and sickly, and was wearing at least three layers of clothes under his denim jacket.

"Are you all right, boy?" Darl let go of the back of the taller one's shirt, turning his attention to the sluggish boy supine on the grass. He was trying to stand, with little success, falling back to the ground with a grunt and lying there for a moment before speaking.

"I'm fine." The shorter boy huffed and crawled to his knees. "He attacked me, sir."

"Frankly, Officer, I think that this kid is drunk." The taller kid was no stranger to talking to the police: he was keeping his tone defiant and insolent, but his words respectful. "I think he may need a ride home and a night to sleep it off. I'm not going to press charges, though. He's been through enough."

"But, but," the battered kid in the denim jacket began to stammer. Darl had gotten tired of watching the kid struggle and flop on the lawn. He hooked his good hand under the kid's armpit and lifted him to his feet. The boy looked as if he'd been turned, but there was something else there too, and Darl figured it out after he spoke. "But he...he attacked me, your honor."

"Your honor?" This kid's got a screw loose. Darl snickered from behind his own eyes. *Ha! Some invasion force you alien pricks have got together: a queer, busted-up old cop, a couple of geriatrics, a psycho teen girl and now a spastic that don't know his ass from your honorable elbow.*

The kid's eyes were rolling around in his head, and Darl guessed that they had been like that before the bigger kid started walloping him. To be out here in the cold, even with all the layers the kid had on, was not something that an effectively turned human would choose to do.

That's because he's defective, you asshole.

"Hey, Officer." The crazy kid smiled wide, a spark of recognition entering his shaky eyes. "I think I know you, your honor. I recognize you as part of the family."

Darl held on to the boy's arm and gave him a sharp pinch, trying to implore him to shut his mouth. Darl shielded his eyes against headlights as a car pulled into the empty driveway. The street was becoming a little too crowded for his liking, and he needed to shuttle this kid away before he blabbed anything more incriminating and less vague than "part of the family".

"I see what you mean, boy." Darl turned to the teen, the James Dean rebel-looking one. "This boy here is drunk as a skunk on St. Paddy's Day."

"I told ya, man. Uh, sir," the tough guy said and started walking backward. The kid was still flying high on the fight. Despite the cold, there was a sheen of perspiration on his head and neck as he sucked in breath. The kid was so fixated on Darl that he hadn't even noticed the pizza guy pull up behind him. "Can you handle this from here, Officer?"

"I sure can. You stay out of trouble tonight, you hear?" Darl said, calling on his old self's faux-western twang. "And don't forget your pizza."

The bigger boy gave Darl a perplexed look before backing into the pizza guy, who had been busy exchanging a knowing glance with Darl. The pizza guy's look said, *Don't worry. This kid won't be troubling anyone else tonight.*

Darl started walking away from the house, dragging the crazy kid with him.

"Aren't you going to do anything about this? Can't we just go back there and fuck him and his friends up?" the kid whined, loud enough for the whole block to hear.

"Shut your goddamn mouth," Darl whispered into his ear and nudged him to walk even faster across the street. Hopefully Rhonda would know what to do with him, because Darl sure as hell didn't.

"Keep the change," Tom said as he pushed a few folded up bills into the old guy's palm and took the pizza box. The pizza guy didn't get it yet, but Tom was only joking with him. It was the kind of joke you got once you were in the car on your way home. Tom had given the guy exact change and pocketed the twenty that Billy had given him to pay with. The pizza man had it coming: he had a thick mustache that only exaggerated his sour puss. He was probably a dickhead.

Tom stomped up the front steps, hoping to make it there before the delivery guy could count the wad of bills. He didn't need any more headaches tonight. As soon as he stepped back inside, he was greeted by a walking, talking, whopping headache.

"Oh, my baby boy!" Darcy squealed. "Are you awright?" She wrapped her arms around his head and neck and hugged him tight: an annoying Long Island mother in training. "That gawd-damn animal."

"Could you fucking stop it? I'm fine. The kid never even touched me." The voice and accent were bad enough, but when she started molesting his head, he couldn't tough it out any longer. She recoiled from him. The concern dropped out of her expression and was quickly replaced with anger.

"Fine. I hope you have a fucking concussion."

"Look, I'm sorry. Let's not do this here," Tom said and waved one hand to emphasize that they were standing in Billy's foyer and that he was holding a pizza.

Darcy looked at her feet, probably contemplating what emotion she wanted to level off at.

"Did you see me beating on Manfred?" Tom asked, leading her to the basement door and stepping back so she could open it for him.

"Yeah." Darcy smiled. She was back in the game, at least for the moment. He saw her bite her lower lip as they started down the stairs to rejoin their double date. "It was pretty sexy."

Chapter Fifteen

As he walked into the living room, still holding on to the kid by his ratty denim jacket, Darl realized something. The kid had been right: why didn't they go across the street and fuck those remaining kids up? Darl clicked his tongue in frustration. It was a human sound. The more time it spent in this body, the more comfortable it got with these fat, hairy animals and their little tics.

"Honey, I'm home!" Darl shouted upstairs. Sarcasm dripping from his voice and he hoped that Rhonda would pick up on it. But would she realize it was there because of how sick and tired of this house he was? All this sneaking around was for nothing. The pizza guy got to drive around and be proactive, so why couldn't he? There was still something utterly persuasive about her. In life she had been a smart girl, but now she was something else entirely. Was cunning too strong a word? Commanding?

Who wears the pants in this family? Your old lady has you barking like her little poodle bitch in heat, don't she?

"Shut it. I don't have time for you now," Darl said to himself.

"What do you mean?" the kid asked. His pupils had stopped doing the Watusi, but his eyes were still too wide.

That's 'cause they're crazy eyes. I used to see that kind of look all the time when I was a rookie and would land all the shit jobs. They would call me down to the loony bin if one of the nuts wandered off and they needed the sheriff's help to track him down. It happened more than you'd think. This kid may not have been crazy before your little bugs got a hold of him, but he sure is now. Your method of indoctrination doesn't work as well as you thought it did. If it did, how come I'm still here and you can still hear me?

"I wasn't talking to you." Darl ignored the history lesson and debate going on in his own head and answered the kid. Darl left the kid standing in the living room and then ducked into all the downstairs rooms to check for the girl. She was probably with the children in one of the upstairs bedrooms.

"While we're here, we should go on a panty raid." The kid was inspecting one of the pictures in the living room, one with both Rhonda and Rachel together. "Eh, old man?"

"Quiet," Darl said and shushed the boy. There was movement at the top of the stairs. "Rhonda, we have a guest. Would you kindly join us?" No answer. "Please?"

As if saying the magic word had done the trick, there was a creak at the top step. "Our house guest is one of us, so there's no need to pretend." He felt his own jaw grow slack and his words jumble as he looked up and saw Rhonda take the last step. She was completely naked, but that wasn't the spellbinding part.

"That is fucking awesome," the kid said. It was more words than Darl could find.

"Beautiful," was the only thing Darl could say, and he couldn't even do that properly. The word got caught, dried up and flaked away in his half-open mouth, barely audible in the silent room.

"Thank you, Darl," Rhonda said. Without her fleshy human mouth, her speech sounded harsh, but it was still not without a certain feminine music to it. "And who are you?" The tips of her fingers were a lighter shade of green than the rest of her hand, and she pointed one at the kid.

"Terry. Terry Manfred," the boy said, not looking the least bit afraid of the creature standing before him. If anything, he was fascinated and possibly aroused by her bizarrely appealing body, a quality only exacerbated by her nudity.

Jesus Christ. It just keeps getting worse and worse. Darl could feel himself scream and then pull deeper into his own mind. The sight of the new Rhonda was too much for both Todd Darls to handle.

Everything about her was streamlined, most noticeably her facial features, which were barely recognizable and yet somehow still very much Rhonda. There was something angelic about the new curves, something classical. It was as if this body had been hiding inside of Rhonda her whole life; she just needed help to enter her natural state. Musculature was sharper, more defined now that the top layer of skin had been shed and the tissue beneath was repurposed into a tough, smooth exoskeleton. At her joints, the places in her new armor where the plates met, the color of the tissue was a dark jade, complementing the lighter hue of the plates themselves.

The novelty of the change must have been gone for Rhonda. "Why is he here?" she asked Darl, the tone of the words all business.

Darl stammered for a moment, still trying to take in her exquisite new form before speaking. "Can we talk about it in the kitchen, please?"

Darl followed her into the next room. When she turned, she revealed the flip side of her new body. She'd sliced off her buttocks, and with the absence of flesh, her reconfigured coccyx had curled out. She now had a small, delicate tail. Her backside was easily the least humanoid part of her new body. It was not strange that Darl also found it the most enticing.

"Caught you staring," Rhonda said. It was impossible to tell if she was joking or not. Darl had not yet acclimated himself to her new voice, and it was difficult to read expressions when a person had no lips. Once in the kitchen, she stopped short and leaned in to talk to Darl, her face so close to his that it made Darl churn with both arousal and unease. "So," she whispered and clicked an impatient finger against her exposed hip bone.

"The kid, he is turned, but he's..." Darl struggled to find the word.

"He's what?" she said. Her voice clicked as she raised it to ask the question, and her breath still smelled of festering human tissue. Darl wondered what was going on inside of her body, whether the changes had completely finished or if there were human lungs still inflating and collapsing in there. He doubted it.

"He's defective," Darl said, borrowing the term that his mental guest had used earlier.

If the shoe fits and all of that shit. The old Darl was able to manage a feeble joke, but he sounded weak. Maybe soon he would be gone for good.

"Defective how?" Rhonda looked perplexed. At least Darl assumed that was what the slight movement of the exoskeletal plates on her forehead meant. "Is he injured?"

"No, not like that. He has too much free will. When I caught him, it was because he was fist-fighting with another boy. Getting his ass kicked in, actually." Darl rubbed his chin with his good hand. The skin on his neck felt cool, slack and thin. It was happening to him too. "Brawling on someone's front lawn is not what I would consider 'sticking with the plan'. Plus, if you try talking to him for more than a minute, you realize that there's something not right. When he's not gabbing, he stares off into the void looking like he's ready to drool all over himself."

Rhonda looked down, pausing to consider her phrasing before speaking. "The hosts are problematic. Their minds are overly complex, there is a lot of variation between them, there's no set way to infiltrate them, to take them over entirely." Her tone was still impossible to decipher, but the words could only mean one thing: frustration, with the possibility of fear. "Enough about him. Who was he fighting? On whose lawn?"

"Big kid with a tough-guy attitude." Darl motioned through the doorway, back into the living room. "Probably around the same age as our Terry. He looked like a thug. I can't believe I've never arrested him before."

"Were they across the street?"

"Directly."

"That's the friend of the kid that lives there. I don't know his name. And you're sure he wasn't turned?"

"Positive," Darl said, letting his exasperation be heard. He was growing tired of the question and answer session Rhonda had going. Was it another pointless part of the plan or just something to make him feel stupid and subservient?

She made a show of counting with her slender but monstrous fingers. "That makes four that we know of. Four inside of that house. Rachel mentioned her friend Darcy."

"There's one more thing," Darl said, smiling as he laid down this trump card. "As I was leaving, the pizza guy pulled up. He was looking especially green around the ears, and delivered a large pie. If you can see where that one is going."

Rhonda made some clicks in her throat with her mouth closed, the noises sounded either disappointed or irritated. Maybe it was the alien equivalent of a *tsk*. After a moment of what resembled concentration, she spoke. "I know how this is going to sound, but I was hoping that Rachel was going to get a few more hours with her friends."

"Too late for that now, I guess. Look on the bright side: maybe she'll only be turned and not, you know, explode from the inside out." He was happy that this somehow displeased Rhonda. It was the kind of thrill that Todd Darl used to get when spitting into a guilty suspect's coffee.

"It's a pity. She would have been gorgeous," she said, catching a glance at her own reflection in the glass of the kitchen's wall clock. She looked back up at Darl. "No use decrying pure efficiency," she said and left her momentary lapse into sentiment. "Let's go see if we can't fix what's wrong with our new friend Terry, all right?"

"I hope that you two were good while we were gone," Darcy said, poking Rachel in the shoulder, eliciting a light blush and a dirty look.

Shortly after Tom had left to go get the pizza, Darcy had excused herself to the bathroom. They had both looked as if they knew what she was up to, but she wanted to get out of the basement anyway. The low ceilings and the constant hum of the trunk freezer made her claustrophobic.

"That pizza smells delicious," Billy said in his best goofy *Leave It to Beaver* voice. Darcy could tell that he was trying to defuse at least some of the awkwardness of the situation, but to her he'd just made himself look like more of an ass.

171

"I've got plates and napkins over there." Billy pointed behind Tom. Billy signaled for the taller boy to set the pizza box down on top of the trunk freezer, but instead Tom laid it down on the coffee table, refusing to cross the room. It was in these infrequent moments of quiet defiance, when Tom showed that he wasn't Billy's lackey, or vice versa, that Darcy respected the two boys' friendship the most.

Most of the time she found their boy-talk boring, but she couldn't deny that there was a certain sweetness to their odd-couple match-up. Opposites in so many ways: brains and brawn, rich and poor, painfully polite and dangerously unpredictable. There were areas where Billy towered over Tom—knowledge, money—but there were even more places where Tom was top dog.

Tom opened the lid of the pizza box, and Darcy watched as the warm air gushed upward in a cloud of steam, carrying the comfort-food scents of oregano and pepperoni to her nose.

Darcy stood behind Tom, groping for his hand and tangling her fingers together with his. She gave him a peck on the cheek, enjoying the light prickle of his stubble, and then whispered "Ladies first, hon," into his ear.

Gino's always did a shitty job when they cut their slices. The pizza roller never seemed to make it all the way through to the cardboard underneath. Tonight the roller must have been especially dull, because when Darcy grabbed for the first piece, half of the cheese and pepperoni slid off of the neighboring slices. "Sorry," she said and watched as Billy quickly grabbed a plate and napkin and ran them over to her. He was a tad late; she'd already dribbled some grease and a globule of cheese onto the carpet.

It was only Billy, Tom and Rachel, so Darcy decided that she wasn't going to stand on ceremony and wait for them to take their own pieces. She folded the pizza, tilted the point toward her mouth and took a large bite. Even though she'd had pizza with Rachel last night, she was absolutely starving. Besides, this was Gino's—the good stuff, not the crap that her parents insisted on ordering from Mama Mary's.

Despite the steam, the pizza itself was only slightly hotter than lukewarm. It didn't matter much to her, though. Darcy was halfway through her piece before Tom had taken his first nibble.

Darcy slowed down and allowed herself to luxuriate in the cheesy tomato and pepperoni blend that she tucked into her cheek like a wad of chew. Gino's was a rare treat, and because there were four people in the room, Darcy bet that she'd only be allotted two slices instead of three. She savored the bite. It was meant to be enjoyed.

Tom yelled out a muffled curse and spit a glob of half-chewed pizza back onto his plate. Rachel looked at him with disgust, obviously turned off of her own pizza for the moment. Darcy swallowed her cheekful before asking what was the matter.

"Fucking black olives, they must have dropped some under the cheese," Tom said and wiped at his tongue with his paper napkin. "I just squished a big juicy one with my teeth. Fucking gnarly. Tastes like moldy dick."

"Your favorite variety of dick," Darcy said, catching Rachel's eye and then Billy's. Both of them laughed, but Billy was audibly more uneasy with making fun of Tom. What a pussy.

"I need something to wash this out," Tom said. Billy held up a can of Coca-Cola. Tom gave him an amused look, shook his head and then walked over to the trunk freezer. "It's still in here, right?"

"What is?" Billy asked.

"The bottle of booze I hid underneath all your dad's frozen peas," Tom said. "You do know about that, right?"

"You're not serious, are you?" Billy said, knowing damn well Tom was serious. "You've got a secret stash in my home that you didn't tell me about?"

Billy's voice was giving Darcy a headache, although she did manage a giggle for the audacity of her boyfriend. *So much for being on our best behavior tonight. The fight probably got him a little worked up.*

"Yeah, because if I told you about it, you would have acted like this and I wouldn't be about to blast away the sliminess of black olive with the tastiness of Jack Daniels," Tom said. He turned his back to Billy and flung open the door to the freezer.

Rachel sidled up next to her, observing the two boys' ruckus.

"They fight like my mom and dad. Maybe we're both barking up the wrong tree, eh?" she said, pointing with her untouched piece of pizza. Maybe Rachel was going to keep it to one slice and Darcy could have the extra piece. At the thought of more food, her stomached twanged. A gas bubble painfully slid along her insides.

Tom began riffling through the frozen contents of the trunk, pushing preserved food goods aside with what sounded like brute disregard. "How much shit do your parents need?"

"Come on, man, that stuff is in some kind of order," Billy whined. His voice wasn't just giving Darcy a headache, but worsening her stomachache as well.

"Shit," she gasped and held her tummy.

"Are you all right?" Rachel looked at her with an expression that worried Darcy. She didn't feel all right.

"You know I just beat the shit out of Manfred the Sped on your front lawn, right? I think I earned the drink," Tom said, confessing his barbarism. Darcy was in too much pain to care about the bombshell. The room was doing loopty-loops now, and she reached out for Rachel to steady herself.

"Wait, you did what?" Billy said. Billy was confused and Tom was indignant and neither boy was paying any attention to Darcy.

"Guys," Rachel said, not in a whisper but nothing approaching the volume needed to break her way into Billy and Tom's conversation. Darcy squeezed the redhead's shoulder and coughed.

"Here we are," Tom said, holding the small, frosty bottle under his armpit and encountering some trouble with the cap.

"Terry Manfred was here?" Billy asked, looking about ready to pass out from the night's combined excitements.

"Billy! Tom! Darcy is going to be sick," Rachel yelled as Darcy continued coughing. The house must have been having trouble with the wiring or something, because Darcy could have sworn that the lights in the basement were flickering. The rhythm of the strobe that was affecting her vision was speeding up, coinciding with the strain of her heartbeat.

Darcy felt about to tip over when Rachel steadied her with both arms, Rachel's large breasts smooshing against Darcy's shoulder. *In case of emergencies, your friend's boobs can be used as flotation devices.* Why did she think that? Had Tom said it once?

She coughed once more and tasted something gross. That was when the pain got really bad.

So this was the way it was going to go down. This was how he was going to react in a crisis situation. On days when he sat with his uncle behind the counter at the liquor store, Tom had always wondered what would he do if he was suddenly called upon to act. He liked to fantasize that if some drug-addict thug came into the store and started waving around a Saturday night special, he would heroically leap over the counter, Don Johnson-style.

Tom wasn't an all-star athlete, but he was pretty big. He wasn't in terrible shape, and he'd been in a few fights before. The problem was that there was still no way to be sure what he would do if he or someone he loved was in danger.

His fingers were so tightly wrapped around the frozen Jack bottle that they were beginning to go numb. He hadn't taken a step since Darcy coughed up the first batch of blood. He just stood next to the open freezer, bottle in hand, whiskey still drying on his lips.

This wasn't the way it was supposed to happen. It wasn't supposed to be some unseen force threatening his girlfriend. It was supposed to be a mugger or escaped mental patient. Something he could punch, tackle and call names.

The coughing was punctuated with abbreviated screams. Interrupted sounds that seemed to be trying to fight their way through a blockage in her throat, only to be stifled mid-yell. Billy stood in front of her with Rachel behind; they both looked panicked. Rachel was trying some variation of the Heimlich maneuver. Tom wanted speak out and tell her that she was doing it wrong, but he couldn't even form the words. *In and up! God damn it!*

The only thing he could do was watch, his eyes fixed on the blood more than anything else. The blood that spattered the front of Billy's shirt as Darcy retched onto his chest. The shirt Billy had taken so long to finally settle on, the one that he wanted to use to impress Rachel, was now matted with bits of Darcy's insides. Tom felt himself flinch. He wanted to blink it all away, this sudden sickness that had taken hold and hurt Darcy so quickly. He couldn't control time or reality: he couldn't even control his feet and knees.

Billy spoke to Rachel at a volume that looked like it had to have been a screech. Tom couldn't hear the words, so there was no way of knowing what it actually sounded like. There was a whooshing sound pressing against the insides of his eardrums now. He figured that it was either shock or that he was about to faint. His mind expected his body to keel over, but it remained rigid, standing by and doing nothing.

Tom began to seriously doubt that he was conscious. This had to be a hallucination brought on by the drugs. The fact that the drugs up until now hadn't done jack shit didn't matter. Maybe they were delayed-action.

Legs were crawling out of Darcy's mouth. Long, smooth spider legs. From behind Rachel couldn't see the legs yet, but her freckled face was already streaked with tears and snot. Billy couldn't see them either: he had his back turned to Darcy, trying to lock eyes with Tom.

"Do something." Billy's words flooded back into Tom's understanding, like the sudden sharpening of a static-filled radio station. "Please move, Tom!"

Tom dropped the bottle to the carpet, his hand red from the cold and still curved. "Look," he said in a whisper. He doubted that his friend could hear the word over the sounds of Rachel's sobs and the wet crackling coming from Darcy's mouth. If any of this was happening at all.

Billy turned and jumped back by reflex, tripping over the coffee table and smearing his jeans with pizza sauce. The thing was almost all the way out of Darcy's mouth now. Her body buckled at the knees and fell back into Rachel's arms: a grotesque trust fall. Darcy's head lolled back and landed on Rachel's shoulder.

Rachel didn't only see it now, she was face-to-face with it. The mewling creature clicked its jaws just centimeters from her nose. Her screams, Billy's shouting, and all the other minute details of the event added up to one feeling: this was not a trip. All hallucinogenic trips were limited by the imagination of the tripper. Not even Tom's deranged psyche could dream this shit up.

The creature was poking its legs at Rachel now, and she had no choice but to push Darcy forward, sending the girl's body face first toward the basement floor. Tom acted, taking a running step forward and closing the distance across the small basement in only a few bounds, but it was too late. Darcy didn't put her hands out to slow her descent, and her body bounced up against the slight cushion that the carpet provided.

As her head snapped back against the floor, the creature tumbled out, getting to its feet with some disorientation.

Billy was still flat on his back beneath the couch, his jeans spotted with pepperoni slices. He met Tom's gaze with what must have been a mirror of his own expression: abject fucking horror. They both watched as the small animal began to jitter and click. The thing ran in small circles, pausing and looking up at Tom, Billy and Rachel, regarding all three of the room's inhabitants with a frenzied caution.

As it turned, the thing produced a long, spear-tipped appendage that it held above its body like a periscope. It stopped pacing with what looked like its front end facing Tom (it was hard to tell if there was a face beneath all those spikes). It began clicking more rapidly and moved its legs in place with a rhythmic flourish. It was a pattern of behavior that told anyone who'd ever seen a nature documentary, "You better run because I'm getting ready to attack you. You prick."

Tom saw Billy slowly climb to his feet behind the animal. Tom looked back at the gibbering monstrosity as it crouched lower to the ground, and he took a few steps backward toward safety, bumping into the freezer.

Billy gave Tom a somber nod, the most mature look the two boys had ever shared. The creature began running, snagging its pointed legs momentarily on the short carpeting but pulling itself free with almost no effort.

Billy started to run too. His facial expression was serious but his movements were perennially gangly and awkward. He caught up with the animal when both were about two yards from Tom. Billy reared one leg back for a kick, and the critter prepared to leap at Tom. Billy connected, but just barely. It was the kind of a sideways kick that had gotten him picked last for kickball in grammar school...and every sport in high school. Instead of sending the creature careening into the wall, the blow only served to enhance the creature's jump. As an added bonus, Billy lacerated his foot and calf.

The thing lashed out with its stinger as Rachel yelled for Tom to move. He whipped his head back and felt the wind as the knife missed his neck by less than an inch. The blade burrowed into the basement wall, and the creature had no choice but to follow it, rebounding off the back of the trunk and falling into the freezer.

Nobody moved for a moment as the creature's screams changed pitch into a squeal. It made more of a racket as it tried in vain to scramble up the smooth sides of the freezer, its feeler still stuck in the wall beside its new prison.

Tom could not stop his pendulum stare, pointing his attention first at the animal and then back at Darcy. He hadn't even seen Rachel move, but she had crossed the room and muffled the creature's screams by slamming the freezer door closed, imprisoning the damn thing and severing its feeler in one strong motion. Brownish-green fluid slid down the side of the white freezer and dripped from the end of the still-twitching limb.

In the first minute of the aftermath, no one spoke. Billy sucked in air through clenched teeth, holding on to his ankle and trying to kink off his bleeding toes.

Tom paid little attention to his wounded friend. *He'll be all right.* He crept to the center of the room to be close to Darcy. He then unbuttoned his shirt, wiping the some of the blood splatter from the dirty button-down onto his white undershirt. He held the shirt by its edges and folded it once. He crouched by Darcy's side and closed his eyes as he gently turned her over.

Without looking, he placed the folded shirt over her face. Then he picked her up, held her and cried.

Chapter Sixteen

"Scalpel," Rhonda said, mimicking a surgeon on a TV show as she put out her hand, palm up. Darl handed her the paring knife she had used to carve off her own skin. When she attempted to giggle at her joke, the only sounds to come out were a few hollow clicks. Her new body wasn't made for giggling.

"I simply cannot believe what a good patient you're being, Terry," she said and placed one hand on his shoulder, using the other to align the blade with his scalp.

"It's going to make me a stone-cold killer. Ain't that right?" Terry asked, looking straight forward at Darl, his spine planted firmly against the back of the chair. The chair was just small enough to fit both of Terry's legs in the bathtub with room for Rhonda to crouch behind him.

"Yup," Darl said and nodded to him with an expression that, if Rhonda hadn't known any better, would have looked a little squeamish.

"Then let's go. Bring on the pain. This is going to be fucking metal!" Terry shouted. He'd obviously forgotten what she had told him about keeping his head steady, because his fidgeting had caused her to cut a big, uneven line across his forehead.

From the looks of the blood steadily dripping from the wound, Terry's body had only begun to undergo the change that afternoon. The flow was slower than a normal human's would have been and the blood was a darker shade of red as it gushed forth, but it still managed to coat Terry's face in a matter of seconds.

"Sickening, but totally rad," Terry said. The blood dripped into his mouth and outlined his teeth in red. The blood-streaked look gave an even more insane quality to his wide, toothy grin.

"Are you sure about this?" Darl asked as Rhonda finished cutting and let the majority of Terry's scalp slog to the bathroom floor with a wet smack.

"Not really, but it was either this or..." Rhonda pantomimed twisting his neck and ripping Terry's head from his body. She did this while Terry remained blissfully unaware, doodling on the shower wall with his own blood. She was trying not to alarm the lunatic, something which seemed increasingly implausible.

Rhonda used a wad of toilet paper to wipe off the excess blood and try to find the area on Terry's skull that she was looking for. She found it and placed one pointed finger at the intersection of two plates over his frontal lobe. "The hammer, please," she said. She took great care not to move her finger from the spot, even though Terry was wiggling all over the place.

"All right, hold still," Rhonda said, steadying the claw end of the hammer over the kid's forehead. After he'd found it in her father's tool belt, she'd had Darl give the hammer a rinse in the sink. There were still remnants of what smelled like motor oil on the end, but it would have to do. "If this doesn't work, then it's been very nice meeting you, Terry."

"Same here," Terry said, unengaged. He finished up the penis he'd graffitied onto the pink bathroom tile in his own blood. "Wait, what?"

Rhonda moved her finger and brought the hammer down as Terry began to turn around. There was a crack like a soggy gunshot and Rhonda let go of the handle. Instead of clattering into the tub, the hammer stuck out of Terry's forehead. Terry put one hand on the tile and then slumped, leaving a long, smeared handprint in his own blood.

Rhonda had bull's-eyed her target, more or less. Both she and Darl stood silent for a moment. "I think I killed him," she said and reached down to pry out the hammer. She'd barely touched the wooden handle when Terry sprang up in the chair and began coughing and heaving, sounding like someone who had just narrowly avoided drowning.

Darl lunged forward to help the kid and Rhonda put up a hand to stop him. "Wait a moment," she said.

As Terry shifted, trying to stand, the hammer wiggled free from his wound and finally fell to the floor of the bathtub. The shock of the sound disoriented Terry and set him on his face, his teeth mashing into the polished chrome of the tub's spout.

Rhonda squeezed out from behind the chair, giving him some room to recover. On his second try, still slipping slightly on blood and uneasy legs, Terry stood up and stared at Darl and Rhonda. His eyes were dead, a lot like they had been before the operation.

"Terry, can you hear me?" Darl asked. Terry was unresponsive. Then the corner of his mouth briefly twitched upward into a half smile and just as quickly fell slack again.

"If you can, speak," Rhonda said. It was not a question, but a command.

Terry made a muffled cough. It might have been a "yes" or it might have just been reflexes.

"Well, that's not going to be a valid form of communication. Can you nod, then?" Rhonda said.

Terry shook his head with great enthusiasm. Flecks of gore flew off his exposed skull and speckled the walls.

"Well, there you have it. He's cured," Darl said, laughing and taking a step toward Terry, hands outstretched to help him out of the tub. Once he was within grabbing distance, the boy growled and pressed his back up against the shower wall, baring his fingernails as if they were the claws of a grizzly bear. "All right then, I won't come near ya," Darl said. "Jeez." He looked back at Rhonda.

"Come along now, Terry; let's go," Rhonda said. Terry nodded and signaled for "one second". He bent down, steadying himself with the back of the chair, and picked up his scalp, plopping it back on his head as a mushy toupée.

"Good as new," Darl said to Terry, rolling his eyes. "May I be excused to go check on the kids across the street? I bet they're dead or turned by now. I've had about all of Fluffy here that I can take."

"That's not a bad suggestion," Rhonda said. "Terry and I should be able to entertain ourselves, shouldn't we, dear?"

Terry smiled and chuckled, nodding until his hair slogged off and landed in the open toilet.

The bleeding had slowed to a stop, and Rachel applied some antiseptic to Billy's wounds while Tom paced the living room. The antiseptic had come from a small first aid kit that Billy's parents kept under the bathroom sink. The kit was old, the metal box itself probably dating back to the seventies, but the contents were fresher and still useful.

"It should be okay now," Rachel said. "It looked a lot worse before I cleaned it off. There was a lot of blood, but none of the wounds were very deep." Billy's lower leg looked like he'd been in a hunting accident. Birdshot, thankfully, not buckshot.

"You sit down and I'm going to call the police." She patted his shoulder as she rose from her spot in front of the couch. All three of them were shaky, but Rachel was the only one who was with it enough to talk on the phone, so Billy didn't offer to do it. "The phone is in the kitchen, on the wall," he said.

As she left the room, Billy caught Rachel taking a quick glance at Tom, obviously trying hard not to stare. Tom stopped pacing and sat down on the arm of a recliner, hands compulsively rubbing the stubble under his chin. The areas around his eyes were red and puffy, but dry.

Billy spoke when Rachel left. "I'm sorry. I know she really did mean a lot to you."

Tom kept feeling his slight beard, making a soft, rhythmic crackle when his nails passed over his neck. "It's not so much that I loved her or anything. More..." His voice trailed off and the only sound was Rachel using the rotary phone in the next room.

"It's more of a 'what the hell was that'?" Billy said, wincing as he toyed with the Band-Aids on his ankle, trying to look at his friend but failing to make eye contact with anything other than the carpet.

"Yeah," was all that Tom said. There was silence for a moment before he added, "Nice kick." They made eye contact for the first time since coming upstairs, Billy and Rachel first, Tom following behind after he'd had a few minutes alone with Darcy. Rachel had wanted to prove to herself that nothing could be done, so before they came upstairs, she had very gingerly taken Darcy's wrist away from Tom and squeezed for a pulse. There was nothing.

Rachel came back into the room, phone in hand with the cord pulled taut around the corner of the doorway. "How can 911 be busy?"

Rachel ducked back into the kitchen, and Billy heard her hit the receiver down and dial again. Billy took the moment to exchange a worried lift of his eyebrows with Tom, who returned the look. If anything, Tom was at least closer to normal than he had been in the basement.

"Fuck," Rachel said and slammed the phone down. Billy winced at the sound.

"Don't worry, it didn't sound to me like she broke it," Tom said. Even if his voice was an even monotone, at least he was talking and joking.

"Well?" Rachel said, reentering and steadying her shaking hands by leaning on the couch's end table.

"Well, the only way 911 could be busy is when something seriously big is going on," Billy said.

"Big how? Like Russia invading big?" Rachel said.

"Yeah, but, I think what we just saw..." Billy started to speak his thoughts but couldn't find the nerve or the words to articulate them, not even to himself, never mind out loud. The past few days' events swam around in his head, each strange strand of information tangling up with another and another until he could no longer distinguish what was his imagination. It was a feeling similar to those hazy moments in the morning when you're not exactly sure if what just happened in your dream really happened or not.

"He thinks what we just saw happen to Darcy is connected to 911 being busy. And not just that, but to the pills we bought," Tom said and stood up from the arm of the chair.

"What, why?" Rachel said.

Billy turned to Tom, continuing the list. "And to all of the absences at school, and to Terry Manfred attacking me, trying to make me eat something, and to Russ looking like a zombie."

"This is crazy," Rachel said and stormed out of the room. They could hear her trying the phone once again.

"One too many screwed-up movies, eh?" Tom said and chuckled, but not in a way that sounded like he was having any fun.

"We need to go back downstairs, check some things out," Billy said.

"I don't think I can," Tom said. All the levity, no matter how much of a put-on it had been, was gone from his voice. He looked down at the dried blood on his undershirt. Some of it was Darcy's, but most of it was the goop from when the tentacle had been severed in his face. Tom didn't want to have to look at Darcy again.

"It's okay, man. I can do it." Billy got up, trying not to bleed on the carpet or limp too noticeably.

"What are you doing? Sit back down," Rachel's third phone call hadn't ended in success, or they would have heard her. Now she was back in the living room as Billy tried to hobble his way to the basement door.

"I have to go downstairs," Billy said, reaching for the doorknob.

"Don't, wait, what if it got out?"

He hadn't thought of that.

"It didn't," Billy said, not convincing even himself. Tom had been tending to Darcy as Billy had held down the lid to the freezer and Rachel had piled nearly everything in the room on top of it. While she was stacking, the creature's scratching and clicking had grown fainter, until it had finally stopped shortly before the friends headed upstairs. Was it just biding its time, or had it bled out inside the freezer? "You can close the door behind me, just to be sure."

"Don't be an idiot. I'll come with you," Rachel said, looking at Tom and expecting him to join up as well. He didn't. "Do you have, like, a baseball bat or something? For protection."

Billy didn't, and for the first time in a long while his aversion to sports embarrassed him.

"You do have something," Tom said and smiled again. Billy wasn't getting it; his mind wasn't as sharp as usual. "From your trip to Disneyworld?"

"Here, put this in your mouth." Rhonda handed Terry the end of the hose, which he shoved about four inches into his mouth and bit down on. "No biting," she said and wagged her finger in his face. She undid the fuel cap on Darl's patrol car and fed the other end of the hose down into the gas tank.

While she worked at opening the gas can, Terry nibbled on the hose slightly. "Now suck," she said. Terry stared at her, slack-jawed and dead-eyed. She wondered if he had forgotten that he had a length of garden hose halfway down his throat.

"Suck!" She made the sound of sucking in air. She would have puckered up her lips and collapsed her cheeks if she had any.

After a moment of quiet deliberation, Terry sucked in hard. He gave himself a lungful of gasoline and dribbled more than a mouthful down the front of his tacky denim jacket and Metallica sweatshirt.

"Jeez, don't drink it all!" Rhonda grabbed the hose and yanked it out of Terry's mouth, spilling some more on his sweatshirt and jeans. He gagged and coughed up some of the gas that had been caught in his windpipe, but his expression was not one of disgust, just passive enjoyment.

Rhonda put the hose into the canister and the garage filled with the trickling sound of liquid hitting tin. "After this one's done, we can get to the other car," Rhonda said, talking to herself as much as she was Terry. "Then we can move on with the plan. Getting close now. Almost time for the big show."

She looked up at him, and Terry smiled a big, goofy grin that only served to make his already ghastly appearance even worse. The hole in his head was only partially covered by his scalp-toupée. From what she could see, the hole wasn't healing well. The jagged cut on his forehead had begun to grow green around the edges in the less than an hour's time since the "operation". Still, he was her puppy, her smiling and mute slave.

"I wonder how Darl is doing?" Rhonda said out loud, the way a young Rhonda might have talked to a favorite stuffed animal or her mother to a plant in the garden. "You're not a mouthy, disobedient prick, but you're not exactly up to doing complex tactical maneuvers," she said to him and nodded. Terry nodded back, still smiling. He had no idea what she was talking about.

Billy gripped the hilt of the samurai sword. His hands were slick with sweat and blood against the carved faux-ivory handle. If he had to swing, it slipping through his fingers was an all-too-real possibility. Against his better judgment he still felt self-conscious about how stupid he looked in front of Rachel, waving around a display sword he'd picked up at Epcot Center as a kid. *You're beyond that now. You could be wearing a tutu and a bikini top and she wouldn't give a crap. The game plan for the night has changed.*

Opening the basement door a crack, he listened and pointed the end of the sword downward before continuing down the first few steps. Rachel followed and closed the door behind them. Even though he was expecting it, the sound still made him jump.

The familiar paint and acrylic carpet smell of the basement now had a new scent. It was a tangy, metallic accent that you could taste on the back of your tongue. Billy had read enough Stephen King to know that this was the coppery smell of blood.

The lights were on, bouncing off the white walls of the basement. The well-lit setting did nothing to soothe the chill of fear. Billy felt the cool tremor start at his lower back and work its way up his arms until the tip of the sword was vibrating.

"It'll be okay," Rachel assured him from behind, but she had no way of knowing that. He jumped again in surprise at his own exhale as he turned the corner of the stairway to see that the freezer was still sealed. The pile of junk they had piled on top was undisturbed. Books, a lamp, the VCR, one of the cushions from the couch: everything was as they had left it, meaning that the monster was still trapped inside the trunk.

"Do you think it's dead?" Rachel asked. She was standing close to him, her hand on the back of his shoulder. It did wonders for his bravery level.

"I don't know," he said. "Let's see what this does." He took one hand off of the sword. His fingers were sore from his prolonged kung fu grip, and it took effort to uncurl them fully. With his free hand, he knocked softly on the side of the freezer and waited. There was no movement.

Rachel stepped forward and rasped with considerably more force. If it was in there, then it was lying completely still, waiting for them to open the lid so it could jump up and bury its spines into both of their brainpans.

"Maybe we shouldn't open it yet," Billy said, walking toward the center of the room and trying not to look directly at Darcy, but making sure not to trip over her either. He wanted to take a look at the pizza, which he had mashed into the carpet and couch when he tripped over the coffee table.

"Take a look at this." Billy crouched, wincing through the pain in his foot, and picked up a more or less intact slice of pizza. He put the sword down on the table and looked closely at the cheese. Nothing out of the ordinary on the top. "Remember what Tom had said, right before it happened?"

"About him beating up Terry Manfred?"

"Not that, but that is interesting too," Billy said. He had forgotten that bit. "He was freaking out over there being a black olive on his pizza."

"Yeah, I do," Rachel said, sounding like she was losing patience with his master detective act already.

Billy peeled back the layer of cheese, starting at the crust and working to the tip. It came away easier now that the pizza was room temperature. Revealing the tomato sauce and fleshy dough reminded

188

Billy too much of Darcy's hacking, bloody coughs, and he shivered. Under the cheese, embedded in the dough, were two small, black pills.

"Those are the same things Darcy and Tom took," Rachel said, picking up what Billy was putting down. "But does that mean that Tom's going to..."

"No," Billy interrupted her, not wanting to think about his best friend dying as well. "I think when they cut them in half, they broke them somehow. Look." Billy carved one of the black lumps off of the pizza with his fingernail and laid it on the table. Taking up a serrated plastic knife that had come with the pizza, he began to cut the pill longways down the middle. It took some sawing to get through, but when he was done there was a squirt of viscous liquid. He wrinkled his nose in disgust. Inside was what looked like a small, white insect. Billy had seen something like it on nature shows: it was larva.

"It's like a cocoon, see?" Billy said. "When they cut it in half, they killed the bug."

"Who would put these in there? Why is this happening?" Rachel looked at Billy now, her eyes pleading for him to make sense of the senseless. *When science fiction burrows its way out of your friend's girlfriend's throat, it becomes science fact.* Billy was as close to an expert as Rachel was going to get.

"That thing lost a lot of blood," Billy said, changing the focus of the discussion. "You cut off its, um, squishiest part. It's either dead or dying." He smiled because it felt like an okay thing to do. "Let's try to open up the freezer and see what we can figure out."

Instead of calling him nuts, laughing in his face or bursting into tears, Rachel simply nodded. They stood to turn, and both looked at Darcy. Rachel reached out and took his hand as they walked around the hooded body. It was hard to believe how both of them were keeping it together. Maybe it was shock, or maybe it was only in books that people were reduced to useless mounds of grief when their friends died, or maybe Rachel was taking it worse than Billy realized. Maybe she was torn up inside and the real despair would come later.

They unpacked the lid of the freezer, speaking only when they needed help lifting something heavy. Rachel took a spot at the far end of the freezer, away from where the creature had originally been pinned.

"Ready?" Billy asked, raising the sword, getting ready to slide it under the door and impale the clicking fucker. "One, two..."

Rachel opened the lid and Billy plunged the sword down before he could see inside of the dark freezer. He'd stabbed where he thought the creature must be, and unlike the kick, his aim was true.

"Okay, it's dead." Billy waved her over to the edge of the freezer and they stood staring at the thing. Its color had changed. It was now pale, more of a tan than the dark brown it had been when it jumped out of Darcy's mouth. Many of its spikes were broken off, and the contents of the freezer were littered with pointed shards of bony chitin.

The sword was stuck through the top of the creature, impaling it against a box of frozen hamburger patties. The weapon had only done some of the damage. Most of it must have been the result of the creature's frenzied last attempts at escape. It must have done some major damage to itself by thrashing around in the dark.

"Look, frozen solid," Billy said, picking up one of his mother's antiquing magazines from the floor and rolling it up tight. He used it to poke at the creature, and one of its legs broke off. "I barely touched it."

"It's only been in there for fifteen minutes, tops. It can't be frozen," Rachel said, getting into the detective/scientist mind set herself. "Let me try." She took the magazine from Billy and whacked the dead thing. It disintegrated into a pile of spines, legs and crystalline dust like a lightly packed snowball.

"My guess is they don't like the cold," Billy said. He was racking his brain trying to figure out which movie this was most like when he was interrupted by a knocking from upstairs. The knock turned into a frantic banging, and they both jumped.

"Somebody's knocking on your door," Rachel said, probably sounding more panicked than she intended to.

Tom listened at the basement door, not really focusing on

deciphering the murmurs of Rachel and Billy. He couldn't make himself care. They were talking, not screaming, and that was enough to put him at ease.

He was propped up, half-sitting on one of Billy's mom's expensive pieces of junk. It looked like an umbrella stand, but didn't have any umbrellas in it. The banging on the door caused him to fly up and knock over the stand. It rolled, and he stopped it with his foot.

Tom held his breath. The knocking came again, firmer this time.

He opened the basement door a crack and yelled down, "You hear that?"

"Yeah, we're coming up," Billy said.

Tom didn't wait for them. He began to approach the front door. All of the first-floor lights were on, so there was no way to approach the mostly glass door without being seen. Tom walked proud and strong; if the person at the door was a raving lunatic ringing in the apocalypse with some door-to-door massacres, so be it. Tom was through with being scared and useless.

Of all the feelings he expected upon approaching the door, disappointment was not one of them. It was only the cop who had broken up his fight with Terry Manfred. *That seems like days ago*, Tom thought, standing in the foyer, staring at the cop.

The old guy knocked again, his wrinkles looking even more pronounced in the porch light. His face was drawn tight, his jaw clenched, as if it were the dead of winter outside instead of the beginning of fall. Tom just stared, not knowing what to do. Even if he hadn't just witnessed Darcy's death, he still wouldn't have wanted to answer follow-up questions with the cop.

He thought of more reasons the cop had for being at the door. What if he had really hurt Manfred? Good; that kid had it coming anyway. He didn't much care anymore.

The cop looked at the blood on Tom's undershirt, and instead of alarm, his expression softened to a smirk. "Open the door," the cop said, taking his hand out of his jacket for the first time. No, not a hand: a weapon. Three long, sharp talons that the cop used to knock on the window, scratching while he knocked and leaving marks that could never be buffed out of the glass.

How could Darl have been so stupid? Assuming that because the kid looked pale and his shirt was bloody that he had been turned. Darl should have stayed in character until he was sure that he saw a puncture wound. There wasn't a mark on the kid; Darl could see that as the kid turned and ran deeper into the house.

If it weren't so fucking cold, he'd be able to smash through the glass and finish off the rest of the kids inside without Rhonda ever knowing about it. It would be something if he found her sister alive, then twisted her head off after he carved up the boyfriend. Not because he'd enjoy it per se, but because it sure would go against Rhonda's quiet, orderly and covert plan.

As it stood now, all Darl could do was wrap one arthritically frozen hand around the doorknob and try it. Locked. He wasn't surprised. Before he turned tail to run back to the warmth of the Krieger household, he stood looking at his reflection peering back at him in the window, silently damning himself.

Yeah, you really fucked that one up, champ. Letting the kid see your Creature from the Black Lagoon *hand? Rookie mistake. I mean, absolute alien invader amateur hour.* His mental passenger reveled in Darl's failures. These were now the only times that he gained enough morale to speak up.

"You're a coward," Darl whispered to himself, quite literally.

And you're a moron.

Darl focused his attention inside the house now. There were more kids in there. He could see their hunched shadows dancing across the wall.

"Kids, I know you are in there. I can see you!" Darl yelled, knowing they could make out his words through the wood and glass of the door. The street behind him was dead, the entire neighborhood was quiet, but it wouldn't be in a few hours from now. "I think there's been some kind of misunderstanding. I'm really badly hurt. You can see that for yourself if you come here. I need to use your phone to call for backup."

No answer, but a slight shifting of the shadows. They were conferring among themselves. He wondered how many there were. Maybe one had even been turned and the others didn't know it yet. Darl could use some help on the inside.

"Please. I'm bleeding badly, and I don't have the time or energy to get to another house," Darl said.

You're laying it on a little thick, buddy, his inner voice goaded. *Maybe tell them that their mommies and daddies have been hurt and you're here to take them to the hospital. Get real: they're teenagers, not idiots.*

Darl paused a few moments, ignoring the voice in his head, his eyes locked on the source of the shadows. Out from around the corner came one of the kids. It wasn't the one he'd caught fighting; it was a smaller, wimpier-looking one. The kid approached the door slowly, searching Darl's face. Darl made sure to turn his neck wound outward, hoping that the bandage looked bloody enough.

"Oh, thank God," Darl said as the kid took another step toward the door. He added an artificial pant to his voice, pretending to be out of breath.

No! You stupid little bastard, Darl felt his inner voice churn in dismay. He wanted to smile, but he couldn't risk scaring the kid, not when the kidwas this close to opening the door.

The boy stopped a few steps away from the door, extended his hand and then threw a second lock, a deadbolt from the sound of it. The kid wore a scowl on his young, oily face and flipped Darl the finger from the other side of the glass.

Darl's anger coursed through his body like lava. Toes that moments prior had been numb in his boots now felt like they were heated through pure force of rage. The vitriol surged up from his stomach and ended in his fingertips.

Before he could think about the consequences, he smashed his still-human fist against the glass, cracking it but not shattering it inward. The pain was immediate and substantial, but he was surprised that he was able to crack the glass at all in his weakened state.

There was a rush of activity on the other side of the door, but Darl was blind to it. He could not afford to waste the momentum he'd built up. He stuffed his throbbing hand inside his jacket pocket and then turned his shoulder to the glass. Using the weight of his body, he dropped his shoulder and elbow against the broken glass, bending the small, decorative metal frame out of the way and sending most of the window crashing to the inside of the house. Shards of glass stuck in his jacket and ripped up his elbow, but it hardly mattered.

Darl had successfully punched a hole in the window. He prayed that it was large enough to reach the lock on the doorknob, and shoved his claw inside to try, disregarding the remaining bits of glass that pricked his useless human skin.

It was only then, with his arm halfway inside, that he saw what the taller kid was holding. *Where did this kid get a fucking Chinaman's sword?* Darl's inner voice shrieked, elated at the boy's bizarre choice of weaponry.

There was no time to retreat, so Darl lashed out, flattening himself out against the door and taking a last, desperate swipe at the kid with the sword. He heard the shrill cry of a young girl and took note that there were at least three of them inside the house: two boys and the girl. The follow-through of his attack was largely unsuccessful. The tips of his claws caught fabric, but no skin as the tall kid jumped back, taking a swing at the same time.

This quick first strike carved through the battered layer of rotting human flesh on his forearm. The nerves of this old tissue were dead, and Darl could barely feel what he assumed was a small nick in his new and tougher hide.

The smaller kid was sneaking up on the other side, taking advantage of Darl's blind spot and readying what looked like a busted table leg. Darl tried waiting until the geek kid was close enough and then slashing out at his throat, but something was wrong. His arm wasn't responding. He turned to look at the taller kid just in time to see him finish winding up and take another smack with the sword. Darl heard the wood of the door splinter from the force and knew that he was in trouble.

That didn't sound so good, chief. There was that familiar, aggravating laughter as his legs buckled. *I think you might have fucked up by not listening to that boss of yours and sticking to the plan.*

Darl heard the girl scream again as he fell backward, dragging the small stump that remained of his arm with him. He hit the concrete steps and had all the anger knocked out of him. What he felt now was embarrassment, a low, pitiful feeling that he had been worthless with two arms and would now, no doubt, be even worse with just the one.

Billy noted that the sound Tom had made as he chopped the cop's arm off was almost an exact reproduction of Han Solo's "Yahoo!" from the end of the first *Star Wars*. It was the scene where Han shows up at the last second, blasts Darth Vader's ship, and makes it possible for Luke to destroy the Death Star.

"Fucker," Tom said and wiped a long string of brown blood from his eyebrow. He pushed his head close to the busted window, hocked and spit onto the front steps. Billy should have been worried about the fragile mental state of his friend, but it was good to have the old Tom back, even if he was streaked with monster gore.

"Rachel, are you okay?" Billy turned to her. She stood agape just beyond the entrance to the foyer. Luckily, she had been far enough away to be spared the splash when Tom lowered the sword a second time, but she'd still seen a man being grievously wounded in front of her eyes.

"People don't bleed that color," Rachel said, her eyes fixed on the half arm that had fallen inside the house. Tom had separated it cleanly at the elbow.

"Yeah, and people don't normally have honking monster butcher knives for fingers either," Tom said, standing over the arm and poking at it with the tip of the sword. The first hack had taken off a huge flap of skin and sliced a greenish tendon right below the elbow. The second, which Tom made with both feet planted firmly on the floor, had sent the arm tumbling to the hallway tile. The second swing had probably been wholly unnecessary, but Tom had taken it as if he wasn't going to

195

be satisfied unless he got something to take home with him.

Tom lifted his foot, the heel of his shoe hovering over the cop's mutant pinky finger for a second before setting down. He leaned his weight onto it. The finger gave way with a pop. The tip of the finger squirted a brownish-white fluid onto Billy's mother's handmade welcome mat. It was the kind of mat that visitors are not encouraged to wipe their feet on, and now it had quite a stain.

"Come on, man, don't do that," Billy said, noticing Rachel's unease. "It's morbid."

Tom paid him little attention and kept staring down, both eyes and expression slack. Tom was a child invested in immolating every last ant under his magnifying glass, and no words could reach him. He put the tip of his Converse over the knuckle of the elongated middle finger, and was beginning to press down when the hand curled up, ensnaring his foot in its dead grasp.

"Holy shit," Tom yelled, sparking to life as if the grip had woken him from a sound sleep. He lifted his foot high, almost tossing the hand to where Billy and Rachel stood before slamming it back down to shatter the two remaining mutant fingers. Tom panted, swallowing hard and giving Billy a wild look that said, "Did you just see me almost shit myself?"

"Maybe next time you won't horse around," Rachel said. The foyer was quiet while they thought about that. Her remark was sobering, not only because it stressed seriousness, but because it implied that there would soon be a next time.

Chapter Seventeen

Rachel was trying the phone again, Billy was looking for something to cover up the gaping hole in the door with, and Tom was left with the sword, keeping watch.

Tom watched the yard, standing behind the door but angling his body away from the broken window. The cop lay at the bottom of the steps, motionless for a moment before flipping onto his stomach and attempting an army-man crawl with his one remaining arm.

"Where ya going, pal?" Tom asked. The cop didn't answer. He just grunted in exertion and tried to rise, giving up on the crawl and slipping in his own blood. The cop mashed his nose into the concrete. It looked painful.

Tom looked down the hallway and saw Billy's shadow. He was probably breaking the remaining legs off of the end table, ready to use the boards to barricade the door. Emergency or not, Billy had almost pissed himself when Tom first broke off a leg and handed it to him to use as a club.

Tom turned back and was surprised to see the cop had gotten to his knees. "Good job, slugger."

The cop steadied himself, let go of his wounded elbow and used his good hand to rise to his feet. He took a series of shaky footsteps before falling again, but not before making it to the sidewalk. *Are you headed where I think you're headed?*

"Billy," Tom said. "Could you come in here for a moment?"

"Just a second." Billy huffed in exertion. Why wasn't he keeping watch while Tom did the manual labor? The cop was up off the asphalt. He had caught on quick to how to stand with one arm. He crossed the street to Rachel Krieger's front yard.

"Now, please," Tom said as Billy entered the foyer. Billy pushed his body against the opposite wall and shimmied toward the door, avoiding the glow of the streetlight through the hole in the door and trying not to be seen from the outside.

"Look," Tom said as Billy peeked around the broken glass in time to see Terry Manfred swing open the front door to Rachel's house.

"My God," Billy said. Tom couldn't tell if Billy was reacting to how fucked up Terry looked or the very fact that he was in the Krieger house to begin with. His head was a bloody mess, a mixture of rust-red human blood and the darker stuff that now painted the hardwood of the foyer. Odder yet was his distinct lack of hair. "What is he doing over there?"

Tom shushed him. "Let's try not to get her too excited," he said, hooking his thumb back into the house.

"This is the first movement I've seen over there, even though I did notice that the lights were on," Tom said, pulling his leather jacket closer around him. He'd put it back on after the cold night air had crept through the busted window and cooled down the house. They watched as Terry helped the stumbling officer to his feet, clamping his hand around his stump and offering the injured cop his shoulder. Once he had a hold on him, he partially dragged, partially carried the cop inside and shut the door.

"This is unreal," Billy said. It was a phrase that Tom had heard him use often while poring over the pages of the most recent *Fangoria* magazine. For once, Tom agreed with him completely.

"Can you see anything else from your side?"

"There's a light on in the Dobson house." Billy squinted. "I see Geraldine."

"The fat one who always has the sweatpants?" Tom knew who she was, but the insult made him feel somehow more human.

"Shit, I think she's staring right at me."

"Does she look like she's calling or going to call the police?"

"No," Billy said, ducking down out of her sight. "She looks like she's watching the most entertaining TV show of all time and really wishing that she had some popcorn."

"Maybe you should get Rachel and turn on the TV. Maybe the news can tell us something for once. I'll stay here."

Terry made a series of excited gasps and grunts. Rhonda gave him her partial attention, and he pointed an eager, curved finger toward the window. He'd been staring out at the Kriegers' front lawn for the last ten minutes.

"What's that, boy? Timmy's stuck in a well?" Rhonda said, her new voice ill-equipped to handle either humor or sarcasm.

Rhonda approached the window to witness a huddled figure limping across the street, leaving a steady trail of dark fluid in his wake. Darl held his human hand over the stump of his elbow, but it did little to stop the flow.

"Motherfucker," Rhonda said.

Terry made a low whine. He was obedient but easily frightened.

"Go get him," Rhonda said, miming picking up an invisible parcel and putting it down on the floor of the living room. It took him a moment of critical thinking, the wound in his skull pulsating with the beat of his heart, but finally he walked to the door to go get her wounded lieutenant.

While he stepped out, Rhonda went into the kitchen and clicked on one of the stove-top burners.

What was she hoping to achieve? If she ever got through to 911, she suspected the odds were good that the operator would be sprouting claws and spewing black blood. The tick of the rotary kept her sane by keeping her occupied.

When it had first happened, all she had wanted to do was get across the street. Go home to her mother, father and sister. Then she remembered Rhonda's pale skin, Jake's mysterious death, and,

199

suddenly, the fact that she hadn't seen her parents in two days. She began trying desperately not to think too hard about what it all meant: she wanted to stay put. They were connections her conscious mind didn't want to make, so she instead focused on dialing the three numbers, removing her finger from the rotary and waiting for the busy signal.

And then—a voice. "Nine-one-one, what is your emergency?" Rachel could feel her pulse throbbing in her fingertips as she tightened her hold on the phone.

"Hello?" the operator asked, sounding about ready to hang up as a stunned Rachel assessed the situation.

She couldn't stand hearing her own lonely breath on the line anymore. "Hello, I'm here. Don't hang up," Rachel pleaded with the operator.

"I wouldn't hang up, darling," the woman on the other end of the line said. "Now tell me what your emergency is." Rachel got a clear picture of the woman in her head just by listening to her words and voice. She saw a matronly woman, a caring grandmother-type who'd secretly be offended if you thought she was old enough to be your grandmother.

"It's hard to explain on the phone," Rachel said, desperate for a way to explain what had happened to Darcy without having this nice old lady hang up on her. "But please send the police. My friends and I have been attacked and the man is still outside the house."

"Is there anything else?" the woman asked, her tone still cheery, down-home apple pie.

"Sorry, um, I don't understand the question," Rachel said.

"What I mean is, have there been any other strange occurrences?" the woman asked. Rachel swallowed hard. The question had to mean that this, whatever the hell it was, was a widespread event.

"Yes, ma'am. We've actually had a fatality here, and that's why you need to send the police and an ambulance right away."

"Oh, my, well then."

Rachel didn't need to hear the old lady's wonderment. She needed her to do her job. She interrupted:, "The address is 67 Mo—"

"I'm afraid that won't be necessary, dear," the woman said. There was something else there now, something much colder than Granny's hand-squeezed lemonade.

"What do you mean?" Rachel was losing what little cool she had left. She wanted to scream at this old bag.

"What I mean is that I advise you to stay in your home and wait for the final stage of the plan to take effect, dearie. Now if you'll excuse me, I'm the only person manning this call center. Have a good night." The woman spoke in one long, hurried speech. Her voice dissolved into a dial tone and then silence.

Rachel didn't understand what the old lady was talking about, but she knew that her time of finding solace in compulsively dialing 911 was at an end. There was a tug in her throat as she tried to hold back the tears that she knew would come if she let them. She wanted to let them. Before she got the chance, Billy called to her from the living room.

"Rachel, come look!"

"I want you to drag his useless ass in here, right now." Rhonda's voice sounded like it was coming from the kitchen. Darl couldn't be sure of her exact location, because none of his senses were working half as well as they used to. Now that he'd spilled himself across two lawns and two lanes of blacktop, he was finding his faculties to be incapacitated.

"I've been very patient with you," Rhonda said. "You do realize that, don't you?"

Darl choked on a bit of congealed blood, not up to answering the question. It sounded rhetorical, anyway. His head throbbed along with the clangs Rhonda made as she rearranged some of the pots and pans. He was in the kitchen.

"And you know what? I'm going to give you one last fucking chance," Rhonda said, laying something down on the stove next to her.

201

His vision was blurred and discolored; he could see nothing but vaguely suggestive shapes. Rhonda may have been preparing him a steak dinner for all he could tell.

You're in trouble now, my friend. The old Darl tried to sound tough, but he could feel him slipping away. The little bastard was finally losing his grip on Darl's mind, the only problem being that it was because Darl was losing his grip on being alive. His neuropassenger was still connected in some rudimentary way to his old body. If the old, human Darl could feel a tenth of the agony that losing an arm involved, then his body was having nearly as rough a time as he was.

Darl refocused his attention on the here and now, muting the ongoing drone of his insulting inner monologue. That was perhaps the only good thing to come out of having his arm hacked off by some hoodlum with a samurai sword: the promise of mental peace and quiet.

From behind him, Terry whimpered. The lobotomized kid was more scared of the sounds Rhonda was making than he was of her words. Darl could feel Terry's strong hands locked around his stump. Either Terry was doing a much better job slowing the bleeding than Darl had done himself or he had no more blood left to give.

"I explained the fucking plan to you. It's not a difficult one to follow," she said, waiting at the stove. Was she really giving him the "plan" lecture again? He knew the plan; in fact, he had known it long before she had ever told him about it. It had been in the back of his head every moment since she plunged into his neck, turning him into a creature like her. Only, when he heard it repeated in his own mind, in his own voice, it had sounded more like a series of suggested guidelines than the absolute gospel. The plan was part of his nature now, part of his molecular structure—the molecules that were pooled all over the street outside and now splattered the kitchen floor.

"We stay hidden," Rhonda began, reciting the rules. She paused, picking something up off the stove before continuing. "We turn as many people as possible. And we do it as quietly as possible." She stepped forward until she was inches from his face and Darl could see what she was holding: a metal skillet. "And then we step back and watch as the whole fucking thing collapses and burns. That,

Lieutenant Todd Darl of the Suffolk County Sheriff's Department, is The Plan. Any questions?"

She put the skillet to his stump and held it. The smell of his own cooking meat was nauseating, and the pain would have been enough to put him under if he had still been human. But there was another sensation as well: pure ecstasy.

The crackle and pop of his boiling blood and seared flesh became the soundtrack to his own personal porno movie. Complete, hedonistic euphoria accented with slivers of utter agony. It was a sensation that no human could comprehend, and one that Darl would have liked to keep going infinitely. He felt the burn in what used to be his arm and could not shake his desire for the wound to burst into flames. It would be heaven, his body encased in a cocoon of oppressive warmth.

"What's so bad about that?" Rachel asked Billy. They stood in the living room, both staring into the glow of the television. An episode of *Sanford and Son* heralded the apocalypse.

"It's prime time, and this is News Channel 12 Long Island. This should be the news, not an episode of a show that was popular ten years ago," Billy said. Redd Foxx held his heart in mock surprise. It was a joke every human being with a television had seen at least once. He flipped the channel a few times. "Look. Here's what channel four looks like."

"It's *Cheers*. What's so weird about that? Isn't it supposed to be on right now?"

"This is the same episode that they played last night. Watch: Woody is going to open that door and Carla's going to drop that plate full of glasses." Woody did; the glasses smashed. Carla was stoic, saving her rebuttal until after the laughter of the studio audience had subsided.

"What does it mean?" Rachel said under her breath, possibly the first person to ever be chilled silent by Woody Harrelson.

"This is a national station, showing a rerun from last night. All the stations are like that; nothing but canned material and commercials. Not even so much as an emergency broadcast test. It's as if..."

"Someone was trying to stop people from knowing what was going on," Rachel finished his thought. That was more or less what Billy was going to say.

With a considerable amount of Terry's help, Darl was able to lie back on the couch, placing his smoldering stump on the armrest. Rhonda had cauterized the wound well. Taking her time, reheating the frying pan and going back for seconds once it had lost the heat needed to scald and sizzle. On his drooping face he wore the slack smile of an opium fiend.

"Very good," Rhonda said, patting Terry—her new right-hand man—on the shoulder. Despite his capacity for independent thought, Darl had been demoted. Terry could do all of the things that Darl couldn't. She was just going to have to make her instructions explicit and easy to understand.

Those kids across the street knew about them. They had survived an attempt at indoctrination and would now pose a threat, even if it was insignificant in the larger picture. "Not in my sector," Rhonda said. "We won't have holdouts on my fucking block." She was resolving, then and there, that the adolescents would be crushed. No mercy. They would become a footnote in her campaign.

Terry looked at her, momentarily distracted by her muttered words. They seemed to make him no more or less confused than he was by his own every sound and movement. Darl coughed and giggled and Terry went back to arranging him on the couch. Terry brushed the speckles of drool from the crags in Darl's wrinkled face and placed a pillow under his crispy stump. His actions reminded Rhonda of a video she had once seen when she was human: a mother gorilla coddling and caring for a plastic baby doll.

While he was busy with that, Rhonda plucked something quietly off the mantle piece. She'd placed it there after returning home from Heckscher Park. That seemed like a lifetime ago. Everything in its place, everything a part of the grand plan.

Rhonda touched Terry on the arm, approaching him slowly from behind, careful not to startle him. "It's your time to shine, Terry," Rhonda said, taking his hand and interrupting him as he smoothed out Darl's hair. Terry turned to her. He contorted his bloody face into his customary smile, signaling he was ready to listen.

Instead of just issuing orders, Rhonda went further. She put her other hand under the bottom layer of his clothing, slipping her long fingers beneath the elastic band at the bottom of his sweatshirt and making sure to stay under his T-shirt. She stopped when she reached a soggy, crusty mound. "What's that?" Rhonda said, gently groping with her sharp nails. She gripped and pulled her fist out. It was a collection of bloody gauze and paper towels, Terry must have been covering up his conversion wound.

"You don't need this anymore. You're all healed up," she said, indifferent to the fact that he probably could not understand a single word and definitely couldn't form words in response.

She tossed the bundle of semidried blood and paper to the floor. They didn't have to worry about making a mess anymore; Darl had made that decision for them by bleeding all over the place.

She caught Terry's attention with a wave and then mesmerized him with a quick magic trick. Palming her lighter (the one she'd set fire to Jake's van with), she flicked it on in front of Terry's eyes. He giggled and pointed a dirty finger at the flame, pushing the tip of his nail into the fire and scorching the human flesh. Rhonda took it away, noting that Terry still reeked of gasoline. She didn't want him immolating himself. Not yet.

Walking him over to the kitchen table, she explained what she wanted him to do. It was the most complex set of instructions she had given him yet. She took her time, even drawing a simple map on the Formica table, using the tips of her fingers as a pen and Darl's blood as ink.

When she drew the final X, Terry spoke for the first time since his operation.

"Rile," Terry said, slurring his words but unmistakably making an effort to speak. "Billy Rile," Terry said, switching his perennial smile to a look of exaggerated anger and disdain. He smudged the diagram on the table with the back of his fist, trying to wipe the neighbor's house off of the map.

"Perfect," Rhonda said. "I'm so glad that you understand."

After nailing a few pieces of the broken table over the window, doing a passable job of sealing it, Billy and Tom discussed their options in the living room.

"We need to stay put. I think you freaked her out enough with the TV trick. Telling her what we saw across the street is just going to make her worry about her sister," Tom said.

"Of course it will, but she's going to be worried and want to go over there anyway. We have to tell her," Billy said, raising his voice despite the need for discretion.

"Tell me what?" Rachel asked. The damn carpeted floors made it impossible to hear her sneaking up on them.

Tom glared at him and then punched Billy in the bicep.

"Ouch," Billy said, rubbing his arm. The punch was all the convincing he needed that telling her was the right idea. If he didn't warn her, she would insist on going over there, and that would increase the likelihood of something else terrible happening. "We saw the cop go over to your house."

"He was able to stand up?" She didn't let a word in. "Oh Jesus, Rhonda! We have to go over there and check on her."

"Well, that's not all we saw," Tom said, taking over for Billy. "Terry Manfred opened the door to your house and helped him in, and he didn't look..." Tom was at a loss to find the words, but Billy was glad that he was the one that had to find them. Coming out of Billy's mouth, it might have sounded too fantastical, too much like the product of science fiction. "He didn't look human, either."

Chapter Eighteen

"Either we're leaving or we're staying here. Regardless of which one we choose, we need to be able to defend ourselves," Rachel said. She surprised herself with how level-headed she was being about this new development. She got the feeling that she was surprising Billy and Tom as well. They seemed as if they had anticipated her either trying to fight her way to the front door or just breaking down and sobbing. They did not expect a calculated and rational reaction.

"You mean, like, board up the windows?" Billy asked. That mean, secret part of her suspected that the real question was, *You mean, like, fuck up the house?*

"No; I mean we need better weapons," she said.

"Well, this one isn't bad," Tom said, swinging the samurai sword and taking out an expensive-looking lamp, sending it crashing it to the floor.

"Just because the world's ending doesn't mean you can destroy the house," Billy said, throwing his hands up in the international pantomime for "I give up".

"Sorry." Tom shrugged as the dust cloud from the crushed lamp flew up. The humor in it finally broke Billy down, and both boys unsuccessfully suppressed a chuckle. Maybe it *was* the end of the world, but at least it had gotten Billy to finally lighten up. It would be a shame if all he needed was time, not cataclysm, to come around. Rachel would have liked to get to know him under better circumstances.

"I see what you're saying though," Billy said to Rachel. "We only have one badass sword, and I think Tom should hold on to it." He held up his own weapon, the leg of an ornate, antique coffee table. Two-and-a-quarter feet of polished, etched wood that curved in such a way that it looked impossibly unwieldy to swing with any accuracy.

"As 'badass' as the sword may be, I can think of something that could possibly work better," Rachel said. "And it will definitely work better than that thing," she added, pointing at the table leg.

"Yeah, I guess it is a bit dinky," Billy said, lowering his hand and letting the leg wilt. He blushed, taking a minute to get his own joke, and Rachel felt a tiny rush of blood to her own cheeks. *What a schmuck.*

"So what is it?" Tom said, taking the opportunity to both ruin the moment and fray the carpet with the tip of the sword. He was anxious and started to say something else.

"If you'd shut up and listen," she cut him off. "When Billy and I were in the basement, we opened the door to the freezer and found the monster frozen solid. Not only that, but it turned to ice dust when Billy touched it." Watching Tom, she saw the knot above his eyebrows knit itself tighter. He spun the sword in his hand in quick, anxious circles. Rachel hadn't meant to take such an attitude with him, hadn't meant to answer his swipe with her own. She had forgotten the very justifiable reason Tom hadn't gone down into the basement with them. Darcy was down there.

"These things don't like cold," Billy said, picking up Rachel's slack and trying to get Tom's mind off of Darcy.

"Where is your linen closet? We're going to need a couple of pillow cases," Rachel said.

"I'll go get them," Billy said and rushed off. He was giddy to get Rachel what she asked for.

Billy left them alone for only a minute. Rachel had no time to engage Tom in a deep philosophical discussion about where their lives would go from here and who they would be sharing them with. She didn't even have time to work up the nerve to tell him how sorry she was for what had happened to his girlfriend. The only thing they had time for was a charged silence and a lone question. "How bad do you think this is going to get?" Tom asked.

Rachel didn't have time to answer his question before Billy came bounding back into the room, holding some folded pillowcases.

"Now what?" Billy asked. The excitement in his voice and on his face was both palpable and inappropriate. It didn't bother Rachel at all.

Terry had to use two hands to carry the big red can. The big red can was very heavy. The big red can was full of smelly liquid.

Terry was very cold. It was dark and cold outside.

Rhonda was very pretty. Rhonda had told Terry to do a lot of things.

Terry liked the last thing she told him to do very much.

The last thing was to kill Billy Rile.

He used to think that would be bad, but Rhonda told him to do it. So it was an order.

Terry turned a corner. Boy, was the big red can heavy! Terry had to lift it all the way over the fence. Terry had to pick it up again after he had climbed over the fence himself.

He walked through a stranger's backyard. The stranger had a pool. Terry used to like pools.

The pool looked cold.

Terry had to lift the big red can over another fence. After the second climb, Terry was where he wanted to be.

Billy Rile's backyard was where Terry wanted to be.

Billy's backyard didn't have a pool.

Billy's house was about to burn down.

Terry was very excited.

"This is both stupid and dangerous," Tom said. He was holding his new weapon (a pillowcase that was mostly filled with frozen peas) and his old weapon in his crossed arms. Billy noted that he looked like a giant toddler with very odd taste in playthings and very liberal parents.

A few moments ago, Billy and Rachel had gone back down to the basement to scavenge the freezer. Tom had not been invited, not only because of Darcy's corpse but because they needed a lookout. The three of them were gathered in the living room now, debating going over to Rachel's house. Billy knew the stubbornness that Tom was capable of, and he was very happy Tom was being so resistant to Rachel's desire to investigate her house. The two of them had been arguing for five minutes, but Tom's enthusiasm for believable rhetoric was starting to flag. He was beginning to just stare at her with a sullen, you-ain't-gonna-get-me-to-budge look.

Without saying anything, Rachel tied a knot into her pillowcase full of frozen food. It was somehow a very intimidating maneuver, and Billy found that it lent her a bit more authority. "I say we go over there, not only to find my sister, but because: if I'm going to die, I would rather do it while taking offensive measures instead of standing here and playing whack-a-mole as monsters bust in through the doors and windows."

Billy swallowed hard, imagining an army of claws busting through the walls.

"Two measly monsters," Tom said, as if it were only a slight uptick in the number he saw every other day of the year. Billy moved to the window for a better lookout spot. "Two is all we've seen. Not counting the pizza guy, who you two have suspicions about. Who's to say there is some kind of invasion force getting ready to come and attack the house?"

"I don't know about an invasion force, but there is one standing on my front lawn right now," Billy said, stepping back from the window and flicking off the light. The figure was tall and wore a large, hooded jacket that blocked out its face. Billy ushered his friends down to the floor and told them to turn off the rest of the lights on the first floor. He didn't want the hooded figure looking in at them to be able to keep watch on their every movement.

They ducked to the floor in unison.

"Hey, you! The creepy bastard on the lawn! What are you doing out there?" Tom crouched beneath the windowsill and yelled out to the trespasser. There was no answer. The streets were quiet.

"Did you see who it was?" Rachel whispered. She hunkered down, ear pressed to the wall, listening for any movement.

"I couldn't tell," Billy said. "We need to know where it's headed and what it's doing." Billy crawled to the living room's far window and stood, trying to remain hidden while peeking around the corner. The figure was still there, standing motionless in the same position, a creepy, lifeless scarecrow stuck in the middle of his lawn. The face was shrouded in complete darkness. With the hooded jacket and the streetlights at its back, there was no way of knowing who it was. The only thing Billy could see were the tips of its fingers. They seemed to extend much further beyond the cuff of the jacket than was normal.

"He's not moving, just standing there. I can't tell if he sees me or not," Billy said. It was a man's jacket and the baggy jeans looked masculine, so Billy upgraded the figure from an "it" to a "he".

Billy didn't see her do it, but Rachel must have looked over the windowsill. "That's my dad's jacket," she whispered and then raised her voice. "That's my father!"

"We don't know if that's your dad," Tom said. "We saw Terry Manfred in the house. It's probably him wearing your dad's jacket just to screw with us." Billy admired Tom's quick thinking; even in the low light he could tell that Rachel was seriously considering calling out to her father, maybe even thinking about making a break for the front door. That would be bad.

"Didn't you say that your father works nights?" Billy said. He was holding his pillowcase-weapon against his leg, and he'd barely noticed that his knee had gone numb from the cold. "Tom might be right. Your dad is probably at work."

"'Probably'? 'Might be'? What if you're wrong? Then what is he doing?" Rachel said, a tremor in her speech. "Is he standing on the grass outside, ready to skin us and eat us?" The person on the lawn didn't seem to react to her raised voice. Billy had no answers to her questions.

"Why isn't he doing anything?" Tom said. He was standing now too. The figure on the lawn was no less intimidating, but the group was tired of hiding. "He knows we're here."

"Dad!" Rachel yelled, sending Billy and Tom jumping to her side. Billy squeezed the top of her arm and shushed her. Tom was less accommodating, leaning his sword against the wall to free up a hand and then pressing his fingers over her mouth.

The three of them stood close in the silence. They watched the shadow man intently. Rachel's breath was the only sound. She took big inhales and exhales through her nose, Tom's hand still pasting her mouth shut. Billy considered asking Tom to remove his hand, but he wasn't quite sure that gagging Rachel was that bad of an idea.

The man on the lawn took a single step forward and lifted his arms. He didn't speak, but his body language said "come give Daddy a hug". The face remained totally obscured, his feet toeing the outer limits of the porch light.

Rachel let out a sob and they all saw the reason at once. Raising his arms had revealed more of his hands, the sleeves of his jacket receding to show his sharp claws. The figure gave his fingertips a soft flutter; the ten daggers on the tips of his fingers danced under the streetlights.

"What the fuck is going on?" Tom said, Rachel wiggling beneath his grip.

"Whoever that is, it's not your dad," Billy said. "I mean, even if it is him, it's still not your dad." He then loosened his grip on her arm and tried to turn the maneuver into a soothing pat. She took the opportunity to use the freed elbow to jab Tom in the ribs, freeing her mouth while he moaned and swore, still taking pains to stay quiet.

The creature on the lawn raised one arm even higher and began to wave. It was a "come on out, I won't hurt you" motion.

"Not on your life! Asshole," Rachel screamed out the window. Billy was relieved that Rachel felt that way. He really didn't want to go outside to meet this guy.

Before the monster could entertain them further by responding to Rachel's insult, there was a sound from the back of the house.

"You hear that?" Tom said, putting a finger up to his lips. He didn't need to quiet them; they were holding their breaths, listening as well. There was a moment before the sound came again, a sloshing accented by plodding footfalls. Tom's eyes widened. The whites seemed to collect and refract every bit of light from the street. It was the crazed, wild look of an unhappy epiphany. "This fucker is a distraction." He pointed out the window. "They're coming around the back!"

Rhonda struggled to keep her hands outstretched in the cold. It was much harder than it should have been. Before she left the house, she had stuffed the inside pockets of the jacket with potatoes she had microwaved. They retained their heat well and kept her chest warm, but her arms remained susceptible to the cold.

Rachel yelled at her, calling her an asshole. She looked into her past and remembered that Rachel had always been a clever little bitch; it was one of the reasons she'd grown apart from her sister. Rhonda had suspected as much, but having Rachel run out to join her father wasn't necessary, even though it would have been an unexpected perk to the plan.

There was a flurry of motion and voices inside; they must have heard Terry coming around the back. Rhonda was thankful that he had at least found the house all right. The biggest contingency had been whether or not he would be able to count the number of yards and houses correctly and find Riles' backyard.

"Stay here," Tom said, pointing at Billy and Rachel. "If it tries to get in here, you start whaling on it. I don't care if it turns out to be wearing your Aunt Mildred's favorite nightdress. Fucking kill it." He was barking orders, taking charge, and attempting to right the ship. *Where is this coming from?* Tom thought, and he suspected that Billy and Rachel were asking themselves the same question.

It's coming from your guts. It's coming from a lifetime of not giving a shit and finally getting pissed off enough to do something. It's coming from watching Darcy's head split in half at the jaw and watching a

213

fucking alien crawl out of her neck. It's about that same monster then trying to tentacle-fuck you. It's the feeling that your best years were high school, and even those sucked the big one.

Tom slung his pillowcase over his shoulder and picked up the sword from where he'd leaned it against the wall. Rachel was a smart girl, but he had some serious doubts about her invention. He hadn't seen what cold had done to the creature. Billy vouched for it, but that didn't mean that the human-sized ones had the same weaknesses. At least Tom's pillowcase was heavy enough. He had put a whole frozen chicken in his bag. It could probably do some major damage before it thawed out and went soft.

He ran through the doorway and into the short hallway that connected the living room to the kitchen. After he turned one more corner, he would be able to see outside and into the backyard. The sloshing sound continued; he could hear it bouncing off the back windows. He didn't know what he was going to find when he broke through the back door, but he was hoping that it was more than one of those things. Tom was feeling strong and out for blood.

Turning the corner, Tom was greeted by Terry Manfred, his face perfectly framed by the window over the kitchen sink that faced the backyard. Luckily, Terry did not see him. His face and eyes were pointed down. The gimp seemed to be concentrating on his hands. With his head down, Tom could see that the back of his scalp had begun to sag. The flap of skin peeling away from his discolored skull looked like soggy wallpaper.

Tom walked as quietly as possible while still trying to retain his rage-fueled momentum. He reached the back door without being spotted and unlocked the door, throwing the deadbolt. Sucking in a quick breath, he turned the knob and shouldered his way into Billy's backyard.

Losing his footing the moment he stepped outside, Tom's speed worked against him and he slammed sideways, falling half onto the grass and half still in the doorway. Scrambling to his feet, he cursed himself for the clumsy exit, and prayed that his slip would not cost him his life.

Tom struggled to stand. He wriggled his nose, gagging as the strong smell of gasoline burned his lungs and throat. The side of his body glistened with gas in the moonlight, beads of it dripping off of his forearm hair. He was up, but covered in flammable liquid.

Terry hadn't moved from his position near the kitchen window. He threw Tom a goofy smile.

"You crazy bastard, what are you doing?" Tom said.

Terry's only response was to raise his gas can and give the side of Billy's house one more splash. He then turned the can upside down and began to douse himself. Tom opened his eyes wide in a terrible moment of realization. The gas made his eyes water, and the teardrops collected in the stubble on his upper lip.

"Don't," Tom said. He stretched a hand out, unsure if the move was self-preservation or Terry-preservation. Ducking low into a dead run, Tom dropped the pillowcase and the frozen chicken. He closed distance between him and the psychopath, but not before Terry had dropped the canister and begun rummaging around in his pockets. Tom held the sword out at his side, letting it drag across the lawn, petrol-saturated mud flecking the blade.

Terry had the lighter out of his pocket now. Tom was close enough to catch its semigolden glint, close enough to hear the familiar *click* of a Zippo being flipped open. Terry was primed for action. There was another sound too, an insane giggle, filtered through a not-quite-human throat and lungs.

Tom was running so fast and his thoughts were so hurried that he had no time to think to use the sword. Instead he barreled into Terry at a full sprint, both boys falling to the ground and sloshing into the puddle of gas around Terry's feet.

Tom had seen this kind of thing before. It was a football game played in a downpour, messy and lacking any semblance of finesse, but exciting as all hell to watch. Terry had the ball and here they were, under the pile. Tom was going to do whatever he could to get it away from him.

And, just like that, it walked away. The thing in her father's jacket lowered its arms, took several steps back, turned and crossed the street to Rachel's house. She watched as it closed the door behind it, but her concentration was wrestled away by the sounds of the struggle out in the backyard.

"We need to do something," Billy said. His hand was still resting on her upper arm from when he had tried to keep her from running out the front door (something she really had had no intention of doing in the first place).

She looked at him, trying to decipher what it was he was saying. Then she remembered how Tom had stormed off to defend the back of the house.

She looked back out the window to Billy's empty front yard. "There's nothing out there anymore," she said and grabbed on to Billy's hand. The touch made him jump, and she saw his grip tighten around his pillowcase.

They ran together toward the kitchen, Rachel pulling him along and leading the way. They got there just in time to see the flames spread out like a carpet, blocking the doorway. The blast bathed the room in a hot orange glow.

They clashed together in a whirl of sprawling limbs. Gasoline and Terry's clotted blood splashed up into Tom's face. Terry landed the first hit, his forearm connecting with Tom's jaw in a gas-soaked smack. It clacked Tom's teeth together and sent a painful reverberation from his forehead to the bottom of his neck. Trying to ignore the shock, Tom snatched for the lighter. He clapped both hands over Terry's fist in an attempt to stop him from flicking the thumbwheel on the open Zippo.

Under his grip, Terry's strong fingers tried to wiggle their way free. When he was moderately confident that he could remove one hand without Terry flipping the wheel and sending them both up in flames, Tom reeled back his left fist and brought it down on the bridge of Terry's nose. The cut from their first fight was still there, so when combined with the fact that Terry had been scalped since then, the punch did some real damage.

Tom felt the skin of Terry's nose slip below his clenched fist. The flesh of Terry's face rolled down his skull and bunched up all the way to his neck. The tops of Terry's eyelids were pulled down. The skin of his forehead was a blindfold, covering his eyeballs and obscuring the world. Terry let out a garbled shriek, unable to work the sound through his sagging lips and cheeks.

Tom redoubled his attention to the lighter, trying his best to ignore the bizarre nature of the fight. Pausing to admire Terry's rumpled face would mean certain fiery death before he could say "holy shit".

The sword was lying tantalizingly close to the scuffle. It was easily within arm's reach, but attempting to grab for it was too much of a liability. Terry could have them both medium-well by the time Tom could grab the hilt, never mind make an attempt to swing it. Wiggling under his knees, Terry kept on screaming and finally used his free hand to stretch the skin of his face back into position. He aligned his eyeholes and glared at Tom. With great effort, Tom brought a knee up and down into Terry's stomach. The blow should have winded Terry, but instead it just served to kick the two combatants further apart.

It wasn't that he totally disregarded personal hygiene, but Tom rarely clipped his fingernails, and Darcy had always given him grief about it. He thanked his own laziness and used his nails to dig into Terry's clenched hand. Terry's skin tore easily, and Tom worked his fingers under the cool flesh like a torn glove.

Terry grabbed Tom's shoulder with his free hand, apparently trying a Vulcan nerve pinch. It was a maneuver that Billy had once tried on him in middle school. Back then, all Billy had earned himself was a bloody nose. Tom started to chuckle before he felt something poke through the tips of Terry's fingers. There was a sharp pain in the meat of his shoulder. Terry's fingers felt like needles.

"God damn," Tom said, and the warmth of his own blood began to soak his shirt, sticking the material to his chest. Reaching up to dislodge Terry's claws, he was forced to let go of the lighter, bringing forth a giggle and a crooked smile from Terry.

"Foooosh," Terry said, slurring, drool pouring out of his crooked mouth. It was the sound a child makes to indicate an explosion. There was no time left. Tom jumped away as he heard the first click. The Zippo must not have given off much of a spark, otherwise his face would have been melted. Tom clawed at the grass, pulling himself farther away from Terry and the back of the house. The light bounced off of the tall white fence and into Tom's eyes before he could feel the fire begin licking at the bottoms of his feet. He'd had no time to switch back into his shoes and had run out of the house in his socks.

Tom sprang to his feet, not extinguishing but at least dampening the flames that had formed on the underside of his socks. Taking no chances, Tom made an extra few jumping steps before turning to look Terry.

Dead already, Tom thought, watching as the flames spread away from Terry's motionless body and climbed the siding of Billy's house. He had to squint, but he watched as the charred flesh flaked and blew away as the wind caused by the inferno passed over Terry's face. It looked like it had been a peaceful death: Terry had simply laid down and let the flames walk all over him.

He felt it then. *I'm on fire*. His jeans were covered in short wisps of flame. Tom was too busy stopping, dropping and rolling to notice Terry sitting up, his old flesh turning into ash and blowing away into the night.

At first Rachel was running in front of him, holding his hand and pulling him onward toward who-knows-what. After the blast of light and heat, she was on top of him and pushing him back into the hallway. He caught a whiff of burning hair, some from him and some from her. The kitchen was ablaze and Billy was fairly certain his eyebrows were gone in the initial explosion.

Rachel wriggled on top of him, and he was relieved to find that she wasn't dead. Grabbing the molding of the hallway for support, Billy pulled himself up. The light from the fire may have flickered, but there was so much of it that the kitchen was just as well-lit as if it were the middle of a summer day. Amid the shadows cast by the ebb and flow of the flames, there came a deeper darkness—something walking through the back door and into the house.

Billy gripped Rachel's shoulder as she stood up, as much for her support as for his own. Not only was he still in shock from the blast, but his foot ached and the shadow frightened him. He needed the human touch.

Tendrils of smoke began to peek around the corner from the kitchen. To Billy they were blind snakes, intent on seeking out more of his house to incinerate.

"Tom, is that you?" Billy asked, and the shadow stopped its approach. Rachel and Billy stayed in the middle of the hallway, bolted in place, eyes fixed on the shadow.

"No," a voice said. "Guess again." It was an inhuman voice, but Billy could also detect the sense of bemusement in it. Slowly and with the deliberate nature of a striptease, smoldering fingers wrapped their way around the corner of the hallway. The burned-up hand used the wall for support as the creature rounded the corner and revealed itself.

Billy couldn't be sure if Rachel screamed out from behind him, because he deafened himself with his own yelp. The figure was vaguely human and still on fire in places. The tip of the creature's snub nose and the points at the end of its sharp cheekbones glowed a deep orange. It was a color that reminded Billy of the end of a cigarette during a deep drag. At its forehead, a few inches above where its eyebrows should have been, was a smoking gash, a large, burning divot in its skull. Billy had seen a similar wound before. All it took was for the creature to speak his name to recognize it as Terry Manfred.

"Rile," Terry said, raising one claw to his chest and flicking off a piece of charred skin from the tip of one nipple. Terry's shirt had been the first thing to go in the fire, but the bulk of his jeans had (thankfully) fused to his melted waist and thighs. The creature took a step forward, and Billy matched it with one backward. Billy could see the resemblance now: Terry's zonked-out eyes moved a step closer and forced Billy and Rachel to retreat to the end of the hallway, up to the threshold of the living room.

"Terry, you're sick and you need help," Billy said.

Terry didn't respond vocally. Instead he raised one hand and raked his elongated fingernails across the wall, leaving behind burns and gashes in the chipped white paint.

The heat began to reach unbearable levels as Billy watched the fire steadily spread further into the kitchen. Terry's burning footsteps singed prints into the hallway carpet. Billy felt beads of perspiration drip down his forearm, landing between his clenched fingers and then soaked up by the pillowcase that he was still holding with a death-grip.

Placing his palm squarely between her breasts, Billy pushed Rachel back, urging her into the living room. Too frightened to be embarrassed, he then made his own less-successful attempt to turn and run.

Before he could get clear of the hallway, Terry bent low and leveled his shoulder at Billy. Terry looked like a frenzied animal readying itself for a charge. He sprang at Billy, who took a halfhearted swing with the frozen pillowcase. It was a glancing blow at Terry's wrist.

Terry backed up, shaking out his hand. He had reacted to the light blow as if Billy had burned him. It was a slight relief to see that the cold did *something*. Billy gripped the pillowcase with his other hand, beginning a two-handed wind up and preparing to bring the frozen peas and berries down with greater force. Terry was much faster, slamming into Billy with his shoulder and lifting him off the ground. Terry's follow through launched Billy into the living room. It was a feat of miraculous strength, and Billy's chest throbbed with pain.

Billy was no stranger to being knocked around by bigger kids, but this was otherworldly. Terry was now the strongest bully alive. Billy landed in an awkward position, the living room carpet helping only a little as his own fist knocked the wind out of him. Gasping for air, he tried to regain his bearings.

The carpet crackled and hissed as Terry walked over to him, getting close enough to let Billy get a good smell of his new odor. Billy's nose wriggled at the scent: burned fabric accented with overdone burgers that had been forgotten about and left out on the grill to turn to charcoal.

"Rile, you still good now?" Terry said, crouching to talk into Billy's ear.

"What?" Billy asked, unable to decipher Terry's cryptic message.

The creature formerly known as Manfred the Sped made a short, frustrated grunt and slowly repeated the question. "Are you still better than Terry? Billy Rile?"

Billy looked up. He tried to ignore Terry's exposed teeth, his purple gums, and instead focus on his eyes. The eyes were the only human thing left. Beyond Terry's cold, unblinking expression, Billy thought that he could see a scared and confused boy of his own age. Terry was a boy who had been dealt a far worse hand than Billy. Even now, locked away in this monstrous body, he wanted an answer as to why life was so unfair.

"I'm not better than you are, Terry," Billy said to the creature as it reared back a claw, still ready to rip his throat open. Billy imagined bleeding out, his elevated heart rate sending the majority of his blood spilling onto the carpet, where he would hear it sputter and burn as the flames spread over and through it. "I was never better than you."

It could have been his overactive, too-many-movies imagination, but he thought he saw Terry hesitate. The classic misunderstood monster.

Before Terry had the chance to follow through with his attack—to finish what he had started with Billy—the tip of the samurai sword burst through his chest. The sword sang as it dug into the floor, centimeters from Billy's ear.

"I'm sure-as-shit better than you are, Terry," Tom said, gritting his teeth and pressing his weight down onto the weapon. Tom's body was smoking and Rachel leaned in behind him, her hands against his back to support his attack like the soldiers of the Iwo Jima Memorial.

Tom's toasted leather jacket was too hot to keep her hands against. Rachel pulled them back and allowed herself to fall backward onto the living room couch.

She covered her ears once Terry started screaming. Rachel's father had once clubbed a rat that he'd cornered in the downstairs closet. It had taken two blows to kill the animal. The first hit had only wounded it, and the animal started screeching so loudly that Rachel could not believe such a tiny animal could have so much pain. Terry, impaled through the chest and pinned to the floor, was making that same sound, only proportionate in volume to his size.

Terry's arms thrashed as he tried to shake off Tom. Manfred's range of movement was limited by the steel blade pinning him to the floor, but his enthusiasm was not. At first Tom was a rodeo cowboy, hanging on to the end of the sword, expecting Terry to stop moving. Tom's strength visibly waned after a few more moments of struggle, and he slumped on top of Terry, Tom's weight pushing Terry down the blade, toward the floor.

Wiping a large gob of Terry's dark brown blood from his face, Billy slid out from underneath the two boys. His eyes were wild. He was probably having even more trouble processing the last few minutes' events than Rachel was; she hadn't been the one under Terry when Tom rammed a sword through him.

The majority of the blood on the carpet was the brown, dead blood gushing down the sword from Terry, but next to it was a growing spot of brighter, redder blood that she traced up to Tom's shoulder. Tom wasn't only charred and fatigued: he looked like he was bleeding to death.

Tom went slack and Terry was finally able to buck him off. Darcy's boyfriend rolled to Billy's feet without as much as a groan.

Thoughts surged to the front of Rachel's brain and were scrambled by the noise still streaming from Terry's mouth. *Is Tom dead? Will Terry snap that sword in half and get free? Are we all going to die tonight?*

Terry reduced his screeching to a low whine and took hold of the blade sticking out of the back of his burned exoskeleton. With considerable effort, he was able to pull himself closer to the carpet, passing the blade through his body far enough that he could grab it and pry it free where it met the floor.

"Do something!" Billy yelled, sounding on the verge of tears. Rachel knew just what he meant and picked up the pillowcase from beside the couch.

Terry had just begun to sit up when Rachel sent the twenty-plus pounds of semi-frozen food down on top of his head. There was no scream this time, only the crack of his skull. His head smashed open, looking like a ceramic vase filled with strawberry Jell-O as the contents splattered to the floor.

Terry's body bucked to a halt. The only sounds in the room were the crackling of the fire mingled with Rachel and Billy's sobs. She had hit Terry so hard that his shriveled scalp flew against the far wall and slid down with a wet splotch that echoed with the weight of finality.

Chapter Nineteen

Geraldine Dobson watched as the first flames began to lick the insides of the windows at the Rile household. She looked over at Kenny, who was sitting in his old chair and staring, eyes unfocused, at the blank television. *"Old habits die hard." That's what Geraldine would have said,* she thought, and then said, "Kenny, get the cat. We're leaving soon."

She walked from the front window to the back of the house, stopping to gather her coat from the hallway closet before entering the kitchen. She had set the oven to 450 degrees and left the door open to better heat up the house after Lieutenant Todd Darl had left, but now she set all the burners to high as well. She flipped past the *click* of the starter and let the burners pump the house full of gas.

Kenny appeared in the doorway, Spartacus resting in the crook of his arm. "It's cold outside," he said, not sounding too passionate about it either way.

"Well, there is going to be an explosion in here in a few minutes. So I don't think we have a choice, do you?" Sarcasm came quickly to her. It was one of the old Geraldine's most dominant traits, especially when dealing with Kenny.

Billy soaked his balled-up T-shirt in the bathroom sink. When he was done with that, he held a dish towel under the tap. He unfurled the shirt and tied the sleeves around the back of his head. Then he handed the towel to Rachel. She wrapped it around her own face like a bandanna. He nodded to her and they hurried back into the living room. He kept his mouth shut tight, trying to hold his breath and not waste precious oxygen. The flames had spread to the end of the hallway and were climbing up the wall, primed to overtake the couch.

Both of them knew what they had to do. Rachel turned Tom over onto his back and grabbed his legs. Billy climbed over Terry's body and positioned his hands under Tom's armpits. They lifted Tom up. The tall boy was at least twenty pounds heavier than Billy.. "Muscle weighs more than fat." Billy remembered that Tom had said this once when he was in a more playful mood. Tom had crunched down onto Darcy's lap, giving her a big kiss as she protested that he was too heavy. Billy and Rachel were feeling that muscle now, and it was nothing but dead weight.

Please don't be dead, Billy pleaded. Warm blood oozed out of the wound in Tom's shoulder and between his fingers, loosening his hold on his friend. There was a crash from the kitchen. Chunks of the walls, ceiling or both must have begun to give way as they burned. A rush of wind from behind them filled the air with sparks and delicate embers that floated down onto Tom's unconscious body—and, thankfully, died out seconds after landing.

When they reached the foyer, Rachel motioned that she needed a free hand, and she set down Tom's legs to open the front door. The smoke stung Billy's eyes and his mask wasn't doing a fantastic job of keeping the black, poisonous air out of his lungs.

Once they had placed Tom on the grass outside, Billy ripped the shirt from his mouth and gagged until he puked onto the lawn. His vision swam and he narrowly missed vomiting on Tom's face. As if the kid didn't have enough problems.

Rachel's mask seemed to have functioned slightly better; she was able to speak with only minor interruptions for coughing. "Are you okay?" she asked. "I'm going back in. I'll be right out."

Before he could make any move to stop her, she ducked back into the house. An uneasy second passed, but then she walked through the doorway and onto the lawn. She tossed the samurai sword down onto the cement walkway and then shook out her hand, cursing and wringing the wet towel out over her fingers. The hilt must have been hot enough to take off her fingerprints.

There were two lines of black soot leading into Tom's nostrils. It was a good sign. It meant that he was breathing, or at least he had been when they were still inside the house. Rachel pinched his wrist and felt for a pulse.

"What do you think they are doing?" Billy said. Rachel looked down the street to where he was pointing. There was a group of people walking down the sidewalk and spilling over onto the street. Dots of flickering light began appearing in the distance: small bonfires sprouting on the hoods of cars and on front lawns.

Rachel turned at the close-by slam of a screen door. It was Geraldine and Kenny Dobson, walking with haste out their front door.

She began to reply that she didn't care what anyone was doing, that they needed to figure out if Tom was still alive and get off of the street, but the explosion came before she could speak. The sound of breaking glass accompanied a fireball that lit up the street as it rose out of the windows of the Dobsons' house.

Tears, not of sadness but of shock, spilled over Rachel's eyelids and immediately evaporated in the heat of the air around her.

Tom was jolted awake by the sound of thunder. Or that was at least what he assumed it was until he collected his thoughts, realized he was lying on the front lawn and felt rush of warm air waft over his body.

His left side was numb. He reached a shaky hand to his shoulder and was unsurprised when it came back bloody.

Billy's face was floating above him, a little too close for comfort. Tom's eyes focused on the tip of his nose, then his off-white teeth, and then the world went black again for a moment. Billy was saying something. Rachel was too, but their words blended together to form an unintelligible mush that failed to push through the constant rush of blood whooshing in Tom's eardrums.

"What?" Tom tried to ask. The question was blocked by something before reaching his mouth and died in his throat. He turned onto his less-injured side and pushed a large glob of blackness out of his lungs and onto the grass. It tasted awful: a mix of gelatin blood and one of those synthetic fireplace logs.

Tom tried to repeat himself, but nothing came past his lips but a bubble of tar. Billy cradled the back of his head and stuck two fingers deep into his throat. Tom felt the release of pressure like the removal of a cork from a bottle as Billy pried some of the goo free from his mouth and flicked it onto the concrete walkway.

He felt it as the fresh air was finally able to flow past his teeth, filling his lungs and cooling down his veins. The world was racked back into semifocus and he was able to discern Billy and Rachel's chatter.

"Is he going to die?" Rachel asked. Her voice was so small and defeated that it sounded like a rhetorical question. Tom didn't like that one bit.

"No." Tom coughed and squeezed Billy's arm. He didn't want Billy to answer for him. "I am not going to fuckin' die."

Darl stared out the window as the pillars of flame across the street reached higher, boosted by the wind from the explosion at the Dobson household. After he was through lying on the couch and had gathered enough strength to stand, the first thing he'd done was find his hat. He now wore it, cocked to the side, as he stared out the window.

As the fires started to break out across the neighborhood, Rhonda was worried she would have to physically restrain Darl to stop him from charging outside and bathing himself in the flames. He had tasted the thrill of the fire, and he would want more. If he managed to get outside, he would have to choose which one to throw himself into; there were a lot of fires.

The fire she had ordered Terry to set had simply been the signal flame. It let the rest of the neighborhood know that the time had come to make their presence known. It was not every house. There were holdouts; there would have to be, but by morning there would only be a few homes and businesses left standing. Those remaining buildings were good. Her people would need these as places to stay warm after the initial fires burned out. There also had to be enough infrastructure left to operate the rebuilding out of. They needed to make this place less human and more…habitable.

Darl sighed, and the sound brought Rhonda's attention back to the here and now.

Rhonda sidled up next to him, her long toenails snagging and pulling fibers free from the living room carpet. She watched his eyes flick back and forth, as if he were watching an invisible tennis match.

Laying the tip of her forefinger on the end of his cauterized stump, she dug into it with a low, deliberate pressure until her claw hit live tissue. Darl spun around, looking surprised to see her. "What did you do that for?" he asked, holding the end of his amputated bicep. His eyes were still quite distant and unfocused. She assumed he was deep in thought, fixating on getting the kids across the street, the ones who had taken his arm away from him.

"It was your own fault, you know," Rhonda said. "You lost that arm because you couldn't follow orders."

Darl grunted and turned his back to her, returning to stare at the fire and the kids spread out on the grass in front of it.

"The tall one's not dead yet," Darl said. "It looked like he was, but he's not."

"You say that like it's a good thing."

"It is. That's the one who cut me," Darl said. "I'm going to turn him and have him suffer like I suffer." He hooked a finger to his temple, pointing to his brain.

"You mean suffer the way that Lieutenant Todd Darl has suffered," Rhonda said, trying to remind Darl to keep his current self at a distance from his human past.

"I have suffered plenty," was Darl's only response.

"We have to get off of the street," Rachel said. She took hold of Tom's arm, motioning that she was ready to lift him up with Billy's help, and then added, "They are burning everything down! They feed on the heat. It makes them stronger like Terry!"

She was right. At the end of the block, a mob of people was marching toward Billy's burning house, the tallest and fiercest of the blazes. As they approached, small groups would occasionally break off in order to stop in front of another of the fires. They would stand for a moment, basking in the flames, before gathering themselves and wandering back to the bigger group. They were recharging themselves like batteries.

They formed a grotesque parade, firelight bouncing off of the vacant eyes that were fixed on Billy's house. Billy could see that around the corner, another crowd was already staggering away from somebody's car that had gone from a blazing inferno to a burned-out husk in a matter of minutes. The air was so thick with smoke that he doubted he would ever get the taste of burning plastics from the back of his tongue.

Tom sat up, pressing a finger to each of his nostrils. He took a deep breath into his mouth and shot long, black snot-rockets out onto the grass. Despite all of his macho bravado, his movements were sluggish and uncoordinated. He had lost a lot of blood, and Billy wondered if his friend was going to make it. He frowned as he realized how unlikely it was that any of them were going to make it.

Rachel took a knee, dropping to eye level with Tom. "Can you walk?" she asked.

"Yeah. Shit, I can probably run," he said, wheezing.

"Well, you might have to," Billy said, his eyes widening to the point of tearing as he watched the approach of the crowds from both ends of the street. The car fire had completely burned itself out, so the crowd had now redoubled its efforts to make it to Billy's house.

The people walking toward them, glistening in the firelight, were not George Romero's zombies. They did not have the pale skin of the vampires Charlie Heston fought in *The Omega Man*. They were not puking fountains of pea soup or bleeding Karo syrup out of their eyeballs. They were simply his friends and neighbors. They also all wore subtly twisted half smiles that told him both that they were intelligent and that they wanted him and his friends dead.

"Let's get him across the street to my house," Rachel said.

As soon as she said it, Billy recoiled at the idea. "How do we know it's safe?" It was a stupid question.

"It's not, but I have the key and you've got the sword and there doesn't seem to be any better option."

Billy glanced behind her to the crowd. Geraldine Dobson had walked to join the closest group and was leading them onward. In one arm she held an orange tabby cat, stroking it before pointing ahead and giving her troops the "forward march!" signal.

"You make an excellent point," Billy said, picking up the still-hot sword and trying to look strong as he helped get Tom to his feet.

Chapter Twenty

In his past life, Todd Darl had detested expressions such as "my mind's going a mile a minute" or "I've got mixed emotions". For Darl these were non-issues. Darl could not abide indecision or ambiguity, and he tried to avoid succumbing to bewilderment whenever possible.

As he looked out the window and watched the kids hobble their way across the street, he was indecisive, bewildered, and his immediate course of action was ambiguous even to himself.

His injury, the blood loss and the subsequent cauterization of the wound had fucked him up good, more than even Rhonda's parrot-beaked mouth-tentacle had. But in some small way it had nudged open the door to freedom, if only a crack.

Rhonda stood behind him, taking a step back as the kids reached the curb. The group paused so the smaller boy with the limp could take a swing at Geraldine Dobson with the sword. He missed her as she jumped back to avoid injury to her cat, but the swing had bought the kids some time, and all three dived forward onto the grass.

"They'll be at the door in a minute," Rhonda said. "Would you like to do it or should I? Are you feeling up to it?"

"I'll do it," Darl said, trying to quiet the screaming in his mind by fitting and refitting his Stetson. There were two distinct voices roiling inside him: the old and the new. "I want to do it," he added. He was trying to convince every part of himself that it was true.

"Use the gun. At least to take care of the boys," Rhonda said. "No reason to leave yourself open to unnecessary risks."

Darl laughed. It was a small, derisive snort that would have been uncharacteristic in his old life and was in his new one as well.

Rhonda had started to say something, probably prepared to chew him out for his open insubordination, when he cut her off by raising his hand, palm out. *Shut your face and don't tell me what to do,* he screamed in his mind, wrestling the urge to say it aloud. "I'm okay," he said. "Give me a break, all right? It's been a long day."

He lowered his gimme-a-break hand and used it to unclip the top strap of his holster. The gun felt cool and foreign in his hand, not just because he hadn't wielded it in so long, but because earlier in the night he'd had his shooting hand completely severed. Holding it in his left just felt clumsy.

Rhonda gave him a look with her dead reptilian eyes that let him know that he had now gone beyond thin ice. Behind those eyes she was likely weighing whether or not she should just kill him now and take care of the three teenagers herself. After a moment of their staring contest, her body language softened and she took several more steps back toward the kitchen, partially concealing herself in the shadows.

There was a shuffling at the front door. The group had made it that far. *Let's see if they can slide headfirst into home, shall we?* the old Darl thought, not screaming this time but usurping his battered master. The thought was strong, confident, and it carried every ounce of hope that he could afford to throw behind such a dog-shit situation.

During life's pivotal moments, all your senses are heightened and time begins to slow down. At least that was the way Billy understood it. He had never been in a fistfight, never endured a traumatic car accident. He'd never even asked his biggest crush to junior prom. Those high-stress events had passed him by, or he'd avoided them by virtue of his introversion. Because of this, he wasn't quite sure if what his mind and body were experiencing was authentic. He stood supporting Tom's deadweight on the stoop to Rachel's house. She fumbled for her keys and tried to open her front door. He felt like he could count the milliseconds.

The physical feeling was a vague lightheadedness accompanied by a steady adrenaline hum in his extremities. What he noticed most distinctly was after they had reached the curb on Rachel's side of the street, and after he had taken a lunge at Geraldine Dobson, everything had become impossibly loud. The jangling of Rachel's keys, Tom's shallow wheezing in his ear, the laughter and mutterings from the larger crowd as they pushed and shoved to get a good place next to the fire: every sound had undergone a tenfold increase in decibel level.

The smaller group of neighbors formed a loose circle around the three friends. The members of the circle could each take one giant step and be within arm's length of Billy and company. Preparing to defend himself, however feebly, Billy was ready to prop Tom against the house when he heard the turn of the doorknob and the creak of hinges.

"The thing wasn't even locked to begin with!" Rachel yelled out. Billy could not place her emotion: was it surprise, gratitude or pure terror? On a scale of one to screwed, how screwed were they?

Billy half-carried, half-dropped Tom over the threshold as Rachel picked up her semithawed weapon from the stoop, pulled it inside and slammed the door. The crowd outside must have taken Billy and Rachel's sudden movements as a cue. Vaulting forward, they slammed their bodies against the door, fists beating down until the door visibly shook in its frame.

It would hold. The door had modern construction on its side, with the only window being a small, security-conscious porthole near the top. These creatures were smart though; if they wanted to get, in they would. Billy and his friends had to keep moving. Although they were physically safe for the moment, the cacophony of curses and muffled threats from outside the door was enough to bring tears to Rachel's eyes and a chill to Billy's lower back. The wispy hair above his ass tingled and stood on end.

"Are we there yet?" Tom's head lolled to the side as he spoke. Billy could not tell if he was kidding or if he was that out of it.

"Yeah, we're here," Rachel answered, flicking on the foyer light and jumping at the sound of movement farther back in the house.

"We're also not alone." Tom coughed. He was right.

Rachel heard them before she could see them. The tips of their six spindly legs tapped and tore against the hallway as the creatures jockeyed with each other for position. All three of them were eager to reach the kids. Their metallic spears dangled behind them, bouncing off the carpet and ready to lash out and stick someone.

Billy gave a quick scream as the first one rounded the corner and took a small hop toward them. Rachel concluded that their skinny legs were not built for jumping. Hand outstretched, she pushed Billy through the entryway to the living room. In his excitement, Tom lost his grip on Billy and stumbled down, becoming the easiest prey.

The small monsters were now a few feet from the prostrate Tom, but they slowed their movements as they approached. They were taking a more cautious attitude toward the three humans than the other one had done in the basement. The flaps at the tops of their bodies began to taste the air frantically as they took hesitant, jerky steps forward. The beasts looked like they were not only confused by the banging on the door, but also trying to assess how much of a threat the teens posed. Rachel worried that a sword and two soggy pillowcases would not be enough to stop their advances.

Billy dropped the blade, which he had been using as a walking stick to support Tom's weight, and grabbed hold of Tom's outstretched hand. Billy started to pull him along the carpet, straining until his small muscles bulged with exertion. He made progress, but not fast enough.

Rachel held Tom's other hand and helped Billy hoist as they backed farther into the house. Tom's jacket and pants scuffed the gray carpet with ash and blood.

They had made it a few feet into the living room, steadily pursued by the clicking things, before their momentum was halted by the ear-shattering boom of a gunshot.

The hole in the ceiling was large. Without a support beam to stop it, the bullet had zipped straight through to the second floor. Bits of plaster and vaporized pink housing insulation rained down on Darl's head, bouncing off the rim of his hat, with some small particles gliding gently to his shoulders.

The fingers of his left hand—now his only hand—trembled slightly as he pointed the gun forward. Lowering his forearm, he removed the gun from the textbook "warning shot" position and leveled his sights on the kid in the burned-up leather jacket. To compensate for his lost arm, he kept his legs slightly askew and hunched to the right to keep his arm from sagging. Darl squinted and his body shivered some as he followed the space between the tall kid's eyes with the end of the pistol.

You don't have to do this.

The girl and the smaller boy didn't know whether they should be more afraid of Darl or the children that clicked and babbled at the edge of the room. Their eyes ricocheted between the gun and the children's knives. The tall kid, though, his eyes were locked with Darl's. *There's a nine millimeter in his face: the kid is keeping his priorities in line.*

Darl did not have as much practice talking to the children as Rhonda had, but he was able to produce a few clicks. He demanded that they leave the blood-spattered teenagers alone, explaining to the little creatures that the kids were his to do what he wanted with. For a moment he wondered if they would listen to him, and then they eased up. Their insect legs each took a few reluctant steps away from the three humans. *That was pretty good.* He didn't have the mastery of the creatures that their mother possessed, and even she had trouble getting them to ignore their instincts, their built-in need to implant, to convert.

"What are you waiting for?" Rhonda asked from behind him. She had made her way from the kitchen to the back hallway to release the children and herd them toward the front door. Now she reentered the living room. Darl could not turn to see her, but he knew that she had stepped into the light, revealing herself to the teenagers. He saw the change in the human girl's face. Rachel Krieger, that was her name; she had been Rhonda's sister.

Rachel's mouth hung open, grasping for words, but she was disturbed beyond speech. Pushed beyond the capacity for screams of disgust and anguish. *I know the feeling, Rachel,* Darl thought, his voice coming easier again. She stood silently and took in her sister's new form. The two boys were disturbed, but Darl bet that they didn't even recognize the alien shape in front of them as Rachel's sister. Their minds would also snap once they made the connection.

"Darl, I asked you what you were waiting for," Rhonda said. "That boy took your arm away from you. Don't you want to shoot him?"

Darl's mind reeled. *Don't listen to her.*

"Maybe the trauma of the attack damaged your hearing," Rhonda joked. Darl watched the color drain from Rachel's face as she hunted for some shred of her sister's voice in the remark. "Darl, I am giving you permission to shoot."

It's now or never, big guy. What do you say?

Rachel, such a pretty little redhead, made a low whining sound. It was a stifled scream bubbling up from her knotted stomach.

"The hell with permission," Rhonda said. "I am ordering you to shoot. Shoot!"

"You asked for it." Darl mouthed the words, but he lacked the strength to make any sound come out. From the deepest chamber of his mind, he willed his lips to form the words. Using the words as a pry bar, he tore open his cage and ran to the surface of his own mind. *Victory.*

"Mind over matter, motherfucker," Darl said and squeezed out three quick shots, filling the room with gun smoke, blood and thunder.

Tom was surprised how much he was sweating. Considering all the blood he had lost, he would have figured that there was no more moisture in his body. That he was all dried up. When the cop started shooting, he found out just how much moisture he had left. He pissed himself, the warmth spreading out over his crotch into the already unbearably warm living room.

It was an odd thought, but when the creature had appeared

behind the cop and started imploring him to shoot Tom, with the smaller creatures at their feet anxious to nibble on their insides, Billy suddenly heard the voice of Vivian Leigh in *A Streetcar Named Desire*: "Only Poe. Only Mr. Edgar Allan Poe could do justice to it."

That was what Blanche had said in the movie. Billy thought Poe was one of a few names who could do justice to this situation, the one that had developed here on Long Island, in his town, on his street, and was now concluding in Rachel Krieger's living room. Craven, Raimi, Carpenter, Gordon, maybe Henenlotter or even Ed Wood, the guy who made those terrible flicks: any of those guys could also have constructed a scene like this. It would not have been nearly as scary, though.

He then took one last look over at Rachel—her pretty face was very red—closed his eyes, and prepared to die as the twisted thing at the back of the room yelled, "Shoot!"

Rachel could see what was left of Rhonda's face in the monster, but the differences were so staggering that they enabled her to feel nothing but fury toward the thing. It was not her sister. Looking into those big, black eyes, she could see that her sister was dead, and had been for a while.

The shots didn't frighten her; she knew they were going to happen and she didn't care. They came, and the crack of gunfire did hurt her ears. As she watched the smoke curl from the barrel of the one-armed sheriff's pistol, she was shocked that he was unable to hit them at such close range.

Even though he'd been aiming at Tom since they'd entered the room, he didn't even graze him.

Three shots had been one more than he needed: Darl was that good. The first bullet had torn through two of the spiked children, spraying the walls with brown blood, exoskeleton chunks and shattered spines.

He had taken the shots as quickly as he could pull the trigger, and as soon as the third bullet had left the chamber, he felt control being wrested from him. *No, not yet,* he pleaded, but the alien force was already resuming control, starting with his legs. It was a pity. He wanted to put one in Rhonda's skull too. Gunpowder had never smelled so goddamn sweet.

Once he had taken power over his arm and trigger finger, getting his lungs, mouth and voice box to work was a cinch. "You've got ten fuckin' seconds to kill me and then the bitch behind me before I lose control," he said, spitting his words out as fast and clear as he possibly could.

His speech was met with three blank stares from the teens. Darl smelled piss and saw that the tall one had wet himself.

"Kill me," he screamed, his new volume jarring the smaller boy awake. The shorter kid reached over and took something from the girl, something that looked like it had some heft to it.

"What are you doing?" Rhonda asked. Her lungs and throat were no longer fit for anything approaching human sounds, so her English was blocky and shrill. As much as he wanted to, he could not find the strength to raise the gun again and fire at her. He was thankful she was not already upon them.

"Billy," Rachel said. So that was the small one's name.

The boy lifted both arms, his skin drawn tight and glistening with sweat. Adrenaline looked like it had a lot to do with his strength, because the kid looked like he weighed ninety pounds. Darl saw that the bludgeon was actually a half-filled pillowcase. It reminded him of the kids who came around his apartment on Halloween, The young innocent ones, not the older, meaner ones who yelled "homo" and pelted his front door with rotten eggs.

Attaboy, Billy. You done good, was Darl's last thought as the bag came down, collapsing his monstrous new skull beneath the rotting skin of his face, like a crushed lightbulb stuffed inside pantyhose.

Lieutenant Todd Darl was happy to be finished serving the people of Suffolk County. *Good riddance.*

If she were able to concentrate, she would have searched through the old Rhonda's memories and found the cliché, *you can't find good help these days.* But as it was, Rhonda could only think of murder and feeding her own blind rage.

Rhonda shrugged off her shock and inertia and ran. She intended to swipe Billy Rile's head from his shoulders before Darl's body could even hit the floor.

She was met and intercepted by the tall, bloodstained boy. Tom Mathers, always the minor-league troublemaker. He attempted to tackle her but soon found this attempt woefully inadequate. Lowering her head, she flipped him over her shoulder. His body slammed into the coffee table behind her, smashing the glass top under his spine. After this slight delay, she pushed past the couch to murder Billy Rile, who stood in awe of his own stupidity, Darl and three of her children dead at his feet.

Billy had picked a great time to become an all-star athlete. Rachel watched the sheriff's head buckle and then crumple inward as his neck snapped to the side, breaking with an audible crack.

She only took her eyes off of the Rhonda-monster for a moment.

If he can do it, then I can too, Rachel thought, lunging forward as the cop's body began to slump and fall.

Tom moved too, his long stride allowing him to move much faster. He crossed the room and tried to grab at the monster, which shrugged him off with preternatural strength.

It may have been the hit that finally killed him, he could have broken his back as he landed on Deborah Krieger's coffee table, but he had given her the extra second that she needed to reach for the gun.

She lifted the cop's dead hand. It was clammy, soft, and the flesh felt slack. She fumbled for the trigger and found it just as Rhonda caught sight of her. Her reptile eyes went wide with fear. She would never see anything again with those eyes. Rachel pulled the trigger and blew her sister's mind out of the back of her misshapen head in an explosion of oily brown gore.

After the final gunshot, there was a fierce silence. It was a quiet like Billy had never heard. The neighbors had quit banging on the door; they were either scared away from the shots or had gotten bored when they couldn't get in. The only sound in the living room was their breathing.

What felt like hours were probably only two minutes. Then Rachel spoke.

"That was my sister. That was Rhonda," she said.

"I'm sorry," Billy said. It sounded lame.

"Don't be. As of right now, I'm kind of cool with it. I don't think it's shock; I just think I'm already used to living in a crazy world."

"Well, that was quick."

"See?" She gave a snort of laughter. "You're used to it too, or you wouldn't be cracking jokes."

"Shit." Billy remembered Tom and ran to the table. Tom rolled over onto his side. Bits of the crushed glass table-topper speckled his jacket.

Tom groaned. "Is everything dead?"

"Almost." Billy smiled and helped his friend to sit up. Billy only thought about what Tom had said for a second, frowning when he thought how far this thing must have gone, how many people were probably dead: friends, neighbors, teachers, mailmen...parents. If he gave it more than a second's thought, he wouldn't be able to stop.

The three of them rested on the couch for a long time—maybe an hour, maybe a few—before going to the window to see what their new world looked like now.

Chapter Twenty-One

Tom drank an entire carton of orange juice, convinced that the healthy fluids would both allow him to knit his mutilated shoulder back together and cause the beasties on the front lawn to disappear. The orange juice did neither of those things. In fact, the strong smell of the warm juice may have caused even more to gather outside of Rachel's house.

There were dozens of them that they could see, sitting patiently and waiting for the flames next door to die down. When they were done basking, they would try again to get into the house, and this time they would do it. That's what Tom and the others prepared for, but it never happened.

After a few hours, most of the creatures either became too cold or too bored and walked away, searching out new fires to warm themselves by. Their numbers diminished until there were about ten. Those ten chose to wait it out.

Among those ten were a few that were developing what Billy classified as nervous skin conditions. These folks used their fingernails to peel away the flesh of their faces, their hands and the rest of their bodies. They were trying to reveal the monster underneath, and a lot of them were succeeding. One of these neighbors, Kenny Dobson, had used his car keys to strip his entire body of flesh, even his pecker.

"What do we say?" Tom said. All three of them gathered at the window. They had to get out of the living room. Even though Rachel had turned down the heat, the bodies were beginning to stink.

Billy lifted his weapon, and then gave Rachel a quick kiss. He had wanted to do it an hour ago, after they were halfway through a bottle of wine that Rachel's parents had kept under the sink for special occasions. But he had been too scared. Now that they were risking life and limb again, he thought, *The hell with it.* Her lips were warm and soft. Afterward, when he ran his tongue over his own lips, he could taste her salty sweetness still on them. Billy said, "What do you think? Should we try a *Butch Cassidy and the Sundance Kid*?"

"That's not even a horror movie," Tom said, even though Billy had intended the question for Rachel.

"I know, but it's the movie most applicable to our current situation." Billy tried forcing a half smile with only moderate success. He was very tired. Both boys looked back at Rachel, who, after a moment, gave them a solemn nod and lifted Darl's pistol. A few hours in and she was a regular deadeye.

"We really want to do this?" Tom asked. He hadn't even tried to wash off the soot and grime.

"What other option do we have? They know we're here. They'll come for us eventually," Rachel said. "Why not try fighting back while we still can? We'll find a new place to hide." Billy could read the undercurrent of *let's take out as many as we can before we go.* He agreed.

"Well, all right," Tom said. They took a few steps, Billy and Rachel holding hands.

"One." Tom unlocked the front door.

Another quick kiss, this one with mouths parted ever so slightly. She pulled him close and he could feel her heart. It wasn't beating as fast as his.

"Two." Tom turned the doorknob.

On the count of three, Tom ripped the front door open.

They emptied out onto the lawn, slashing, shooting and cursing as the monsters closed in, their mouths open and clicking. It had been one hell of a night.

Epilogue

Billy flicks on the television. The screen is snowy at first, but some fiddling with the antenna soon straightens the picture out. Reception underground truly sucks, but at least he's not missing much. It's this same old shit again. The message has been the only thing broadcasting on every station for the past week.

"My fellow Americans," the speaker says straight at the camera. Tonight the president's new face looks more smug than usual, but it may be Billy's imagination. "Today we officially enter a brave new era in our history," the monster says. "An era that not only continues the age of unchecked prosperity we have been enjoying for my time in office, but also one that ushers in what I hope you have already recognized as one of new community-building and togetherness. The next few months and years will be glorious, but make no mistake: they will not be easy. I want you to focus on the future and to rest assured that we have a plan. We have always had a plan."

"Turn that shit off," Tom says as he walks downstairs. He sticks out his tongue and makes a long raspberry as loud as he dares, flipping off the television with great enthusiasm. It took a bit of recuperation, but he finally looks like he's not going to keel over and die at any moment.

"We don't watch TV anymore?" Billy asks.

"We do," Rachel says in a low voice. "But we try and stick to the classics."

Billy smiles and presses the cassette into the end of the VCR. The machine takes a moment to load. There is a whir of gears as he adjusts the tracking, rewinds to the start of the movie and presses Play.

About the Author

Adam Cesare is a New Yorker who lives in Massachusetts. After studying English and film at Boston University, he decided to stay in the area to work and write.

His work has been featured in numerous publications, including *Shroud Magazine*. His film writing has appeared in *Paracinema*, *Fangoria* and other venues.

Where only terror lives!

Jin Village
© *2013 Vincent Stoia*

For generations, the inhabitants of the remote Jin Village in China had almost no contact with the outside world. Nearby villages whispered of murder and odd disappearances. Then the Jin villagers vanished.

Now, one hundred years later, American historian Malcolm Wang and a team of archaeologists arrive at Jin Village to excavate the ruins. They uncover evidence of a long history of human sacrifice and cannibalism. What Malcolm and his companions don't know is that Jin Village is still very much alive. There is something out there, a dangerous remnant of a forgotten past...and it has woken up.

Enjoy the following excerpt from Jin Village ...

The old woman moved through the black forest. There was no wind, and the trees were still. She glided slowly, her feet inches above the ground, dissipating into nothing whenever she came to a tree, and materializing again on the other side.

The moon was fat and strong tonight, not that it mattered to Mother Chen. She saw perfectly well in the dark. The Jade Mountains were her real home, but she had stalked these woods for centuries. She knew them well.

Ahead she saw a small clearing in the woods, almost invisible to the naked eye. Mother Chen smiled. She came to the edge of the clearing and landed on the grass. A jolt of pain shot through her limbs, out to the tips of her fingers. Mother Chen bared her teeth, felt a surge of energy that climaxed with the pain and disappeared seconds later.

It had been more than a century since she was last here, in her

Jin Village. There wasn't much left. The temples were little more than piles of rocks on the ground. Animals had made their home next to the stone wall. She saw no traces of the wooden huts.

No matter. Mother Chen loved this tiny place, the village of her birth. She had loathed it as a child, when she ran away, broken and frightened. But then she had returned, had punished the guilty and thrown their sins back in their faces.

And what she had created after that was...marvelous.

It had been a pity to leave this place, but Mother Chen had no choice in the matter. Unbidden, the face of the man who drove her out surfaced in her mind. Thinking of that small peasant with the frightened eyes made Mother Chen gag with hate.

No, it was best not to dwell on him. She had greater concerns. New people were coming, people from a world she did not understand. Several had already come. Soon there would be more. They meant to wipe her village from the earth, to sweep it away. Mother Chen looked at a stack of square, metal objects, piled in a spot near the village well. She had never seen anything built with such precision. It made her uneasy.

Mother Chen's eyes drifted down to the deformed parts of her body. Even now she could see the spots where the arches of her feet had broken, the scars where pieces of glass had burrowed into her flesh. She had suffered because she spent her human life living as a frightened rabbit.

No more. She would never accept that again. Let these new ones come. If they meant to take what was hers, she would bleed them dry.

Available now in ebook and print from Samhain Publishing.

SAMHAIN

P U B L I S H I N G

THE BEST IN HORROR

Every month Samhain brings you the finest in horror fiction from the most respected names in the genre, as well as the most talented newcomers. From subtle chills to shocking terror, experience the ultimate in fear from such brilliant authors as:

Ramsey Campbell

W. D. Gagliani

Ronald Malfi

Greg F. Gifune

Brian Moreland

John Everson

And many more!

THE HOUSE OF HORROR

Samhain Horror books are available at your local bookstore, or you can check out our Web site, www.samhainhorror.com, where you can look up your favorite authors, read excerpts and see upcoming releases.

SAMHAIN
PUBLISHING

It's all about the story...

Romance

HORROR

www.samhainpublishing.com

CPSIA information can be obtained at www.ICGtesting.com
Printed in the USA
BVOW041122191212

308680BV00008B/146/P